Aerisia:
Gateway to the Underworld

Sarah Ashwood

Prophecy of the Artan

She is of our world and beyond. From another place, another time, she will come. She carries the burden of tomorrow, and her true essence will be birthed with the moon and the dawn. The Singing Stones once more will sing, and she shall unite those long hated with those who long have feared them. Unity with the everlasting will heal her soul, lifting the eternal from rejection and fear. She will be untouched by man and untainted by The Evil. In her will be met all the Powers of Good, and with them shall she defeat The Evil. The Dark Powers she shall overcome by becoming, yet not. Bound to the past, the bond will be broken that she may pass through the vales of shadow and despair to walk forevermore in the light. Wars may rage, kingdoms rise and fall, and monarchs topple, but the Artan will defend her people. Aerisia by her strength will be kept, and in her time peace will prosper.

The shadows swirling about It veiled the eyes and clouded the senses, but nothing could hide the fact that It was forsaken. Black with the blackness of death, It abode in the shadowed

recesses of Its vast hall, buried deep in a massive cavern that stretched for miles.

This was a place forgotten by most and secreted from any who might remember. The lighting was poor, the temperature cold. However, there was a purpose in using this place. Aside from the wild ones, whose lands It inhabited, and those of Its servants whom It most trusted, It managed to dwell here unseen while seeing all. Or nearly all.

The reek of death filled the air. Bits of corpses, strewn carelessly across the stone floor, rotted in various stages of decay. One yellowed, twisted, bare foot rested upon the freshly severed head of Its latest victim—the latest who had dared defy Its supreme will. Long toenails, coiled into talons, dug into the thatch of red-blonde hair matted with blood.

"It succeeded not, O Great One."

The servant approached on his belly like a snake, his head bowed to the earth. He would not risk looking into that face. A single look from his Master's eyes was death. The merest glance—and skin melted away, flesh blasted from the bones as if by fire and strong wind. There were none, save his Master Itself, who knew even so small a thing as the color of his Master's eyes; for those who saw Its eyes knew that secret for only a few fleeting moments. And in the grave there is no remembrance or telling.

"Of course it did not succeed," the deep voice rasped. "Jonase was a fool! I allow him to inhabit a human body, and what does he do but let his lust lead him into being slain by the accursed immortals?"

"Bu—but, Great One," the servant stuttered, "ha—had he succeeded, our worries would have been over."

"Do you think me ignorant of this, you fool?"

Roaring in rage, It leapt upright, the weight of Its massive form smashing the head beneath Its foot. Livid, It stalked to within inches of Its thoroughly frightened slave, oblivious to the trail of gory footprints defacing the gray flooring. The slender, trembling man dug his nails into the unforgiving stone on which he genuflected. Every instinct warned him to flee, but greater dread of his Master restrained him.

"I shielded Jonase from the Simathe, even as they have somehow shielded that woman from me! I... nay, we," It corrected Itself, "knew nothing of her whereabouts until she approached the cottage—a simpleton, aye, fully as much as the rest of you."

Stooping, It retrieved a huge slab of broken stone, only to rise and hurl the piece violently through the air. The stone crashed against one of the many thick pillars supporting the vaulted roof and shattered, sending bits and pieces of crushed stone showering down upon the petrified servant. He screamed, throwing trembling arms over his head.

"And they think," his Master snarled, either unmindful or uncaring of Its subordinate's terror, "she will one day possess the power to defeat me. Me! A weak, cringing girl, protected by no more than the strength of a Simathe's arm!"

It glared contemptuously at the man quivering on the floor. "One of them must have Joined with her, something the Simathe have shunned for years beyond number. Only by Joining could they have hidden her presence at Treygon. But no longer. Nay, no longer," It breathed. "Despite Jonase's failure, his attempt told me what I desired to know. Now I am aware of where she is and how she is safeguarded—within Treygon's hallowed halls."

It spat the last three words, as if their taste was bitter. Then, Its manner changed swiftly, unexpectedly, from violence to rumination.

"Treygon…" It murmured. "So that's how the game's to be played, is it? Warriors and fortresses. Swords, spears, and mountains. Nevertheless, I can strike a blow for which all are unprepared. Even Treygon has its weaknesses…"

"M—master?" the shrinking servant finally spoke up, his voice shaking as badly as his body. "Th—the Simathe. They a—are immor…immortal and ca—cannot be…be defea—"

"Do you take me for the bloody fool that you assuredly are?"

Wrath sluiced over the cringing slave, making him wish he'd never dared to speak.

"I am well aware that the Simathe are immortal and cannot be defeated, you worthless dung heap! Not in their own stronghold, of all places. Perhaps the fortress itself is invulnerable, but any defense is but as strong as its smallest weakness. And soon, soon…"

The storm of Its fury having once more played out, the creature turned, regressing toward Its gleaming, mammoth throne, fashioned from the polished bones of Its enemies. It sank into the chair, tracing a toe thoughtfully through the bloody paste—all that remained of the smashed skull.

"The Doinum," It muttered thoughtfully, so low Its groveling listener strained to hear. "The Doinum… send for the Doinum, Gont. I would speak with their leader."

"As my Great One wishes."

As rapidly as possible, the slave, Gont, sidled backward from the room, paying scant heed to the litter of human flesh strewn about. Once out of sight of his Master, he got to his feet and ran, hastening to accomplish the Great One's demands.

He was never so cheerful to quit a place as he was to depart these audiences with his master. Speeding down dank, shadowy corridors, he passed creatures unimaginable in form and being, but he paid them no mind. Like himself, these creatures had long ago chosen shadow or fallen prey to the One who led them all. These creatures did not frighten Gont; within, he was as vile as they. He did not look twice as he passed them by. Yet, in some smothered corner of his soul, he wished he might find the courage to flee and never go back.

Part One
Command and *Become*

Chapter One

A Shell

A week after Jonase's attack, Lord Ilgard, High-Chief of the Simathe, sought out the fairy Aureeyah. He found her on one of Treygon's upper balconies, elevated high above the ground. Her gentle glow melded with the moon's, and her exquisite face was serene. Her outward demeanor betrayed no knowledge of the struggle they faced, though he knew she must be aware of it.

"My lady Aureeyah?"

"Lord Ilgard?" She spoke without turning. "Come, join me. The night is beautiful."

Was it? In all reality, the night's beauty was lost on him. The tall warrior went to stand beside the fairy, wordless as he gathered both thoughts and purpose. In the end, she spoke first, making the tactful inquiry, "You wish to speak of her, my lord?"

He stifled the urge to scowl. The case must be serious indeed if the fairy was able to read his intent that easily.

"Aye, of her."

"She did not dine with us this evening."

"No, she did not."

Silence fell. This time, it was the Simathe who broke it. Looking hard at the fairy, he said, "It has been a week. Seven days, and still she will not leave her chamber. I sense only numbness and chill in her— very little life."

"I know."

"What are we to do?"

"That, I wish I did know."

He shifted, leaning his weight against the balcony wall. Folding his arms over his chest, he lifted his face to the brilliant, nighttime sky. Its twinkling stars were like his charge, he thought: beautiful, but distant. Unfeeling. Cold.

"Have you spoken with her?"

The fairy's question interrupted his gloomy reflections.

"She said little."

"I met with no better success."

"You tried?"

"Aye, I did, but to no avail. She has succumbed to despair and refused to meet my eyes or hear my voice. I fear she is lost in a dark place where I cannot reach her."

"Why?" he frowned.

"High-Chief, *think*. Think of all that has transpired since she first came. Nay, even coming to our land was a hardship, for she was required to leave behind all that she knew and all whom she loved upon Earth. Then she left the friends and familiarity of Laytrii in exchange for

4

Treygon, a foreign and frightening place to her. She's been attacked more than once in these few weeks and her life put in jeopardy. Matters have been hard for her. Now, in silence and despair, she seeks a solace from reality."

"She showed no signs of this the night Jonase struck," he protested mildly, thinking of that evening. She'd certainly not been cold and indifferent then. Light save him, but he'd not forgotten her kiss.

"No, not then. I suspect come morning she reconsidered her plight. Perhaps she decided we ask too much. All I know is that her state is brittle, fragile."

"Like a shell."

The fairy's emerald eyes met his, pleading for her friend. "Aye, a shell. A shell into which she's withdrawn as a means of protecting herself."

"What can we do? Will she heal?"

"Heal? She must heal! High-Chief, it is your duty to help her."

Aureeyah glided closer, placing a hand on his forearm and gazing imploringly into his face.

"Why my duty?" he responded tersely, little favoring the idea. He'd done his part by rescuing her from the creature, and far beyond the following night. What more could he do?

"Because you are *Joined* to her. You may be able to reach her when none of us can."

He looked away, recalling Lady Hannah's entreaty that fateful night and his own pledge.

"Ilgard, help me… I don't know what to say or do or think anymore. Everyone wants me to become the Artan, but I have no idea who she is! It's like my life isn't my own, and I don't even know why. I have to know, though. What happened today—it didn't happen without a reason, did it? There must be a reason why. A reason why me.*"*

He had told her there was a reason. He had said, *"One day you will know you are the Artan. You will know your magic, your strength, and your purpose in Aerisia."*

Had he meant that? He had promised himself that night that he would help her discover herself. Help her *be* the Artan. Maybe this was the first step in fulfilling that promise.

"Perhaps you are right," he agreed aloud. Then asked, "How do you suggest I help her? We have both tried reasoning with her and failed."

The fairy's answer was thoughtful, slow in coming. "I think sympathy will not work. Nor reason. As you said, we both attempted to reason with her, and I offered much sympathy as well. If anything, they only drove her further away."

"What then?"

"What is left?" she shrugged. "Anger?"

"Anger?"

It sounded far-fetched—albeit, given their past history, making her angry ought to be easy enough.

"Aye, angry…" the fairy mused. "It could work. Make her angry enough, and she may be forced of her own initiative to shatter the walls of this self-constructed shell."

She stepped gracefully away, a fey smile twitching at her lips. Moonlight glinted on the silvery blonde of her hair, washing her pale skin in ivory. Like all creatures of her race, she exuded magic, entrancing and delicate, at once soothing, mystifying, and gratifying to the senses.

"I believe this may work, High-Chief. It must work. After all, she cannot grow into her role as Artan until this—this lethargy is broken. Indeed," Aureeyah continued, peering off toward distant, mist-mantled peaks, "it is high time I relay the legend of the Artan and commence working with her. We agreed to wait a time before you sent for me, letting her accustom herself to life in Aerisia, in Treygon. But daily strengthens the might of The Evil. The fact that Jonase could have assaulted her as he did underscores this truth."

"We need her," she said simply, lifting her face to his. "Aye, and we need you as well. Time for you to take her in hand."

"Surely you could make her angry."

"Oh no, not if I am to instruct her later. Besides"—Aureeyah smirked—"I am a fairy, and it is hard for us to give offense. You, however, are the Simathe High-Chief. A gentle touch is not needed here. I think this task must be given to you."

There were many things he could have said, but he released the arguments into the void. The fairy had a point. So bewitching was her kind that they were hard-pressed to give offense, even when they tried. As for himself, his very presence was an offense to many. Including the young Artan, much of the time.

"As you say. I see my duty," he promised.

"Soon," the fairy urged. "You must do this soon."

"Aye, soon."

Offering a quick bow, he strode away, leaving the fairy alone on the high balcony just as he had found her.

Chapter Two

First...Kiss?

"Come in," I called at the rapping of knuckles on my bedroom door, and lifted dull eyes to see Cole entering the room.

"My lady." He sketched a polite half-bow. "The High-Chief requests your presence at the training grounds."

"The training grounds?"

I tried to weigh this, faintly suspicious that—considering the source—it might be some sort of challenge, but I found I really didn't care. Let him bait me all he wanted. I wasn't up to dealing with it.

Letting my head sag against the headrest, I said, "Tell him I don't feel up to it this morning."

"My lady?"

Although he didn't exactly show it, the man clearly couldn't believe I'd even consider disregarding orders from his High-Chief.

"No," I repeated, a touch more firmly. "Tell him I said no, I just don't feel like it."

The Simathe hesitated. "My lady, the High-Chief also sends word he will come escort you to the training grounds, if you wish."

A frown slipped across my face. The past several days had been hard. The morning after Jonase's attack, I had been in my room, getting dressed, when a tidal wave of emotions slammed me so hard I'd crumpled to my knees on the stone floor. The homesickness, the agony of losing my family, the fear of facing Jonase, then drocnords, then Jonase again… The horror of nearly being raped…

It felt like my air was shutting off. Gasping for breath, I'd wrapped my arms around myself and hung on tight, focusing on nothing but survival until I calmed. The whole episode probably hadn't lasted more than a few moments, not even long enough for Ilgard to become alarmed and send help. What it had left me with, though, was a lingering sense that this place asked too much. Any nobler aspirations aside, I didn't think I could handle an entire world bent on killing or controlling me.

From that point on, I'd tumbled fast and far into the pits of despair. Maybe I was being a baby. Maybe I had good reason to be. All I knew was that it was easier to throw up walls and withdraw from reality than to face what might have happened. For a week now, I'd lived this way, feeling gloomy, enervated, and incapable of action or deep thought. But I hadn't grown so dense that I didn't recognize a threat when I heard it.

Come escort me to the training grounds, I bet. Come and force me to go is more like it.

Since I still didn't feel like a confrontation, I decided to cooperate. "Fine," I said dismissively. "Tell him I'll be down after a while."

"He requests that you attend him now."

A flicker of irritation—just who did he think he was?

"Well, I have to get dressed," I snapped. "Tell him I'll be down as soon as I get my clothes on, unless he wants me running around in my nightgown."

"Very well, my lady. I shall convey your words to the High-Chief."

Without another word, he was gone.

* * *

When I was in sight of the practice fields, I purposely slowed my pace. The Simathe High-Chief was the only one around, and although my gait was meant to nettle him, I couldn't tell if it was working. It was difficult to tell if anything I ever tried on him worked since his face was as hard and calcified as a statue.

Once I got close, he handed me my usual bow and quiver of arrows, which I accepted without comment. Slinging the quiver across my back, I fastened it into place, nocked an arrow, lifted my bow, and perfected my stance. He waited until the exact instant I was ready to release the arrow and then snaked his foot out, catching my ankle with his boot. One quick tug, and my feet went out from under me. I crashed with a squeal, rolling over onto my hands and knees and spitting the dirt out of my mouth.

"Are you crazy? What the heck was that for?"

"Distraction," he replied. Leaning down, he offered a hand and pulled me to my feet. "Rarely is battle a matter of standing still and shooting. You must learn to keep your aim even while distracted."

I eyed him sideways, trying to figure this one out. Was he being honest? Tripping me seemed a rather extreme way to prove his point, but battle was far more extreme than that, so maybe he was only trying to help.

"Sounds reasonable enough," I finally assented, wiping the dirt off my face. "But you really didn't have to knock me on my butt to prove a point."

He merely shrugged.

The old me probably would've started World War III over that, but today I let it go with a roll of the eyes and a "Whatever." All I wanted was to get this over and done with so I could go back to hiding out in my room. Arguing would only delay retreat.

With that in mind, I readied another arrow and tried again. This time—again, just as I was all set to shoot—he deliberately jarred my elbow. And that was how the next couple hours went, with me trying to shoot and him finding all sorts of ways to distract me. Sometimes I was able to find my target anyway, but few of my attempts were good. Time and again I fell for his tricks, feeling more and more like an idiot as I did.

I'd never seen the Simathe High-Chief quite like this. His behavior was insensitive, unkind, and unforgiving. Severe, actually. Rather than respectfully pointing out and correcting my mistakes, he criticized them with stinging, well-chosen words. I had to pull the walls of my little cocoon tighter and tighter to keep his remarks from hurting. All the same, by the time he finally called a halt to target practice, I was a little sweaty, a little breathless, and more than a little irritated. If I hadn't known any better, I'd swear he was enjoying this, even though his equanimity told me nothing.

"Enough," he said at last. Judging by his tone, he might as well have added, "Because I'm sick of dealing with someone so hopeless."

"Good," I panted, "'cause I'm kinda tired and hungry, and—"

He cut me off with an upraised palm. "We are not finished yet."

With that he took off, obviously expecting me to follow.

"*We are not finished yet,*" I mimicked under my breath, but trailed after him anyway, wondering where we were going.

He led me to the stables, where one of the Simathe's huge, black horses was already saddled and waiting. I'd never seen horses like these. If their unique, Simathe-like coloring didn't set them apart as a distinct breed, the pure, primitive power screaming from every inch of their sleek frames would have. It shouted in the way this one tossed

13

his proud head, shaking his mane and pawing at the ground. Ilgard laid a hand on the animal's muzzle; it calmed instantly at his touch.

I felt a sickening twist in the pit of my stomach. The mere sight of this enormous beast was enough to evoke a flood of memories from which I'd been desperately hiding. Memories involving hideous drocnords, whizzing arrows, and the odors of blood and death. Not to mention the attack on the journey to Treygon, of which I still remembered little. And of the ride home after Jonase—

I began to back away.

"Stop!" The sharp command shattered the peace. "…My lady." He added the customary title of respect as an afterthought. "Come here" was his next order, and I found my feet moving woodenly.

When I was within a few paces, he spoke up, all the while stroking the horse's velvety muzzle in short, relaxing strokes. "It is time for you to ride our Restless."

"R—restless?"

"Aye." He scratched the animal behind the ears. In response, the horse butted playfully at his chest, the huge man and animal completely at ease with each another. "They are ever restless for action." His dark gaze lifted, found mine. "You must learn to ride them."

I stared for several seconds before the full impact of his words sunk in. My stomach twisted again, and I edged another step backward.

"You're not serious."

"I am."

"No—no way! You're out of your mind. I refuse."

"I'll brook no refusals. Come here."

Licking my lips, I flicked an anxious glance between man and horse, trying to determine which frightened me more.

"Come *now*, my lady."

Man won out. I slunk over.

He pointed at the saddle. "Mount."

I tried to obey, fighting queasiness as I stretched a hand toward the pommel. But the instant my fingers touched leather…

"No, I can't!"

Panicking, I jolted away, slamming against something hard. I whirled, only to find myself trapped between warrior and horse.

"I ordered you to mount, my lady."

"I can't," I protested weakly, my eyes pleading for understanding. "I just can't."

"Must I put you up there myself, as I did before?"

He referred to an incident at Laytrii, when he'd pretty much thrown me onto the back of his horse.

Shaking my head, I mouthed a noiseless, *No.*

"Then mount."

Perhaps I would've gone ahead and done it. Unluckily, the horse chose that moment to toss his head and shift his weight from front to back. He nudged me, and I freaked, jumping away with a yelp. The warrior had no pity. He got right up in my face, closing a large hand around my upper arm and tugging me near.

"Mount," he practically hissed, so close I could feel his breath on my nose.

Suddenly, it just snapped. All day his high-handedness, his domineering attitude, had been chipping away at my self-constructed emotional coma. Now those walls crumbled in a rush as anger and fear thrust their way to the fore, taking over in the guise of self-preservation.

I shot a scorching glare at the Simathe lord. "No! That's it. I've had it! I won't do it, and you can't make me."

"My lady—"

"No!" In an abrupt, angry move, I twisted free of his grasp. "You've been treating me like a jerk all day. What's wrong with you? Are you mad at me for some unknown reason? Like maybe you're now wishing Jonase had succeeded, or possibly even killed me, so you could be free of our *Joining* and go back to living your stupid Simathe life? Is that what you want? Or are you just mad that he got to try something you've wanted to do for a long time?"

It was word vomit. I didn't stop to think about what I was saying; it all just came spewing out. The instant I stopped speaking, there was dead silence. A look of wrath like I'd never seen spread slowly across the face of the man before me. I hadn't even known Simathe could look so angry. I blinked, astounded at myself and scared by him as I realized the horrible, horrible accusations I'd just made.

"Ilgard"—I shook my head nervously—"I—I'm sorry. I didn't know what I was saying! I only—"

"Enough." His voice was low, and his eyes blazed black. He shook his own head slowly, like a lion shaking its shaggy mane. "My lady goes too far," he growled.

Before I could think or react, his hands had shot out, capturing my waist. In one swift movement, he had swept me up, bringing my face level with his. I froze, so staggered I forgot to scream or fight. For a split second, his feral eyes bored into mine.

Who is this man? I thought, astounded to see this side of him that I'd never have dreamed existed.

I had no time to figure out the answer—or maybe I did, when he pulled me close, smothering my cry with the harsh kiss he pressed against my mouth. Stupefied with shock, I went limp in his arms, not moving, not resisting. The kiss stretched to infinity, my mind whirling all the while with a million different emotions. When he finally raised his head, I gasped for air, not having drawn breath since he seized me, and relaxed the fingers clenching his shoulders. Unable to meet the bottomless-pit black of his eyes, I averted my face as he lowered me slowly to the earth. When my feet touched dirt, I lurched away, swaying weakly against the horse. Breathing hard, I just stood there, helpless for the disbelief and confusion drowning me.

"Will my lady obey me now?"

At the quiet words, my eyes swung up to his. I seemed incapable of rational thought. He had kissed me. He had kissed me! Never mind what I'd done to start the whole thing. He had no right to do it, but he'd kissed me. He, Lord Ilgard, High-Chief of the Simathe!

The anger I'd felt before the kiss crept back, obliterating common sense.

How dare he? How dare *he? Especially after what I just went through a week ago?*

Just like that, I rediscovered both resolve and voice.

"No, I'm not going to obey you," I spat. "Just who do you think you are? How dare you…you treat me like that?" My hands balled into angry fists. "I'm no idiot— this isn't about me riding your horse! Maybe everything I said *was* true, after all."

The Simathe's eyes were wickedly black, but his tone was deceptively calm.

"My lady will not mount?"

"No!" I shouted obstinately, trying to pry loose the fingers still clasping my arm.

"If my lady refuses to obey, then she must be taught obedience."

"Oh yeah? Who's gonna teach me that? You and what army?"

Actually, that was a pretty stupid comeback, seeing as how he technically did have an army. He didn't need it, though. Although he said nothing, his murderous glare warned me I was pushing too hard. He spun around, stalking toward Treygon's main building, dragging me along behind.

"Where are we going?" I demanded, digging my heels into the earth. It did no good, and I received no reply.

Apparently, I'd really done it this time.

* * *

Hours later, I was down on my hands and knees in a deserted hallway, scrubbing the dusty stone floor with a wet, sudsy brush. Pausing for a brief rest, I used the back of my wrist to wipe a strand of sweaty hair off my forehead. Glancing about, I sighed deeply. *Crap.* I'd been at this for several solid hours and had finished only half the assigned floor.

Who knew scrubbing stone floors on one's hands and knees could be such rough work? My shoulders ached, my wrists ached, my arms hurt, my head ached. My knees were sore from crawling around, and I was soaking wet. If I hadn't been raised better, I would've cussed a certain High-Chief for this.

After dragging me—yes, dragging me—in here, he'd called for cleaning supplies and set me to work. Not only that, but he'd had made sure everyone in close proximity was there to watch. That number just happened to include Cole, Lord Norband, and Lord Contrey, along with half a dozen others. Even Aureeyah and, of course, Ilgard himself had stayed to witness my humiliation.

That's what you get for pushing a High-Chief too far, my conscience chided. *I still can't believe you said those awful things to him.*

I can't believe he made me mad enough to say them in the first place. Doesn't that make this his fault?

With another self-pitying sigh, I dipped my brush into the nearby bucket of soapy water and got on with my work. These floors weren't going to clean themselves, and I highly doubted the guard hovering around in the background could be bribed into doing this for me. Or into letting me go before it was finished.

Being the supposed Artan around this rotten place sure doesn't mean very much. I mean, shouldn't I have diplomatic immunity or something?

Even Aureeyah, whom I'd counted on as an ally, hadn't sided with me, although I'd done my best with genuine tears in my eyes to convince her that Ilgard was "just being mean to me," and wouldn't she please do something? She hadn't, darn it!

Why did everyone around here always assume I was the one in the wrong?

I should've slapped him, I thought for the umpteenth time, thinking back to the forced kiss. *He deserved it.*

No, I amended bitterly, *it's probably a good thing I didn't. If I had, I'd most likely be scrubbing chamber pots instead of hall floors right about now.*

The realization was far from comforting. I couldn't remember anyone ever making me so angry.

Chapter Three

Explosion

It was late when I finally got back to my room. I was wet, hungry, tired, and cross—the exact opposite of Aureeyah, who was relaxing in one of the twin chairs in front of the fireplace, her hands folded serenely in her lap.

She glanced up as I entered. "How passed your day?"

I shot her an evil glare. She offered a sweet smile in return.

Grabbing some dry clothing, I stepped behind a dressing screen to change. I could've used a bath, I realized while toweling off, but I refused to lower myself and ask for one.

"I have sent for food."

"Waste of time. I'm not hungry."

Emerging from behind the screen, I stalked over to the bed, where I plopped down heavily, reaching for a nearby comb.

"You've not dined since morning."

True, but that wasn't my fault. As soon as I'd finished one floor, a Simathe had appeared to escort me to the next. I'd been kept busy all day with no time to rest or eat. Consequently, I was starving; nevertheless, my pride wouldn't allow me to request a meal, bath, or any other favors from my Simathe prison wardens.

Choosing to ignore the fairy's last comment, I gritted my teeth, concentrating on a particularly stubborn knot in my damp hair.

"You'll injure yourself."

Dainty fingers whisked the comb right out of my hand. Seating herself beside me, the fairy gently turned my head and took over the task of combing out snarls and snags. I wanted to protest but was so tired and glum that I couldn't find the energy. Rather than argue, I simply gave up and allowed her to help. Beneath her charmed touch, the comb soon slid through my hair as easily as a knife through heated butter.

After a bit, she stopped and laid the comb aside. "We must speak," she said, all traces of humor gone. I turned reluctantly to face her.

"This past week has been trying for you, I know. First the attack by Jonase, then your subsequent rescue, followed by your difficulties today."

My traitorous mind took a leap, diving through all of it and landing squarely on the memory of Ilgard's kiss.

Oh, if only you knew, I thought wryly.

"You were at odds with the High-Chief today."

"*Were* at odds?"

"Are," she amended.

"That's more like it."

"He was only doing what he judged best for you."

I drew my feet up under me on the bed. "So acting like a jerk toward me all day was for my own good? Hmmm…that's a new one on me."

"Jerk?" she echoed, her green eyes twinkling mischievously.

"Yeah, jerk. It's basically somebody who's arrogant, mean, or rude. Not that the High-Chief has ever been the nicest of people," I said sourly, "but he was way worse today than he's been in a long time. And you didn't even stick up for me," I added, hurt in my voice. "What's up with that? I thought you were my friend."

"So I am," she declared softly.

"Then why'd you—"

"Sometimes," the fairy cut in, "true friendship means doing what is best for another, even if it is not necessarily what your friend would like."

"Oh, so you were in on it with him. For whatever reason, my *closest friends* have decided treating me like crap is for my own good. Wow, I mean, I just feel so loved."

"You would not listen to reason."

"What reason?" I exploded, throwing my hands in the air. "I have no idea what you're talking about!"

"No," she agreed, unruffled as always, "I suppose you haven't."

I took a deep breath and counted to ten before daring to open my mouth. "Okay, so what *reason* are you talking about then?" I asked sweetly, with a fake smile and clenched teeth.

Honestly! These people could make a nun cuss like a sailor.

"Both the High-Chief and myself attempted to speak, to reason with you, my friend. You, however, were too lost in your own misery to pay heed."

What she said hit me like a boxer's fist. I went absolutely still, absorbing the shock.

Too lost in your own misery to pay heed…

Gradually, I began to understand. The more I contemplated it, the clearer it became. Aureeyah was right; I had been lost in deep darkness ever since the attack by Jonase. Oddly, it hadn't helped to wake up and find that the Simathe High-Chief had broken his promise to stay with me that night. Strangely, I had shadowy memories of ghastly nightmares and strong arms comforting me, but waking in an empty room had forced me to face facts. Those memories could only be dreams, for aside from a single follow-up visit in which he'd said little and I nothing at all, I hadn't even seen the man until today. From his aloofness, it was hard to believe he was the same man who'd wiped away my tears and wrapped me in his own cloak to hide my torn gown. The night he'd done all that, the night he'd rescued me from Jonase—the night I'd kissed him, for goodness' sake!—I thought I'd felt a tentative trust springing up between us. However, on my part, it'd been put to the test far too soon. He'd lied to me, breaking my faith, and I was back to disliking him as much as ever. Especially after today's sorry performance.

Well…almost, anyway.

An annoying little voice in the back of my mind insisted that maybe I hadn't minded today's stolen kiss nearly as much I wished I had. Stubborn to the bitter end, I shoved it away, squashing it down deep where I wouldn't have to listen to its foolishness.

"I guess you're right," I finally admitted, returning to the present. "Maybe you and Ilgard did sort of try to talk to me, but I was so miserable I couldn't hear what you were trying to say."

My friend nodded, encouraging me to continue.

"So that's what all this was about today? You two were in cahoots, trying to snap me out of it?"

The syntax may've been unfamiliar, but my meaning was clear. "It would seem we have met with success. Or rather, the High-Chief has," she grinned impishly.

"Yeah, well, he could make anyone mad enough to spit nails," I grumbled.

Aureeyah laughed, but at my ferocious scowl, she smothered her amusement with a hand.

"It's not funny!" I protested. "He was really mean to me."

She lowered her hand, fighting to stifle a puckish grin. "Aye, I am sure he was harsh."

"Harsh, nothing! He was downright cruel. An absolute—"

"Jerk," she finished smoothly.

I tried to steel myself against her infectious humor, but it proved too much. She was right. In a sick sort of way, the situation was funny. Before I knew it, I was laughing hysterically, releasing all of the depression, pain, and anger, letting humor temporarily fill the void in my soul.

When the merriment finally subsided, I rolled over onto my side and faced my new friend, supporting myself with an elbow. Tracing my fingertips over the weave of the blanket, I asked casually, "Do you think the Simathe are handsome?"

She was clearly taken aback. "Why would you ask such a thing?"

"Oh, I dunno. Just curious, I guess."

She tilted her head. "Do you find them so?"

"Uh-uh. I asked you first."

"Which Simathe, in particular, did you mean?"

"I didn't mean any of them in particular. I meant all of them in general, or any of them in particular. I'm asking your opinion of their looks."

"You are from Earth, and you do not find their appearance…strange? I cannot think of a woman in Aerisia who would agree with you."

"I didn't say their looks weren't strange," I said, sitting up. "They are, but—oh man, I must be going crazy. But they're strangely attractive too. Or maybe they're strangely attractive in spite of it. Who knows? I don't know what I mean.

"Hey, how'd we get to talking about what I think of all this when I was asking you what you thought?"

"You haven't the knack for keeping your opinions private," she smirked. "If you'll pardon my saying so, I think it gets you into trouble."

"Gets me into trouble, huh? Ha-ha. There're worse things than being honest."

"And there are better things than revealing all you think."

"Whatever. Okay, so out with it, then—do you think the Simathe are handsome? Or do fairies even think human men are attractive? Or are there male fairies, and that's all you notice?"

Maybe I wasn't very good at nondisclosure, and maybe my train of thought was pretty rambling. She definitely caught the last part, though, because a shadow fell across her delicate features.

"No," she replied, sort of sadly and wistfully. "There are no male fairies. Not in Aerisia. Not anymore."

That was a curious answer, but her demeanor warned me not to push. Switching subjects, I said, "You still haven't answered my original question."

"What?" She shook herself, like somebody lost in thought coming back to reality. "Oh, yes. Well, as for that, were I a mortal woman, I should be inclined to look with favor upon the Ranetron High-Chief."

"Lord Garett? You think he's hot?"

She wrinkled her nose. "Hot? That is an odd expression, and sounds rather improper."

"Being improper is all part of my charm," I snickered.

Rolling her eyes, she shook her head. "Let not Council hear you say so. That sort of charm our Artan can do without."

Before I could protest, she asked mischievously, "Do *you* find the High-Chief comely?"

"Who, Garett or Ilgard?"

"Either. Both."

I shrugged carelessly. "Yeah, I guess I do. Don't get me wrong, Garett's a good-looking guy, but—call me crazy— I actually think Ilgard has him beat…is better," I amended quickly, catching her subtle confusion.

"Ah. I thought as much."

I frowned. "What's that supposed to mean, '*Ah, I thought as much*?'"

Aureeyah slid gracefully off the bed. "I believe you care for the High-Chief more than you realize."

Her observation hit a little too close to home.

It's all fun and games until somebody stumbles onto your most embarrassing secret, chided the little voice, popping up from the dark corner where I'd banished it.

"Furthermore," I came back to myself in time to hear her say, "I believe you will come to know this in time."

All right, it was time to take action. I snatched up a pillow from the stack at the headboard and chucked it at her.

"Hah! You wish. That's never going to happen."

She caught the pillow nimbly. "Mark my words," she warned cheerfully and tossed the pillow back.

I threw up a hand to block it. Suddenly, there was a small, brief-but-brilliant flash. Blue lightning filled the entire room, exploding the poor pillow midair into a mass of singed feathers and bits of green fabric. In the aftermath, downy fluff drifted lazily toward the floor while the fairy and I gaped at one another in unspoken astonishment.

Chapter Four

The Artan After All?

"What was *that*?" I gasped.

"Hannah!" The fairy rushed to my side. "Your necklace—let me see it!"

Trembling with alarm, I reached into my bodice and extracted the necklace given to me by Lord Elgrend, the Aerisian High Elder. The stone was warm: a strange, internal warmth, not derived from my body heat. Its color had also shifted from pink to dark purple.

The fairy reverently stretched out a finger but stopped just shy of actually touching the stone. "Hannah, the Artan…" she breathed. "No doubts remain. *You are she!*"

She sank to her knees before me, bowing her head in reverence.

Panicking, I rose to my own knees on the bed. "Aureeyah, what in the world are you doing? Get up!"

At this juncture, my bedroom door swung open. The Simathe High-Chief stood framed in the doorway. He absorbed the scene with a glance. "Something has occurred."

"High-Chief, come," directed the fairy, and he did, offering a hand to lift her to her feet.

To me, Aureeyah said, "My lady, may we inspect the stone?"

I frowned at the use of the title. She usually called me by my name—a welcome habit, reminding me that to some people I could simply be myself, Hannah. Now, one strange twist of fate had altered our friendship. Forever?

I raised the necklace, lifting the stone for the Simathe to see. He studied it, his deep eyes absorbing the light, before extending a forefinger to touch it lightly. "Warm," he muttered, his black eyes capturing mine. As always, nothing in his expression or pupilless eyes betrayed his thoughts.

"Why did you come?" I asked quietly.

"I...felt something," he responded carefully. "Something curious that bid me come straightway."

"Can you elaborate, my lord?" Aureeyah interjected. "Explain what you felt?"

He shifted his focus to her. "An outburst of power, perhaps? Like energy unleashed."

"What? You mean to say *I* did that to the pillow? And he *felt* it?"

Aureeyah nodded soberly. "So it would seem, my lady."

I couldn't disguise my shock. "But that can't be! I've never done anything like this before. I can't! I don't have any magical…powers…"

The sentence trailed off as I felt a sickening lurch in my belly. Was it possible that they'd been right all along? That it was I who had done this? That somewhere, deep within my being, magic lay dormant?

Am I their Artan?

Remembrance struck—a memory flash of a gigantic, grinning skull. Of blazing luminescence, of blue light springing from my hands. It blanked out, vanishing as quickly as it'd come. I wasn't aware of sitting there, my eyes squeezed shut in concentration, until I felt a feather-light touch on the top of my head.

"Lady Hannah? Are you well?"

Aureeyah. I opened my eyes, surprised to find tears blurring my vision.

"I was wrong. There was something else," I admitted fearfully. "Something I think I did before, on the way to Treygon. When we were attacked during the storm. But I can't—I can't seem to recall it now."

"High-Chief?"

The fairy directed herself to the warrior who, in turn, shifted a step closer.

"She speaks truth. We did not witness it, however."

"It is possible even now for the High-Chief to see what happened, my lady," Aureeyah informed me gently. "In light of this unusual event, giving him permission to proceed is, perhaps, imperative."

Flicking a nervous glance from one Aerisian to the other, I used the heel of my hand to wipe moisture from my eyes. "What does that mean?"

"I mean, thanks to your *Joining* bond, it is possible for the High-Chief to journey within your mind's eye and discover what you've forgotten."

"Journey...look inside my mind? You can do that?" I asked him.

"I can."

He was composed as ever and seemed impervious to my confusion, apprehension, and even embarrassment. I knew he wasn't, though, since he felt all I felt. How could he do that and still preserve that immaculate poise? The man was unfathomable.

Before Jonase, before my life being put in jeopardy, I would've fought the idea of such a personal intrusion tooth and nail. Especially by him. Now? I'd seen the flash, the pillow exploding. Unlikely as it seemed, I'd caused both. Tickling the back of my mind, a repressed memory promised I'd know more if I freed it. An impossible task without the warrior's help. Was I willing to allow it? I knew finding out might change me and my future irrevocably. Once before I'd vowed to become the Artan if it meant taking charge of my own life and destiny. This appeared to be a necessary first step; did I have the courage to take it?

I could find no other alternative. "All right," I agreed, after taking a slow, deep breath. "I guess there's nothing else to do. He can try."

For a moment, everybody was quiet. Maybe they were surprised I'd agreed so easily. What could I say? I'd surprised myself by that one.

"So how do we go about it?" I finally asked.

"We must have perfect silence," answered the High-Chief.

Aureeyah took the hint. "Then I will take my leave. Pray, excuse me—my lord, my lady."

Bowing to each of us in turn, she left the room. It was with regret that I watched her go. I wasn't quite ready to be alone with the Simathe High-Chief. Not after our argument and all the turmoil today. Not after that kiss...

Without being invited, he took a seat next to me on the bed. I shrank back, an automatic reflex. He, however, caught my shoulders and held me in place, bending to peer intently into my eyes.

"Has my lady faith in me?"

I winced. That was Ilgard. He was nothing if not direct. A little too direct.

"I...trust you," I replied cautiously.

He leaned even closer, those consuming, obsidian eyes so compelling I wanted to flee. How could I flee, though, with him right there, his hands holding me still?

"Nay, does my lady truly trust me? If I'm to do this, there must be stronger ties between us than a mere *Joining*. There are mental strongholds I cannot breach unless you've faith in me as a warrior. As your guardian. Your friend."

The last condition, added almost as an afterthought, made me squirm. "Ilgard…" Lowering my gaze, I plucked fretfully at a loose thread on the blanket. "I—I trust you. Sometimes, for some things. But you have to admit"—I left off messing with the thread to clench my hands in my lap—"we haven't ever had exactly the best of relationships. It's hard for me to say we're really *friends*. You can't blame me for not trusting you like I would my father or my best friend or even someone like Aureeyah."

"I sympathize, my lady. Yet know that since we first met I've neither drawn breath nor taken action against your welfare."

"Yeah, well, forgive me if I find that a little hard to swallow."

"What do you mean?"

"What do I mean? I mean like how it was for my welfare that you broke your promise to stay with me that night?"

The question was out before I could stop it. He held his peace—mulling it over, I supposed—while I stared at my hands, chastising myself bitterly.

Stupid, Hannah, stupid! Why did you say that? You didn't want him to know you cared!

No, I hadn't wanted him to know, just as I hadn't wanted to care. But I did care, all the same.

When he finally spoke, there was a strange note of gentleness in his tone, one I'd never heard before.

"You are mistaken, my lady. I was in your chamber until full break of day."

What?

I dared to raise my face. "You mean you were there all night?"

"I was."

Flummoxed, I didn't know where to look or what to think.

"You do not remember? You woke more than once."

I did? Were what I passed off as dreams really memories?

"Indeed, there was no rest for either of us until I took you close."

I glanced up sharply. What the heck did that mean? Had he slept with me? In my bed?

Either the Simathe really could read my mind or else my consternation was written all over my face. He chuckled, gesturing toward the hearth. "In the chair, of course. I did not compromise your honor."

Feeling my face turn red, I ducked my chin, squeezing my fingers into fists. Curse his being able to see through me so easily!

"Lady Hannah." All amusement vanished. "This is your choice alone. If you'd rather I forbear, I will not press it upon you."

For once he won't force me into something? That's a new one, especially after the way he acted today.

"But you think it's necessary?"

He flipped the question around. "Do *you* think it necessary?"

I shrugged in tired defeat. "I don't know. I guess I really don't know what else to do. Yes…I trust you enough. Do whatever you have to do."

Amazingly, it didn't cost me nearly as much to say those words as I figured it would, and I was startled to find myself, well, meaning them. Despite the fact that our relationship had never been good—and might never be—I figured I needed to take this step. Maybe it would help convince me one way or another that I was the Artan. At the very least, maybe it would help me overcome my resentment toward the Simathe High-Chief. Perhaps it would even help the fragile truce we'd formed in the last few minutes last.

Chapter Five

Mind Search

"Close your eyes," the warrior-lord commanded, and did so himself a heartbeat later.

Clasping her face between his palms, he delved deep within himself to find the force uniting them. Once he discovered it, the Simathe allowed himself to be swept into the link and, from there, into her consciousness. She jolted as he entered her mind, her innermost being, but his grip restrained her. Focusing keenly, he swept through the different levels of her soul, seeking and ultimately uncovering a secret place in her mind, hidden even from herself. In an instant, their fusing ties allowed him to demolish the mental walls encircling it and to enter.

What he found caught him unawares.

She saw it too and, with a gasp, tore free. Concentration shattered, he opened his eyes to see her gazing up him, her eyes wide, both wonder and fright on her pretty features.

"I remember," she exclaimed. "I remember it all! It's true, isn't it? I *did* do it both times. Some sort of freak defense mechanism, I suppose. Which means I really do have…some type of abilities."

The dark warrior made no reply; of course it was true. What had been purported from the onset was now indisputable: she was the Artan. Doubtless, now that she knew it herself, under the fairy's tutelage the knowledge and skill to employ her talents would come very soon.

"But how?" she mused aloud, as if she had forgotten him. "How? Nobody on Earth can do these things. I'm from Earth—I am! This is supposed to be impossible. I just don't understand."

"Perhaps when you've heard the legend of the Artan, you shall," he offered, redirecting her considerations.

"Hey, maybe you're right! Maybe I should ask Aureeyah."

"I'll send for her."

He rose.

"Ilgard, wait a second." Her call checked him. Turning, the warrior looked into and was imprisoned by mismatched eyes of brown and green. "What was all that business about my necklace? Why was it warmer after I blew up the pillow? Why did it change color? What does the necklace have to do with anything, anyhow?"

The longer he stared into those strange, bewitching eyes, the greater his odd discomfort. Best he depart. "The fairy will explain all," he pledged, throwing the words over his shoulder as he strode from her chamber.

It was time he sent for the fairy, informed her of what he'd discovered. Also high time the young Artan heard what had been kept from her and learned more of her heritage. This task he would leave to Aureeyah. Better she handle matters of this kind than he. The more time he spent in his charge's company, the more difficulty he had in laying aside the perplexing stirrings provoked by her.

The irony of this did not escape him. After spending so many years in devotion to his homeland, with no woman's presence to soften his life, how was a man to forget a maid when the sole reason for his existence had come down to safeguarding her? How, when it was quite likely for this very purpose that fate had created him? His centuries of silent service to Aerisia notwithstanding, no purpose compared with this: defending the very heart, soul, and future of his native soil.

Ultimately, as *Joined* guardian of the Lady Hannah, he had no loftier purpose in life.

Chapter Six

The Prophecy

Much later I lay on my bed, propped against the headboard with a pile of plump pillows. I was too tired to stay up but had so much to think about I couldn't sleep. Never mind the raw weariness from today's forced labor; my mind was restless and my brain alert, conspiring to withhold rest.

You are the Artan...

Again, I ran the words through my mind, wondering how many times I'd heard them during my visit to this land. How long had I been here anyway? Two months? Three, four? I'd lost track of time; it wasn't that important when I was merely living from one day to the next with no solid goals on which to focus. Especially no homecoming—and that thought hurt worse than the rest. Aerisia still didn't feel like home, and I doubted it ever would.

Laytrii, Artan, Aureeyah. Ilgard, Cole. Rittean, Risean. Elisia, Garett. So many different people, races, and histories. *Me, Hannah Elizabeth.* So diverse, but all of us linked by a common thread: Aerisia, the land and its people. Only, where did I fit into the grand scheme of things?

Of course, as the Artan. The one prophesied to save them all from...whatever it was that threatened. Funny, but I had yet to discern much of a threat. I'd seen drocnords, deathcats, and Jonase (even now that name sent a shudder down my spine), but Jonase was dead, and any other aggravations the Simathe, Ranetron, and Cortain seemed perfectly capable of handling.

There was something more, though. Something I sensed I was being shielded from. Why? Were they afraid their precious "deliverer" would turn tail and run if she knew what she was really up against?

Deliverer. Me—a rescuer, a deliverer.

The Artan.

Closing my eyes, I burrowed into my cozy nest of pillows, recalling the prophecy and legend of the Artan, both of which Aureeyah had finally shared with me...

She is of our world and beyond. From another place, another time, she will come. She carries the burden of tomorrow, and her true essence will be birthed with the moon and the dawn. The Singing Stones once more will sing, and she shall unite those long hated with those who long have feared them. Unity with the everlasting will heal her soul, lifting the eternal from rejection and fear. She will be untouched by man and untainted by The Evil. In her will be met all the Powers of Good, and with them shall she defeat The Evil. The Dark Powers she shall overcome by becoming, yet not. Bound to the past, the bond will be broken that she may pass through the vales of shadow and despair to walk forevermore in the light. Wars may rage, kingdoms rise and fall, and monarchs topple, but the Artan will defend her people. Aerisia by her strength will be kept, and in her time peace will prosper.

This was the prophecy, these beautiful, flowing words. Poetic as it was, I had no idea what most, if any, of it meant. Even Aureeyah claimed ignorance of its entire meaning. It had been handed down through the ages, passed along for so many generations that even the prophet's name had been obliterated by time.

The more commonly known parts of the tale began many lifetimes ago, when the Dark Powers had all but succeeded in blotting out the light of the sun. Destruction loomed, and hope seemed fruitless until there arose a deliverer: a young woman who resisted the shadows, rallying her countrymen to do the same.

Her name was Artan.

After a long and bloody struggle engulfing the length and breadth of Aerisia, a war costing countless lives, this Joan of Arc-like figure and her followers eventually reclaimed what had been lost. Once more, sunlight dispelled the gloom. The Dark Powers were defeated—but not for good. The people knew this, Artan knew this, and although they rebuilt their lives, they continued to watch for any signs that the Dark Powers were moving against them.

Though young, Artan was wise, and she feared the passing of time would subject the Aerisian peoples to forgetfulness. In the forgetting would come inattentiveness, and Artan knew that when this occurred, the Dark Powers would rebuild themselves and send The Evil to consume the land. It was said that she herself foretold of a time when this would happen—a time when the sun would be darkened and all light dimmed. Furthermore, it was believed that the prophecy of the Artan, a prediction of another young woman who would arise to fight the foe, came to light shortly after the first Artan disappeared, never to be seen again. Nobody knew her fate. For years the people of Aerisia sought her, to no avail. No traces of the first Artan were ever found.

Little else was known of the prophecy, and nothing more of the first Artan. According to Aureeyah, some believed her magic would be her greatest weapon, while others claimed it would be the love of her people—a love inspiring them to willingly leave their homes and lay down their lives in her service.

At the conclusion of this incredible story, I'd asked Aureeyah to explain the significance of my necklace to the tale.

"The stone," she'd informed me, "is ages old."

Somehow, it was tied to me as the next Artan, although precisely how nobody could say. The priceless relic had been discovered during the days of High-Chieftess Laytrii by Moonkind stonecutters, hidden in the deep caverns winding their way through Mount Mortane. The stonecutters had discovered it sealed within a transparent box of green crystal, shoved into the shadowy recesses of a stone niche. Also inside was a withered parchment whose High Tongue lettering proclaimed that the piece was linked to the forthcoming Artan and advised that upon her advent it must be given to her.

Realizing the tremendous importance of this find, the High-Chieftess had guarded the jewelry the remainder of her life and, upon her passing, had charged the newly appointed High Elder of Aerisia with its future watchcare. The tradition then began that each new High Elder, when he or she accepted office, swore a formal oath that bound them to the protection of the "necklace of the Artan," as it later came to be called. It was a tradition maintained until the stone could be delivered into the hands of the next Artan. Which meant until my time since it now belonged to me.

In the semidarkness of my room, I laid a fingertip to the mysterious gem suspended from my neck, fascinated that I should be wearing something so ancient, so mysterious, so valuable. I figured that my powers as the Artan must somehow be associated with the pale pink stone. This would explain why using them had altered the jewel's color and made it glow with warmth.

Tracing a thumb over the stone's polished surface, I continued to mull things over.

When I'd questioned Aureeyah as to why my magic had sprung to the fore only twice, why it hadn't come to my rescue during Jonase's attack, she'd carefully replied, "This is not unusual, my lady. Until you master your talents and direct them as you will, the magic will come and go as it pleases. It will be erratic and set in motion by uncertain and varying causes. That is why the High-Chief brought me to Treygon, that I might teach you to conquer your magic—to wield it like a weapon, with dexterity and skill."

Inborn abilities, magic, enchantments. It all seemed so incredible. I couldn't quit asking, why me? How me? How could *I* be the Artan, of this world and beyond?

"Surely on Earth you must have sensed that you were different?"

No, never. Never…except maybe once. One black night so deep in my past that I could scarcely recall it and, when I did, wished I never had. Whatever the truth of that incident, it'd occurred so long ago that I questioned its validity. Was it real or a dream?

Before, I may've had cause to doubt. Now, there was little room for reservations, although part of me hated accepting the fact that I wasn't who I'd always been. That I might be something else, something more. I'd once vowed to find out the truth and to learn to become the Artan if it meant controlling my own destiny and protecting myself from danger. However, could somebody prophesied to a certain fate ever really control her own destiny?

Oddly, discovering I was who they said I was sort of hurt. Maybe I just needed time to accept the full impact of this revelation. I still didn't know why me or how it was possible for an ordinary young woman from the United States to suddenly become the prophesied liberator of some unknown world parallel to mine. Maybe not knowing how I'd been chosen to fulfill the role was part of the problem. Maybe I still needed more answers.

However, when I'd pressed for them, my fairy friend had clammed up and refused to speak. She'd told me the prophecy and much of the legend, but further she wouldn't go. Now was not the time, she said, nor was the remainder of the tale hers to relate. I'd have to be content with the information she'd given me. I'd tried to worm more out of her but got nowhere. For all her soft, ethereal beauty, a fairy could be as cast-iron as a Simathe when she put her mind to it. I'd learned nothing else. And that was why I lay awake in the murkiness of my room pondering, thinking, contemplating, debating, conjecturing.

Sleep was a long time coming.

Chapter Seven

Visitors

Perturbed, I was pacing the perimeter of Treygon's outer wall. Frustration dogged my steps, and even the exercise wasn't getting rid of it. This was my third lap, and I scarcely felt better than when I'd started.

I heard footsteps behind me but didn't bother checking to see who was following. One of them was always there: Kan, Cole, Chief Captain Norband, Lord Contrey, Lord Sarvye, a couple of others. Sometimes the High-Chief followed, though another warrior was usually assigned. Once I left my bedroom's confining four walls, I was never alone. Even when I kept to my room, there was now a guard stationed outside my door, in addition to the pair in the corridor. Apparently, there'd be no repeat performance of the last time I'd managed a few minutes alone, because the Simathe were determined I'd never be alone again.

This place is locked down tighter than solitary confinement on Alcatraz, I grumped.

The whole guards-all-over-the-place thing wasn't the reason for my bad mood, however. Or, rather, it hadn't started it. The underlying cause was the long lesson with Aureeyah that I'd just left. Now I not only had to contend with daily practice sessions with one Simathe or another, I also spent time with the fairy, trying—in vain, so far—to pin down and utilize my powers as the Artan.

Nothing is working, nothing!

Hence the reason for my long walk. Annoyance oozed out of each terse step, each broad swing of the arms.

Archery was the only bright spot in weapons training, but there hadn't been any bright spots with the fairy. I was beginning to consider myself simply inept and inadequate, not only as the Artan, but also as a person. Maybe I was a hopeless case.

At least there'd been no more forced riding lessons. My nose wrinkled as I considered taking on one of those massive beasts. Speaking of which, the clatter of horse hooves caught my ears just then, and I turned in time to witness the last of a large group of horsemen disappearing through one of the courtyard's side gates.

What's up with that?

Those horses weren't Restless; they'd looked far too normal. And even though I hadn't gotten a good look at any of the riders, from what I could ascertain they weren't Simathe either.

Slowing down a bit, I proceeded in the direction of the gate through which the horses and riders had vanished, my long skirt swirling about my heels. After clearing it, I found myself standing just off the weapons ring, where bouts of swordplay typically took place. At least a dozen horses had arrived, and most of them carried Ranetron. I couldn't see the remainder of the group, those who'd already dismounted. The mounted warriors blocked my view.

"What's all this?" I asked the guard who'd come to a halt behind me.

"A party summoned by the High-Chief."

Ilgard sent for these people? Why?

I tossed a glance over my shoulder. Today's watchdog was Kan. Yesterday, Lord Contrey had been my shadow, and the day before—had it been Kan again? Or Lord Norband?

Not that it makes much difference which guard it is.

My shadows did their job as noiselessly as real shadows would. Nobody around here besides Aureeyah talked to me much.

With the fairy in mind, I felt a stirring of apprehension as I neared the mounted Ranetron. The notion had occurred that they might've come to escort the fairy back to her forest home. After all, she'd have to return someday. Unfortunately, with the way my luck ran, it would probably be sooner rather than later.

"Lady Hannah!"

I spun around. "Rittean!"

Laughing, I ran to her, not stopping until we caught each other in a warm embrace. Stepping back, I shoved the hair from my face, laughing and trying to talk at the same time. "Rittean, what're you doing here? I can't believe you came! I mean, I'm so happy to see you!"

If eyes could laugh, hers surely were over my unrefined, unbridled enthusiasm. "And it's a pleasure to see you, my lady, I assure you!" Linking arms with me, she ducked under a horse's nose, pulling me along. "Come, see who else has arrived!"

She waved toward the weapon's ring, where I saw an old man in coffee-colored robes similar to her own. His back was to me, but I knew it her father, Risean Wy' Curlm. Also present were Lord Garett, the Ranetron High-Chief, and, "Is that Lord Elgrend?" I voiced aloud. "And Lady Tey?"

"You are correct. It is the High Elder. And the Cortain Pronconcil, as well."

I found myself gawking at the beautiful noblewoman like a teenage boy in the presence of Miss America.

Merciful heavens, she's beautiful.

The young warrior wore armor styled after the Ranetrons', but no amount of leather and metal could disguise her absurd beauty. Long, silken hair, blonde with delicate red highlights, was pulled back from the sides of her face into twin braids that were woven together in the back. She balanced a helmet with a tufted black plume comfortably against her hip. A sheathed sword in a plain scabbard was strapped to her waist, and her arms—bare except for armbands—had muscle tone any fitness fanatic would envy. She had to be around six feet tall, and her proportions were flawless. She was stunning, like an Amazon queen from Greek mythology.

Contrasting myself with the Cortain, I felt short, dumpy, dark, and plain—then guilty for being so stupid.

This isn't a competition, you moron. Why would you feel the need to compete with her anyway?

Lady Elisia hadn't provoked such envy. Why Lady Tey? Because she was calm and confident as a leader and a woman? Here I was feeling like a dismal failure, and there she was, at ease with herself and her occupation, beautiful, commanding, secure in her abilities.

She's who the Artan should be, I realized bitterly. *Not some plain-Jane nobody like me. She could inspire anyone to do anything—I couldn't inspire a hen to go sit on her own eggs.*

"Lady Hannah?" Rittean's sweet voice crashed my pity party, returning my focus back to herself. "They have come a long journey at the High-Chief's request to see you. Will you not make them welcome?"

Do I have to?

Okay, so maybe I wasn't quite ready to face the Cortain Pronconcil, even though I knew the whole thing of her unconsciously showing me up was stupid. Or maybe my problem lay with Risean. I had to admit, in my heart of hearts, I was still carrying a grudge against the old Moonkind for being the one to bring me here against my will. Nevertheless, keeping all this to myself, I meekly followed my friend over to receive the visiting group.

"Hannah, child." Risean smiled to see me coming. He extended his hands in welcome clasping my fingers within his own. "I see you fare well. This pleases me."

Yeah, and it's all about you, isn't it? I thought as he bent to plant a fatherly kiss on my brow.

Whoa, where'd that come from?

Shocked by my own cattiness, I glanced guiltily toward Rittean, only to see her beaming at the two of us. No jealousy marred her expression. She was just happy—happy that her father cared for her friend.

I felt about two inches tall. If Rittean could be that sweet, that accepting, that welcoming, why couldn't I let go of bitter feelings against her father? It wasn't like he was the only one responsible for dragging me here. Not to mention, if it were true, I was the Artan—which was looking more and more likely—maybe they'd simply done what they had to do. Ashamed of my unkindness, I silently vowed to be more like the Moonkind girl and release unnecessary grudges.

Life's too short for that, I decided, and offered Master Risean as cheerful a "thank you, it's good to see you" as I could.

I almost meant it, too.

Afterward, I turned to the others, and we made polite exchanges. At this point Aureeyah joined us, her gentle aura nearly invisible in the bright afternoon sunshine. That worried me. When I'd first met her beside the stream, during the journey to Treygon, her aura had been one of the first things I noticed about her. It didn't glow so vibrantly anymore, even at twilight. Somehow, I was afraid to ask why.

With everyone's attention now on the forest fairy, Rittean drew me away from the group so we could talk privately.

"My father spake true," she offered. "You look exceeding well."

I quirked a grin. "Why, thank you. I guess I'm doing pretty well on the whole."

"Your appearance has altered since we last met. You no longer look so…young, so bewildered."

I grimaced. "Young—I hadn't noticed, but I guess all the stuff I've gone through since leaving Laytrii is enough to mature anybody. As for bewildered? Hmmmm…parts of Aerisia I'm getting comfortable with, but parts of it I don't know that I'll ever figure out."

"Indeed. Word was sent of all you endured. The Dark Powers, I fear, will not give you an easy time of it. I—I heard of Jonase, and I wept for you."

Naked empathy clouded her happy eyes, making me squirm inside. Did I really deserve such unmitigated kindness?

"Well, it's all over now," I responded a bit gruffly, still loathe to think of that creature and his attack. "Besides, it was pretty much my fault."

At this, her sorrow subsided and the merry Rittean instantly resurfaced. "Indeed, I heard tell of this too! Your independence will be the cause of much suffering," she warned playfully.

"Hey now, I would think that'd be an admirable trait for the Artan," I protested.

"Admirable when used wisely," she reproved with a wink. "Come." Looping her arm through mine, she led me further apart. "In all seriousness…you are well?"

"Yeah, well, like I said—on the whole, I'm doing okay." I shrugged.

Accepting this at face value, she dropped the subject. "And where were you when we arrived? I saw you not."

"Walking off frustration. Or trying to."

"Frustration? Why are you frustrated?"

In her eyes I saw understanding, a willingness to listen. Desperately in need of a sympathetic ear, I poured out the whole story of the past few weeks, beginning with the arrival at Treygon and continuing on to the present. I held nothing back, telling her things I hadn't even told Aureeyah, such as my fears that I would never succeed in learning to wield magic and thus end up a failure as the Artan. Of my annoyance that the fairy always sided with the Simathe High-Chief and that she refused to share all she knew concerning me as the Artan. I explained how frustrated it made me that I nearly always bungled attempts with both weapons and magic. And I told her about Ilgard's kiss.

Throughout my tale of weal and woe, she listened patiently, sometimes interjecting advice, suggestions, or sympathetic murmurs. But when I admitted the biggest secret of all—the kiss—her jaw dropped. She was dumbfounded.

"Surely you jest!"

"Nope, 'fraid not."

Unconsciously I glanced about, seeking the object of our discussion.

"But…the High-Chief? Surely this cannot be!"

"Oh, but it *is*."

And there he was, approaching Lord Garett, the Ranetron High-Chief. His back was to me, his cloak stirring in the breeze. Rittean tracked my vision. Watching Ilgard, she leaned on her moonstone-tipped staff, a frown creasing her ivory brow.

"Well. I must confess myself to be at a loss. Verily, I am so astonished that I, well…I have no words."

"That's because there are no words. I was shocked myself. I mean, who would've thought?"

"Have there been any further…attempts?" she quizzed delicately.

"Nope. Ever since the night my magic appeared, he's gone back to being his regular self. Which means he pretty much just ignores me."

"This was the same night he helped you recover the lost memory?"

"Yes, it was."

"And how did you feel about this…recovery?"

"How did I feel about it? I don't know. It felt weird, I guess. Naturally I've never experienced anything like it. Why do you ask?"

She shrugged evasively. "What is it like, this *Joining*?"

My gaze drifted again toward the Simathe High-Chief. "It's strange. It's like—like I have this kind of awareness of him. It's not constant, but whenever he's close by, I usually feel him right before I see or hear him.

"When he did the memory thing, it was so strange. I could feel him inside me—inside my mind—but it wasn't like an alien presence or anything. It felt bizarre, but not...not..." I searched for the right word.

"Wrong? It did not feel wrong?"

I nodded. "I suppose that's one way of putting it. It didn't feel wrong. Sometimes," I continued, "I wonder what this must be like for him. From all I've been told, the awareness, the sensations, must be extreme on his side."

"Why would you wonder this? Why concern yourself with what he undergoes?"

I scowled at my friend. There was a secretive set to her mouth that I didn't like. "I'm not concerned about it. I'm just curious."

"Ah."

"What do you mean, 'ah'? Why are you asking all these weird questions, anyway? What's gotten into you?"

She flicked a sneaky glance toward the Simathe then back to me. "I am merely conjecturing."

"Merely conjecturing what?"

"If the time you have shared and all you've endured may have altered your opinion of him."

"Opinion of who, Ilgard?"

I peeked his way. When I looked back, Rittean was watching me with a gleeful, cat-that-ate-the-canary smirk.

"Hah—no way! I may not be afraid of him like I once was, but there's no way on earth that I actually like the guy."

"Mmm-hmm."

"Really, I don't."

"Mmmm."

I threw my hands in the air. "You are being so annoying about this—you and Aureeyah both. If I didn't know any better, I'd swear the two of you were trying to set us up."

I didn't trust her full-blown smile. "Set you up?"

"Yeah, you know, like help us get together. Like each other. *Fall in love.*"

"Ah." Her eyes twinkled mischievously. "Nay, we've no such devious purposes. We merely watch and wait. You can hardly blame our interest, after all. Never, you see, has a Simathe spent so much time with a woman as the High-Chief with you. Never before has a Simathe *Joined* with a woman." She winked. "And I have my doubts as to their kissing one, whether out of anger or no. You cannot fault us for speculating on what the final outcome of all this may be."

I groaned. "Oh please! Things are *not* like that between us, and I sincerely doubt they ever will be. He ignores me, and I don't like him."

"So you say."

"Whatever." I rolled my eyes at the cryptic comment. "Let's talk about something else. Why are you all here?"

"Various reasons. The High-Chief sent word that you might welcome visitors and dispatched warriors as guides. I believe there is news from abroad to be shared with the High-Chief, and there was—there *is*—a gift to be presented to you."

"A gift?"

"Aye, my father has deemed it time."

"What kind of gift?"

She smiled. "Come, see for yourself."

She laid a hand on my arm to guide me back to the group, but before we reached them, I paused, needing to voice a question niggling at my brain.

"Rittean, did Ilgard really send for you?"

She looked bewildered. "Aye. I have said so, have I not?"

Pursing my lips, I cast a pensive glance toward the enigmatic Simathe lord.

Wow, that was a nice thing to do. Wonder what got into him? Maybe he's trying to make up for our argument. Maybe he really does have feelings, after all. Hard to believe, but I guess anything's possible.

Chapter Eight

Sword of a Queen

The object was long, slender, and draped in thick, red velvet. I reached for it, feeling all eyes on me. As I took the gift from Risean's wrinkled palms, the scarlet covering slid off, landing in a graceful heap on the grass. I was so enraptured with what I saw that I didn't even notice.

The gift was a sword. Lightweight, sturdy, its polished steel glittered in the fresh afternoon light. Neither long nor short, it was of medium length and almost dainty—clearly, a weapon designed with a woman in mind. Its hilt was shaped into a tree, which was deftly, delicately, intricately carved. I worked my fingers into natural grooves between the branches, marveling at how well it fit my hand and felt so *right* in my grasp.

On both sides of the blade, letters were engraved in a handsome, flowing script. Haltingly, I read them aloud.

"Balos tein apone loy d'afey madross."

"'Using this blade, I vanquish evil,'" the Moonkind Tredsday translated softly. "My lady, do you recognize the sword's hilt?"

Upon closer examination, I realized that, yes, it did seem familiar. "Is it…the Living Tree?"

The old man smiled proudly. "It is indeed. What you hold now in your hands is none other than the sword of Laytrii, crafted by her husband, Lord Ranetron."

"He made it?"

"That he did. The man is reported to have been as skilled a sword smith as a warrior. In this gift to his bride, he utilized the best of both."

"Yes, I can see that."

Carefully, I ran my fingertips across the blade's underside, tracing the engraved lettering. "It's so beautiful," I marveled aloud. "So—why are you giving it to me? Doesn't this belong in a museum?"

Perhaps Aerisians didn't know the word *museum*. Ignoring the latter question, Lord Elgrend answered the first.

"You," he said, "are our Artan, and as such this weapon rightfully belongs to you. With it, may you do as did Laytrii and the first Artan: subdue shadow and deliver our land from the taint of The Evil."

Shrugging, I said cautiously, "Well, no offense, but from what I hear, those two women—great as they were— didn't exactly crush The Evil. If they had, I don't think I'd be standing here today."

"They made war upon The Evil, and they vanquished it for their day, their time, and their people. So much would we all do, and no more may any do. Except yourself," the High Elder added. "You, as the Artan, have been given the opportunity to do far more than they in not only annihilating The Evil, but also mortally wounding the Dark Powers, so they may never again overtake us."

Engrossed by this astounding idea, I couldn't form a reply. This beautiful sword, bestowed upon me as the Artan, held equal symbolism with the necklace I already wore. Both were reminders of Aerisia's two most famous heroines to whom they'd once belonged. Heroines whose examples I was to follow, and even surpass.

In that moment, I could feel the trust, the responsibility, placed in me by these folks as tangibly as I felt the weapon in my hands.

Chapter Nine

Swordplay

Turning from the group, I stepped a safe distance away to test my new weapon. Hesitantly at first, but then with broader, sweeping strokes copied from watching the Simathe, I experimented with the weight and balance, amazed that it felt so *right* in my grasp, as if it had been crafted to fit my hands. I'd never dealt with swords, so this came as a surprise. What should've been awkwardness and hesitancy was instead a growing confidence that made me want to brandish the weapon and test it in real battle...

A quick, half turn sideways. I brought the weapon up, thinking only to slice empty air, but I was met by strength and metal. Steel clanged in my ears as a second blade stopped mine, sending a peculiar quiver through my arms.

"What th—" I stumbled but recovered my balance. "Ilgard, I might have known!" I huffed, stamping my foot. "Is it your personal duty in life to do whatever you can to annoy me?"

He answered with a movement faster than my eyes could follow, his sword snaking out, slapping mine and all but tearing it from my grasp.

"What was that for?" I cried, lunging to recover it before it fell.

He shrugged. "You've a weapon. Use it as a sword, not a plaything."

"I wasn't using it as a plaything! I was getting the feel of it. And this is hardly how you train someone to use a sword," I retorted, but what did I know? Maybe this was an accepted method of sword training.

Refusing to confirm or deny the accusation, he poised with sword drawn, awaiting my next move. Common sense dictated that I back down before I made a fool of myself in front of my friends. My pride, however, was stung, and I'd had just about enough of this man always besting, ignoring, or literally lording it over me.

Maybe it was idiotic—actually, of course it was—but I heard myself snap, "Fine, be that way. Take this!"

With all my might, I swung my sword toward his. As might be expected, his blade blocked mine easily. Nevertheless, the instant our weapons connected in a ringing blow, another odd quiver—different from the first—raced through my body. Simultaneously, what should have been a beginner's attempt morphed into a master's deadly stroke. My blade slipped over and around his in a wicked caress, driving straight for his heart. Only his own well-honed skills prevented a mishap. Leaping backward, swinging at the same time, he deflected the tip of my sword before it punctured his chest.

As he sprang away, so did I, landing in a defensive crouch. "What's the matter, High-Chief? Surprised?" I mocked. Shifting my stance, I set my feet, Laytrii's sword gripped tightly in both hands, held at arm's length and to the side of my face. "Afraid? Surely not. C'mon, let's do this." Fathomless, alien eyes flickered over me—wary, as though he'd never seen such a sight. "Shall we dance?" I taunted him, unafraid.

Then I charged.

If warfare is revelry and the battlefield a ballroom, then our merging was a tango of steel enacted on the bare dirt of Treygon's weapons ring.

The glint of sunlight on metal. The rush of wind past my face as my blade flew to meet his. The jarring of impact. The merging then drawing back of footsteps. The advance, the flight. During all this I was no longer myself, a complete novice with a brand-new weapon. Somehow, my lack of experience meant nothing. Hannah Winters from Earth had been left behind. No longer was I flesh and blood, human, or even a woman—*I was my sword.*

Every atom, every particle of my weapon, I could feel like sweat on my skin. I was tireless, ruthless, fearless. I was cold, inanimate metal brought to life. Possessed, I had abandoned human thought, human feeling, human strength that ultimately turns to weakness. I was invincible, but so was my opponent. For every thrust I offered, there was his weapon to turn me aside—narrowly at times, but he wasn't giving in.

How long we fought, I can't say. I suspect our dance of steel could have been sustained indefinitely. I couldn't tire while so entranced, and I know a mere bout of swordplay meant nothing to the High-Chief of the Simathe. Before it finished, we'd battled all over that weapon's ring and even the training ground itself—back and forth, up and down, in and out. Neither of us could gain an advantage. A detached slice of my mind marveled at how much flesh and blood could endure. Why was he not tiring? When would he make a mistake? Something trivial that I could capitalize on, use to end this match, and come out on top?

But the man wasn't mere flesh and blood. He wasn't even human. He was Simathe. And defeat wasn't in his nature.

The end came unexpectedly. Once again, we were trampling the ground where our skirmish had begun. Faces blurred and clothing was a swirl of color as I whirled to block a blow, came up, and found my blade locked in a straining hold against the weapon of my enemy. That one second of hesitation was enough. Faster than a heartbeat, the Simathe's free hand flashed toward his belt, and there was a dagger at my throat. Unintentionally or not, he pressed too hard and its tip pierced skin. A drop of blood splashed onto my bare sword arm.

That was all it took. I woke up.

As soon as that drop splattered, red, wet, and sticky, the spell was broken. I was human again, no longer my unyielding sword, which dropped immediately from my hand. My knees buckled, and my head drooped, too heavy to support.

What's wrong with me? Am I dying? I've never been this tired in my life!

In a haze of nausea, I stumbled away from the dagger, from my opponent, from Laytrii's sword. Exhaustion slammed me like a bat striking a ball. I couldn't support myself any longer and fell to my knees, panting, gasping for breath, my heart racing a million miles a minute. It was as if time had been suspended for my body during the fight as flesh became steel and steel's stamina became mine. Now flesh was flesh, and I was used up, unable to think or speak or even hold up my head.

Over frantic laboring for breath, I caught the sound of approaching footsteps, followed by the stiff creak of leather boots as someone knelt before me.

"My lady?" A large hand, coarse and weathered, lifted my face.

I squinted, straining to focus bleary eyes. "Ilgard?"

"Aye, me. Are you well?"

If I hadn't known any better, I'd have sworn he almost sounded concerned.

My panting had lessened to the point that I could rasp a few words. "Help me up, will you?" I whispered, and his arm went around my waist, hoisting me to my feet. Lightheaded, I swayed and would have collapsed if not for the warrior's support.

What is going on? I wondered fearfully. *Whatever just happened...is it going to kill me?*

A tumult of voices dizzied me. I couldn't distinguish what they were saying, and I really didn't care. If I was going to die, or even pass out, it wouldn't be out here in the Simathe training grounds. Maybe I didn't have a lot of self-respect, but I had too much for that.

"My lady—"

"Let's just go in, okay?" I pleaded, interrupting whatever my companion had planned to say. Thankfully he didn't argue but tucked me under his arm and helped me back inside the fortress.

Chapter Ten

Classifications of Magic

Seated on a low couch in one of Treygon's inner rooms, I was surrounded by people. The hustle and bustle of conversation about what had just happened finally died away. Briefly, silence reigned.

Time for some hard facts, I told myself, and finally voiced the question I'd been dying to ask: "What's really going on here?"

Even though several different theories had been tossed around, I'd noticed Aureeyah, Risean, and Lord Elgrend had remained strangely silent, keeping their own counsel. I looked right at them when I spoke and caught their subtle exchange of glances. Clearly, they were thinking,

How much do we tell her? What *do we tell her? Can she handle the truth?*

I think I surprised them by stating firmly, "I want to hear everything you're not saying. I'm sure you know what this is all about, and I'm pretty sure I deserve to know too, so please tell me."

Another wordless exchange. Aureeyah, the first to break away, said, "I did not foresee this—though I allow I should have, considering her unique heritage."

"Do not condemn yourself for what we all failed to anticipate. Even the knowledge of fairies is not limitless," soothed Master Risean.

"Excuse me? What's this all about?" I broke in. "You didn't think to look for what?"

"Tell me, my child," said the old Moonkind, setting my inquiries aside. "While observing your fight, the fairy, the High Elder, and myself concluded that you...well..."

"That I what?" I prompted impatiently.

"When you fought, did you feel as one—*overtaken* by your weapon, perhaps? Overtaken, or even that you had...*become* your blade?"

"Overtaken? Yes, I suppose you could say that. I know that sounds strange—"

"Not so strange," the fairy interjected. "We knew this had to be, when you held your ground while crossing swords with the High-Chief."

I stole a peek at Ilgard, who was leaning against the opposite wall, a little removed from the rest of the group. Although the Simathe's face was quiet, his black eyes were reflective. He watched me closely, corded forearms folded over his chest. When our stares caught, I quickly looked away.

"But what happened?" I insisted, turning back to the threesome. "How on earth could that be—me, becoming my weapon? I've never heard of anything like it."

"Hannah..." Seating himself beside me, Risean picked up my hand and clasped it between both of his. My first instinct was to pull away, but I fought it down.

Live and let live, I told myself. Besides, I had more important things to worry about right then than any lingering bitterness between us.

"Permit me to explain," he said, and I was all ears. "In Aerisia, we believe there are two primal forces governing and imbuing all things. One is good; it is light and life and all things beautiful and perfect. The other is evil; it is darkness, shadow, suffering, pain, and death. All things, we believe, subsist by the express result or particular intervention of these two forces—the forces of good and evil.

"Now, there are those among us born with the ability to *Command* a measure of these forces. To not only be empowered by them, but also to *Command* them at will. Do you understand what I say?"

"I think so. You mean people who possess what we might call magical powers are really *Commanding* either the forces of good or evil to do what they want. Which means, I suppose, that people like you *Command* the forces of good, while those like Jonase...evil?"

He smiled, nodding his bearded chin. "Aye, just so. Now, there is a second method of employing magic besides this."

"You're saying there's more than one way of working with magic?"

"There are, in point of fact, two. While we are able to wield magic, using it to accomplish many things, we do not magically *Become* things."

"Not *Become* things?" I echoed, confused.

"An example, my dear. When you destroyed the pillow, you *Commanded* magic, albeit unwittingly, in order to protect yourself. But when you fought the High-Chief, you *Became* your sword. You did not *Command* it to do your bidding, you *Became* it as you wielded it." He leaned closer, intent. "The difference is vast. While some *Command* magic, some use magic to *Become* an object. Can you see this?"

I nodded cautiously. "Yes...I think so. Are you implying that I can do both?"

"Yes, both," spoke up Aureeyah, edging around to stand before me. "Never before has anyone possessed the gift of wielding both. Far more common to *Command* than *Become*. That is why we were so astonished by your earlier display—we did not expect you to be blessed with the gift of *Becoming*. Foolish of us. You being the Artan, we should have known to look for it. Even the prophecy—"

She broke off with a glance at Risean that seemed tainted with fear.

"What is it? What about the prophecy?"

But they ignored me and, after a tense moment, lapsed back into the discussion.

"Aye, because you are the Artan, it seems only right that you of all people should be sanctioned both to *Command* and *Become*. We may have failed to foresee it, but now..." Risean beamed with joy. "Now, we see yet another proof that you *are* our Artan. The evidence is incontrovertible."

Expelling the air from my lungs, I slumped against the back of the couch. As if matters weren't confusing enough already!

Once more, I addressed the fairy. "But Aureeyah, you told me fairies were neither human nor spirit, but sort of a mixture of both. You told me the same life-force that causes plants to grow, mountains to endure, and nature to thrive is what makes the different fairies what they are. If that's true, then shouldn't you also *Become* as well as *Command*?"

"Not so, my friend. You see—" She claimed a seat on my other side, gesturing with graceful hands as she spoke. "We fairies are indeed imbued with the life-force of our realms, as I told you. Howbeit, our capability is still to *Command* the magic in our dominions, for it is us and we are it."

"But if you're a part of the forest—"

"I *am* a part of the forest, yet I do not *Become* my forest when I work magic."

"It is similar with us." I turned back to Risean. "As people of the moon, we wield certain powers, but we do not *Become* the moon or our moonstones in order to do so. Can you not see this?"

"I—I think so. It's all pretty confusing."

He smiled kindly, wrinkles emerging and lines deepening around those tropical-water eyes. "I am sure that it is. Nonetheless, as the Artan, you have proven yourself blessed to employ both forms of magic. You must therefore strive harder and learn to direct them at will."

"But I've tried and can't seem to catch on," I protested, feeling more than a little overwhelmed, not to mention put out.

Work harder, huh? Thanks, like I've been sitting around on my butt doing nothing. You've probably been using magic your whole life. Me? Until a little while ago, I didn't even know it existed! Gimme a break here.

"The first step in learning to do a thing is to understand you've a knack for it. And now that you know how your magic works, I am confident your skills will grow apace. Possibly, the reason for your prior struggles was that the fairy did not know how unique your talents truly were or how to guide you in their use."

I could buy that.

"But what about different degrees of power?" I wanted to know. "If I, as the Artan, have the potential to someday become far more powerful than either you or Aureeyah, does that mean I'm more strongly endowed with the force of good than either of you? Or that I can wield more of it?"

"Both, I should think," spoke up Lord Elgrend, Aerisia's High Elder. "And while we discuss these matters, I should perhaps clarify that the same is true of those who wield evil, commonly called *black magic*. While the Dark Powers are the powers of night, The Evil are those who serve and are endowed by them to different degrees. Some are far more powerful than their fellows."

"And I'm supposed to defeat them?" I bolted upright on the couch. "Me, just one person against the very forces of evil? That's ridiculous! How in the world do you expect me to do that?"

"Because, as the Artan, you've all the Powers of Good at your disposal; you simply must to learn to wield them. As it were, you *are* the Powers of Good—for if you are capable of both *Commanding* and *Becoming*, you are the greatest wielder of magic who has ever been or ever shall be," Aureeyah stated calmly. "It is your destiny not only to crush The Evil, but also to plunge a blade into the heart of the Dark Powers themselves.

"We have pledged our aid. You will learn to *Command* and *Become* as you desire, and when you do, none shall stand in your way."

Chapter Eleven

Progress

Command and *Become*…those two words had taken on an existence of their own these days. I'd had to relearn their definitions and apply them in ways I'd never thought possible. Two simple words, yet they'd come to dominate my life. Now that I knew better the extent of my magic, the easier using it became. I was getting to the point where I could direct it where and how I wanted. At least I was no longer surprised by feats of magic overtaking me unexpectedly.

The lessons with Aureeyah progressed rapidly and well. The emerald-eyed fairy had become a good teacher, friend, and mentor. The more capable I became, however, the greater grew my fear that she would soon return home, leaving me trapped alone inside Treygon's cheerless walls. I dreaded that day.

The party from Laytrii had left the day following their arrival, and no other visitors had shown up. I missed

Rittean and Lady Elisia, who I hadn't seen since leaving Laytrii's palace. Aureeyah remained my only true friend around here. I liked Cole a lot and got along pretty well with Kan. Nevertheless, no one could truly be said to be friends with a Simathe, except the Simathe themselves. I was an outsider at Treygon and probably always would be, but I was becoming okay with that.

I supposed life in Aerisia, if nothing else, was teaching me how to accept the hard things in life, deal with them as best I could, and move on. I was learning to cope—to simply surrender what I couldn't change or control.

Besides being separated from my family, dealing with Lord Ilgard remained the hardest thing to figure out. Our uneasy alliance was just that. Even though we'd had no more temper flare-ups since our last brawl that had ended in me scrubbing floors for hours, neither had we made any gigantic strides toward being friends. I decided he'd taken to avoiding me, because he rarely trained with me now or acted as my bodyguard.

Even though my lessons with the fairy were now going well, I still kept up my weapons training. I wasn't allowed to use any magic, either, not even to *Become* my weapon. The time might come, Ilgard had explained, when I would be prevented from using magic and would have to rely on strength of arm alone. Should that happen, knowing how to defend myself with a weapon would be imperative. Aureeyah had agreed with him, and so I was learning to use a sword as well as a bow. The yedin, the weapon with which Ilgard had taken out Jonase, I wouldn't touch, however. Neither had I learned to ride the Restless, for all that my biggest fight to date with the Simathe High-Chief had been spawned over that very issue.

Ilgard periodically left on those secret little trips he sometimes took, doing who knows what. I was curious about the responsibilities such a man—as both the Simathe High-Chief and a member of Council—must hold, but I knew I'd never find out. Our truce continued to hold, but we weren't really friends. Despite being *Joined*, he went his way and I went mine.

Apart from all this, I couldn't deny that whenever he left, a part of me seemed to leave with him. I chalked it up to our *Joining*; surely it was this and nothing more. It had to be since one element of it was tainted with need—a need for the protection and safety I felt in knowing he was nearby. Still, I also knew that underlying it all could be a psychological reaction to the fact that he had saved my life.

This was a troubling facet of our relationship that I couldn't overlook, along with the fact that he had kissed me. Obviously, that was something I couldn't just ignore. Of course, that was hardly the first time I'd ever been kissed. I'd dated off and on throughout high school and college, but my parents had encouraged my brother and sisters and me to focus on our studies, and I'd liked earning good grades. Maybe my parents were a little strict; maybe I'd been a little sheltered. I enjoyed going out as much as the next person, but I wasn't much of a party girl, and I'd tended to push romance off toward the future. But the future was now, that kiss was the present, and how was

I supposed to react to it? No matter how much I protested internally, a certain, treacherous part of my heart insisted on wondering what it would be like to share a real kiss with the silent lord.

When I could, I sometimes found myself watching him, studying him—trying, almost, to see what made him tick. Sometimes I would glance up from one activity or another to find him watching me closely, an inscrutable expression on his face. Sometimes it unnerved me. Sometimes it intrigued me. Sometimes it flattered me. Sometimes I wanted to stare right back, although I never did. Sometimes I wondered, *Why? Why is he watching me? What is he thinking?*

I never knew, and my confusion remained.

Despite it all, the days slipped by, blending into one another like a stream emptying into a river. As the next season approached, I detected a rising tension in the fresh autumn air. Something was coming; something was about to happen. I couldn't say what or why, but when I saw Ilgard and Aureeyah with their heads together, or Ilgard and his lords conversing in hushed tones with the fairy, I knew something was up. I was never invited to join their little conferences, and if I approached, everybody shut up in a way that told me I wasn't welcome. I knew there were things they weren't telling me. I could feel it as surely as I felt the changing of the seasons. As fall approached, I could sense both the gradual change in the weather and in the people surrounding me. The clock was ticking, but toward what I had yet to discover.

Chapter Twelve

Going Back

It was early that morning. A chilly mist clung to the ground, tingeing the world gray and damp. Thick, low clouds clinging to the mountaintops obscured their lofty peaks from view. The air smelled of wet earth and fallen leaves. Belying the cool temperature, sweat beaded my forehead and dripped from my chin as I went through another series of martial art-type exercises.

A while back, I'd found it possible to tap into the same bank of pure, explosive energy that had served me in my first two outbursts of magic then channel it into my own body. Once I made the discovery, I thought, *Why not?* If it was true that I could someday be caught off guard with only weapons to protect me, what if I were someday caught off guard with only my body to protect me? Back home, I'd always enjoyed kickboxing classes at my local gym. This was like kickboxing on steroids, and I was having fun.

A couple of straw men propped up on wooden stakes were my victims this morning. The early-morning air stillness was broken only by the thumps of a hand or a foot striking the plump bodies, the whip of fabric about my body, and my swift intakes of breath. I knew one of my Simathe bodyguards stood nearby, but I paid him no mind as I forced myself to go harder, faster, harder, faster, until I was panting so hard my breath wheezed in my lungs.

Finally, I let out a flying kick and successfully knocked the head off my battered practice dummy. With a half-spin, I regained my balance and set my feet, only to double over, hands on my thighs, stretching my hamstrings while catching my breath. My head pounded, and sweat dripped off my face, splattering in the dust. Slowly, I let go of the power, briefly feeling fatigue double as the magic left. Staying in place, I deliberately concentrated on slowing my heart rate and breathing, stretching my limbs and quieting my mind—things Aureeyah had taught me that helped speed recovery—not only physical recovery, but also from magic wielding.

Thankfully, the endorphin high from a fierce workout soon kicked in. Within a few moments I was able to straighten, raise my head, wipe the sweat off my face, and roll my neck out. As I did, I caught an appreciative nod from the guard waiting a couple dozen paces away.

"Well done," he approved.

"Thanks." I flashed back an answering grin.

Catching movement from the corner of my eye, I turned to see Lord Ilgard striding across the training grounds, heading our way. Tendrils of fog swirled about his boots, and his cloak was drawn around his shoulders, warding off the morning chill.

Drawing abreast of us, he jerked his chin toward his subordinate. "Leave us."

"My lord." The other man was quick to obey.

"Lady Hannah." Ilgard stopped in front of me, alien black eyes glittering in the pale, weepy light. "Something has occurred that takes me away."

I frowned, puzzled. The man had left several times during the months I'd been at Treygon without bothering to come tell me. Why was he doing so now?

I had to tip my head back to see into his face. He was a very tall man.

"Um…okay."

He didn't say anything right away. I wondered if I should. The wind picked up, sending a fallen leaf skittering across the practice grounds. The chill breeze touched my sweaty clothing, making me shiver and rub my upper arms for warmth. I wondered what sort of news he was planning to break. Good, bad?

Probably not good, I thought, *since he looks so grim.*

Of course, he always seemed sort of grim, so that actually didn't tell me much.

Finally, he broke the silence. "Lady Hannah, today you will depart, as well."

My heart sank to my boots. Leaving? Again?

"Where to this time?" I asked, numb with disbelief. It wasn't that Treygon felt like anything close to home, but the idea of packing up lock, stock, and barrel and being shipped off to yet another foreign place in a foreign world... I just wasn't sure I could handle it.

"Laytrii."

"Laytrii?"

His answer took a moment to sink in. When it did, I couldn't hide my excitement.

"Really? You mean it? I'm really leaving here? I'm going back to Laytrii?"

"That you are."

I smiled broadly—couldn't help it. This was too good to be true. Leaving Treygon for Laytrii? Exchanging the silent Simathe for the company of Rittean and Elisia? I'd take that trade any day.

"What about Aureeyah? Is she coming too?"

The Simathe High-Chief nodded. "She will accompany you partway."

"Only partway? She won't be going to Laytrii? Why not? I need her."

"Perhaps you should ask her that."

"Right. Aureeyah. I'll go ask right now. Thanks, Ilgard!"

I turned to dash off, but had only gone a few steps when something made me stop and swivel back toward the man behind me.

"Ilgard?"

He turned to face me. "This place where you're going, is it dangerous?"

He hesitated before answering, as if trying to figure out why I asked. "For others, perhaps."

Ah, so it was dangerous. But then, the Simathe were immortal—or said to be. I still had a hard time wrapping my mind fully around that. I supposed it was that small, niggling doubt that prompted me to say, "Be careful, won't you?"

He blinked in surprise, just once. On a normal person this would have been the equivalent of a jaw dropping open in shock. Before he could say anything, I hurried on, "Oh, I know you all say you can't really be hurt and all that, but still—just be careful, okay?"

Something flickered in the darkness of his eyes. "We will, my lady. And you do likewise."

Chapter Thirteen

Pain

Be careful, she had said. Whatever could have prompted that?

Standing in place, the Simathe lord watched her hair swing from side to side as she jogged back toward Treygon's main building. He thought of the mix of feelings, both joy and disappointment, that she had felt upon hearing she was to depart Treygon. Once, to leave had been her fondest wish. Once, she would have cared little what happened to him when he left her.

But no longer. She was changing, discovering herself as the Artan and the Simathe as her allies. And himself, how did she see him? As her friend? Her protector? Or still as her enemy, determined to wreck every chance at happiness? The feelings he discerned in her were confused, at best.

As for himself? Deep down, in a tightly locked place, rarely brought to light, he was confused, as well. On the rare moments he allowed himself to think of her as more than merely the Artan, the woman he was sworn to protect, the Simathe was forced to admit there were things about her he admired. Despite all she'd endured, her spirit had not been broken. She was resilient and pliable to needed change. She could bend rather than break. She was sweet as well as stubborn, good-natured as well as unruly. She was clever, kind to those around her. And she was not afraid to contest him, to tell him exactly what she thought, defying his authority even when she knew it was a futile endeavor.

Perhaps it was her stubbornness and defiance that truly set her apart from all the women, and most of the men, he had encountered in his lifetime. She challenged him, had fought him even while she feared him. And, most incredibly, it seemed she had grown to the point where she feared him no longer—at least, not as she previously had.

At times, the warrior found himself watching her, studying her, memorizing her movements, traits, habits, and quirks of personality. The way she made a point of always thanking the underlings who served her; the way she tried so hard to make Cole and Kan, with whom she was most familiar, break habit and laugh aloud. Her easy friendship with Aureeyah. The way she worked so determinedly at her lessons with the fairy and the weapons training with his men.

He could not help noticing the other things, the small things, the things he should not notice. The way sunlight caught in her hair and the scent of her perfume. The grace of her stride and the quick tosses of her head to fling the hair out of her eyes. The way her mismatched eyes glowed when she grasped a new concept or skill, and the sweetness of her smile, warm as springtime itself. Her laughter brought new light to Treygon's halls and her presence a vivid new life. She fascinated and drew him in, despite his determination to resist. She possessed a mysterious strength contradicting her tiny frame; she was a beautiful mystery he wanted to unravel.

In the end, however, she was a woman. The Artan. And he was Simathe. He would not marry, and her future lay far apart from him. Yes, he had vowed to safeguard her, to follow her, and so he would. He would even give his life for her, were that possible. But she could never be his. And at that unspoken realization, a part of him, before unknown and sheltered away, began to hurt.

Forget this, he told himself.

Best to disregard all thoughts of her as anything more than the Artan who commanded his allegiance. They were from different times, different worlds, and faced different destinies. It was never meant to be.

Alas, even when he wanted to forget her, the bond *Joining* them together would not permit it. Day and night he felt her presence, experiencing her joys and fears in a way no one else could. Had she been any woman besides the Artan, had she not been *Joined* to him, had she not been so different from the rest, he would not think such things about her. He would simply overlook her, as he had overlooked scores of Aerisian women during his life. But

Lady Hannah, this one young woman from another world, he found impossible to overlook or forget.

Contrey's past warnings concerning this very thing rang in his ears as Ilgard bent to retrieve the cloak she had carelessly left behind on the training grounds. He would leave it for her in the main hall before going on with preparations for his own journey. Perhaps, in the quietness and distance of their being apart, he could find time to wrestle some peace for his soul.

Part Two
Return to Laytrii

Chapter Fourteen

Fairy Homecoming

We began the return passage to Laytrii later that same morning. It was as uneventful and easygoing as a trip down steep mountain pathways on horseback could be. Peering over sheer drop-offs that plunged thousands of feet, I found myself extremely thankful I'd been asleep the first time we navigated these trails. For somebody from Colorado who'd traveled plenty of hairpin roads in her day, I was having a hard time keeping my head on straight.

Maybe it was the fact that we were on horseback and there were no guardrails. If it'd been up to me, I would've dismounted and walked. However, my Simathe escorts rode along like it was no big deal—which, to them, I guess it wasn't—and I didn't want to betray my cowardice. Instead, I clung tightly to the saddle horn while my horse hugged the cliffside wall. One false step would have sent us both hurtling over the edge. The whole ordeal was harrowing, to say the least, and I was never so glad to reach level ground. At the mountain base we halted for the night, getting up and leaving very early the next morning before the sun had even topped the mountains peaks.

Strangely, I felt a bit depressed, a feeling that deepened with every new mile put between myself and Treygon. Yes, I was excited to be going back to Laytrii and was also looking forward to seeing my friends again. On the other hand, I knew I'd miss the Simathe stronghold in a very weird sort of way. Or maybe it was their High-Chief? The farther from him we went, the stronger grew the pull inside me for him, until it became an ache I could hardly push aside or ignore.

To counteract the depression and the ache, I tried concentrating on my surroundings or my companions. The scenery was beautiful, wild, untouched, and untamed, as only raw nature could be, but my escorts were disinclined toward speech and I didn't feel like trying to draw them out. Even Aureeyah was strangely silent.

The hours passed and the expedition went on. Just before nightfall on the second day, we reached the thick trees signaling the entrance to the fairy's domain. Entering, we passed under silent boughs whose autumn leaves were now painted brilliant shades of gold, yellow, orange, and red. Aureeyah raised her head, drawing in a long, contented breath.

"My home. I have missed it so."

Her smile was blissful, serene, and peaceful all at once.

I tried to smile back, but my heart wasn't in it. After another mile or so, she pulled her horse to a stop, and the rest of us did the same. Sliding gracefully off her mount, she came to me, placing a hand on my knee and looking up into my face.

"Come, my friend, dismount. I would speak with you."

Nodding assent, I climbed down carefully from the back of my own horse, handing its reins to the Simathe riding beside me.

Taking my hand, she led me off the road, away from the Simathe and into the trees. I noticed her aura brightening visibly the deeper we went into the trees. Sadly, I recalled the way her glow had faded the longer she'd stayed with me at Treygon. Now that she was back in her natural element, her health was being restored before my very eyes. She was home, and her aura gleamed brighter than ever because of it.

Just what had she sacrificed, I wondered, to stay with me all those weeks, to be my friend and teacher, helping me come into my own? She hadn't breathed a word of complaint, but I recognized her sacrifice for what it was and felt gratitude.

She now drew me to a halt beside the banks of the same stream where I'd first seen her several months back. Here she turned to face me, taking my hands in her own.

"I have enjoyed this time spent with you, my friend. I have seen you learn, grow, and change. I perceive in you a strength even you do not fully understand. You carry upon your shoulders the weight of both Aerisia's welfare and her future. I know you will not fail but will succeed in delivering all of us from the Dark Powers' curse."

"Aureeyah," I began, but she cut me off with an upraised hand.

"Nay, my lady. Allow me to finish." Her eyes diligently searched my face. "You have been a friend to me, and for this I thank you. I will never forget your kindness to me, a humble forest fairy. I—"

"No, Aureeyah," I broke in, and this time I would not be deterred. "You're the one who's been kind to me. You've been my friend, helping me, teaching me, and showing me how to do the things I need to do. It's I who will never forget your kindness to me."

This pleased her. Without a word, she stepped forward to place a soft kiss, much like a benediction, on my forehead. When she stepped back, her glowing smile spoke volumes.

"Remember all I have taught you. Search inside yourself, for therein lies the strength to perform the feats required of you. To *Command* lies deep within your person. Visualize what you must *Become*, find its elements, and you will succeed.

"If ever the Dark Powers tempt you to abuse your gifts, remember that you are of the light. You are good. Resist, and the Dark Powers shall have no sway over you. You are the Artan.

"Also, I would advise that, for the time being, you keep the extent of your abilities and the progress you've made in discovering them to yourself and those closest to you. Perhaps—I do not say 'tis so, but perhaps—the Dark Powers have found a willing subject in some person residing in Laytrii. The swiftness of the attempts on your life as soon as you were brought to Aerisia certainly suggests this. If such a person exists, you will not wish to tip your hand. Not yet."

"I'll remember," I promised solemnly, trying to take in this unexpected twist.

A hint of sadness—sadness mingled with pride— glimmered in her lovely emerald eyes. "I know that you will. My lady," she went on, "I know that you have endured many painful trials in your journey thus far. It may be that the Powers are testing you to prove whether you are ready for this or not. It may be that they test you to prove to you that you can overcome all in order to fulfill your destiny. Whatever the case, more hardships may come as you struggle to become Aerisia's Artan. It is your duty to rise above pain and sorrow in order to find the greatness within."

I felt tears gathering in my eyes. "I didn't ask for greatness."

Didn't ask for it, didn't look for it, don't really want it now…

She shook her head gently. "No, but you were born for it, nevertheless. Greatness was—greatness *is*—your destiny. Embrace your destiny, and let go of the past."

I realized what she was asking: she wanted me to forget my old life on Earth and embrace a new one with a new future here in Aerisia. Problem was, I didn't think I was ready for that just yet. Maybe I'd see my family again someday; maybe I wouldn't. But I couldn't let go of them, not without feeling like I was spiraling headfirst into the great unknown without any bits of my former self to anchor me in reality.

I swallowed with difficulty and managed a tight nod. It could've meant anything, but the fairy took it as assent.

"I knew you would agree," she smiled. "Come, the time for your departure has arrived."

Once more she embraced me, bidding me a heartfelt farewell. After answering in kind, I'd already moved to leave when her quiet call stopped me.

"Hannah?"

I spun back to her. "Yes?"

"I would have one final word. Your *Joining* with the High-Chief is a bond that cannot be denied or destroyed. It is something unprecedented in Aerisia's history."

I rolled my eyes. "So I keep hearing. What's your point?"

There was no humor on her face. "My lady—open your heart to love. It is possible that what you share now out of necessity will one day became far more."

"You're saying I might fall in love with Ilgard?" A smile tugged at my lips.

"Love's ways are its own," she said evasively.

I had to laugh, despite her earnest demeanor. "Uh-huh. Well, let me assure you, I seriously doubt Ilgard and I are destined to become love's latest victims."

"Not victims, my friend. Love does not torture or kill. Love nourishes and brings happiness."

I remained unconvinced. "Maybe. But I don't think you need to worry about it."

"I am neither worried nor concerned. Perhaps this will happen; perhaps it will not. However, my long years in this land have shown me that sometimes the one a person will love is the one he or she thinks least likely. Love's ways are its own, and a lifetime with the High-Chief may bring you the greatest happiness you could ever hope to enjoy."

I think she's forgetting the fact that he's immortal and I'm not. What kind of lifetime *could we possibly spend together? Not one that would make any kind of sense.* "Now go," she finished, as if sensing the objections I was raising mentally. And before my very eyes, before I could say another word, she had vanished into her surroundings, leaving me to find my way back to my group alone.

Chapter Fifteen

Laytrii Once More

The rest of the journey to Laytrii's palace was uneventful. To wile away the silent hours, I mulled over the words exchanged between Aureeyah and myself at our last meeting and, as I did so, speculated if I would ever see her again. I already missed her glowing smile and optimistic personality. I decided this good-bye wouldn't be forever. We would definitely meet again.

Once we reached the palace, I enjoyed a happy reunion with my friends, including Elisia, who appeared as delighted to see me as I was to see her. The joy of these meetings served to temporarily eclipse my sadness at leaving both Aureeyah and Treygon behind as well as the constant longing for the Simathe High-Chief, which I no longer tried to deny. Accompanying that longing was a vague sense of unease. Not only did I have to contend with Aureeyah's suspicions of a traitor in Laytrii, but I also couldn't help wondering about what kind of situation he and his men were going into. Would they be safe, return to me okay? Naturally, I had no way of knowing. If only they would just appear. Afraid of what my reaction to seeing Ilgard might be, I both longed for and dreaded that day.

The morning following my arrival, I found myself eating breakfast with my Moonkind friend Rittean, her father (who I was slowly making progress in forgiving), and the Ranetron High-Chief. In the doorway, Cole was a silent onlooker, keeping watch over me despite the palace guards all around. I'd asked him to join us, but he'd declined. I shrugged it off.

Too busy playing bodyguard, I guess, I thought, and went on with my business, leaving him to his.

"Where's Elisia?" I asked after swallowing a bite of the cheese and fruit from my plate. "How come she isn't eating with us?"

"Here I am, my lady." She appeared just then in the doorway, magnificent in a scoop-neck, formfitting gown of deep red. The sides were slashed to flaunt a spun silver fabric, and an ornate silver bracelet was clasped on her bare upper arm. Her glorious hair was caught on top of her head, with wispy curls escaping to frame her delicate face.

"Good morning." I gave her an approving smile. "My, don't you look nice?"

She shot a quick peek at Lord Garett and actually blushed. Then, with a soft "thank you, my lady," she slipped gracefully into the seat next to me.

What's all this?

I slid a glance toward the silent Ranetron lord, who was staring back, utterly transfixed, at the beautiful Spinner. By the look in his eyes, the sun had just risen in this room, and for him alone. I smiled to myself. Maybe it had. Garett and Elisia…now there was something to think about. How long had this been going on?

After exchanging warm greetings with the others at the table, the Spinner picked up an ornate silver fork and speared a slice of pear cut in the shape of a flower. She lifted it to her mouth but suddenly stopped, glanced at me with a slight frown, and lowered fork and all back to her plate.

"Lady Hannah?"

"Hmmm?" I mumbled around a mouthful of food, curious about the odd note in her voice.

"There is something I intended to inform you of last evening. However, in the joy of your homecoming, the matter fled my thoughts."

"Oh? What's going on?"

"There are…there are visitors with us in Laytrii," she replied hesitantly.

I noticed she was shuffling the food around on her plate, looking uncomfortable and no longer hungry. The others had also stopped eating.

"Visitors?"

"Aye, besides you and your party."

"Okay, go on."

"These visitors—they claim to have heard of the Artan's arrival. They say they have come out of a desire to pledge their allegiance to *the Great Lady*."

"The Great Lady?"

"That is what they call you."

"Ah, I see. Go on."

She paused, taking so long to speak that I finally prompted, "And?"

"Well…" Her fork stilled, and she flicked a nervous glance at the table's other occupants, all of whom were watching the two of us in silence.

"I think—that is, I feel something is not—not quite proper about them."

I frowned. "You do? What does everyone else say?"

Again that nervous glance. "They do not feel the same."

"You don't?" This time my question was aimed at my other breakfast companions.

Garett, the first to speak, said, "We do not, my lady. No other members of Council find anything amiss with these visitors." He looked at Elisia, and his next words were offered almost apologetically. "Loath as I am to disagree with my lady Elisia, I fear I find no fault with these people."

"Nor do we," spoke up Risean. Beside him, Rittean nodded her head firmly in agreement.

This is weird.

"Okay then, Elisia, why do you feel this way about them?" I probed.

Her smooth brow wrinkled in thought. "It is difficult to say, really. But, for one thing, they seem to know so much of you. How can this be, when you have dwelt in Treygon these past months?"

"Elisia," the Ranetron High-Chief broke in, voice gentle. (It didn't escape my notice that he dropped her title and called her by her given name.) "The Simathe High-Chief continually sent reports to Council of the lady Artan's welfare and doings. Perhaps these were intercepted or overhead by the servants. And servants will talk. News like this cannot remain private for long, nor have we been overly diligent to keep it so."

"I know, I know," she agreed, though she still looked worried. "But that is just it: how did this news reach them, when even the people of Laytrii remain ignorant of much of it?"

"We've no way of knowing, my lady, who overheard what and who spoke which words to whom. Possibly some of the servants have kin close to or among our guests."

This explanation was offered by Rittean, who'd previously sat silent during the exchange.

"Wait…wait," I broke in with an upraised hand. "Just who are these people anyhow? Where do they say they're from?"

"They name themselves as the Adragon and claim to reside in the village of Adrago. It is far west of here," Elisia clarified.

"Adrago? I haven't heard of it. I guess I thought Aerisia didn't have any other towns besides Laytrii."

Seated on my other side, Rittean laughed. "Oh no, my lady, far from it. Laytrii is our principal city, but Aerisia is a large land with many other cities, townships, and villages. We had never heard of Adrago either, but they say it's a small place and unremarkable, save for its fierce loyalty to Laytrii and the Artan."

"So are you buying their story?" Everyone's faces went blank. "I mean, do you believe their story," I clarified, "about being from this village nobody's ever heard of and all that?"

"It isn't so much that I disbelieve them," Elisia started to say, but her explanation was cut short by a stentorian voice from the doorway of the breakfast room.

"My lord and my ladies," intoned Dilk Wy' Kraux, the palace's Chief Steward. I'd met him for the first time last night. "If you have concluded breaking your fast, an emissary of the Adragon awaits. He has requested an audience with my lady Artan."

Glancing down at the food on my plate, I realized I'd been so caught up in the conversation that I'd forgotten to eat. The white cheese and colorful fruit slices—pears, apples, and oranges—had been cut into elaborate floral shapes that were almost too pretty to eat anyway. Finding I was no longer hungry, I nodded to Dilk.

"I'm done. Where can we talk?"

"With my lady's leave, I shall arrange a sitting room."

His thin face and cool manner were as pompous as his voice.

"Sounds good. Lead the way, please, Dilk. And have someone go ahead and bring in the Adragon emissary."

"As my lady wishes."

The sound of chairs scraping over the marble floor, followed by the echo of footsteps behind me, told me my breakfast companions, as well as Cole, were accompanying me to this meeting. With Elisia's words of doubt ringing in my ears, I found myself relieved I wouldn't be facing this stranger alone.

Chapter Sixteen

The Adragon

The sitting room Dilk led us to was spacious and well-appointed. Covering one wall was a massive tapestry embroidered with Ranetron in shining armor mounted on proud white horses. Simple, elegant furnishings were scattered about, including a small, carved table on which sat a delicate crystal vase containing a long-stemmed pink rose. Two huge floor-to-ceiling archways, side by side, led out onto the open balcony. Brilliant sunlight streamed into the room from there, lighting up all four corners, except one. It was there my visitor sat.

He stood when we entered, rising slowly from a large wood and leather chair. "Great Lady," he addressed me, dipping his head in deference. "May it so please you, I am Raycold Wy' Foarage, emissary of the Adragon." His deep voice rumbled in his chest, reminding me of a growling bear.

All this holding audiences stuff was definitely brand-new territory for me. Learning good manners as a kid had never included how to handle suddenly finding yourself thrust into an antiquated-type position of authority in your early twenties.

"Welcome, Lord Raycold, to you and your people," I returned with a friendly smile, doing my best to sound both welcoming and properly formal. "Please, have a seat."

He did so, slowly. His every movement seemed a study in deliberateness.

The rest of us quickly found places to sit, and in the moment of silence that followed, I had an opportunity to study my visitor. He was tall, broad-shouldered, and dressed very oddly. His shapeless robe was some nondescript brownish-orange color I couldn't identify. It wasn't neatly belted, like the Moonkinds', but fell loosely from shoulder to floor, hiding any hint of body shape or even a glimpse of his feet. I couldn't see any jewelry or weapons, but he could've easily hidden the latter under the folds of that robe.

Although his hair was the typical Aerisian strawberry blond, it was dull, shaggy, and looked none too clean. Lord Raycold also sported a long, scraggly beard with a few stray hairs longer than the rest trailing to the middle of his chest. I couldn't help noticing that his hands, the only body parts visible besides his face and a bit of his neck, were smudged with dirt and his nails encrusted with grime.

Part of me was amused by all this. *Maybe the Adragon are the hippies of the Aerisian world,* I thought, smothering a smile. *Wonder if they'll be smoking funny plants in their rooms here at the palace?*

The idea of that kind of behavior within Laytrii's clean, pristine walls was pretty hilarious. However, I also couldn't help a twinge of annoyance.

You'd think he could've at least washed his hands before coming to see me. I mean, that's just common courtesy when you visit anybody.

Elisia, always polite, was the first to break the silence, inquiring graciously if the Adragon had found suitable lodging within the city. That was news to me. I guessed not all visitors were automatically invited to stay in the palace itself, which made me rethink my idea of a smoking fest here in the palace. However, the notion of it occurring within city walls was nearly as outlandish.

Lord Raycold assured the Spinner that they had indeed found lodging. I noticed that while speaking he flashed a sweet smile her way, but afterward his attention instantly returned to me. He'd done nothing but stare at me from the first moment I entered the room. It gave me a creepy feeling, especially since his green eyes seemed so empty and his stare so flat.

A fleeting memory of Jonase flashed in my brain, and I felt a shiver race down my spine. Just as quickly, I reminded myself that I was being judgmental. Just because this man wasn't the cleanest guy in the world, and wouldn't stop staring at me, didn't mean I had the right to take an instant dislike of him. After all, maybe no one had ever taught him better.

Be fair, I warned myself, and launched into the business of trying to make conversation with this stranger.

From him, I learned that Adrago was indeed a small village far to the west, situated along the Swinde River. His people had never forgotten the terrible days when the Dark Powers had ruled the land or the first Artan who'd opposed them. They'd allegedly served her way back when and afterward had remained faithful, watching for the new Artan who was to come. Now that she was here, his people had sent emissaries to come pledge their allegiance, binding themselves forevermore to my service.

During our interview, he appeared polite and eager to please. He answered each question we asked with a smile so sweet, so guileless that it felt almost fake. Not surprisingly, the longer we talked, the more I found myself wanting to agree with Elisia. There was something about this man and his saccharine smile that rubbed me the wrong way. On the other hand, several people in Aerisia had rubbed me the wrong way from the start—including a certain Simathe High-Chief—but I didn't really distrust any of them. Bearing this in mind, I decided to try and give the Adragon spokesman the benefit of the doubt, at least until I found time to study him and his people further.

After an hour or so, our meeting drew to an end, and we all stood to make farewells. As we exited the room,

Elisia leaned close and whispered fiercely in my ear, "I do not care for that man. I just do not like him."

I tossed a quick glance over my shoulder at Lord Raycold. Having risen from his seat for the farewells, he was now slowly following us at a distance and out of earshot. As he crossed the floor, stepping out of the shadows and into the light streaming in from the open archways, I saw him stop, pull the deep cowl of his robe up over his head, and let it fall forward, completely obscuring his face.

Creeeepy, I thought, feeling another shiver snake down my spine.

* * *

Days passed and the weeks went by.

Now permanently ensconced at Laytrii as the ruling Artan—at least, according to them—I was given new duties to perform and roles to play, such as attending every Council meeting. Along with that, a steady stream of people from the nearby city of Laytrii and far beyond had started coming to see me. Every day I sat through long meet-and-greet sessions. The young and old, the rich and poor, the famous and even the infamous—nobody was denied a chance to meet the Artan. Many brought me concerns and grievances that hadn't been settled by Council or the Portex—the city governor or mayor—to their satisfaction, and more and more I found myself peacemaking, placating, mollifying, and even judging.

How well I did the job, I had no idea. There'd been very little in my former life to prepare me for this.

At night, I frequently tumbled into bed worn and weary from another long, trying day. During the final moments before sleep overtook me, the day's events would play themselves out in my head. Had I settled this affair correctly? Made the right call in that one? I second-guessed myself more often than not and wished I had someone wiser and more experienced not only in the ways of the world, but in the ways of *this* world to advise me.

They tried, my friends here at Laytrii, and their help was invaluable. Still, much of the time they were either too kind or else too mindful of my position as the Artan to be painfully blunt, which was exactly what I needed. I couldn't figure out why accepting my role as Artan made everyone think they needed to back off from offering advice. Just because I now knew a few magic tricks didn't qualify me to judge affairs of state, which was pretty much what I was doing. Saying this aloud didn't change much, though.

Desperate, I even approached some of the Simathe attending me here at the palace, but they only let me know that it wasn't their place and these matters none of their concern. I was sure, given the choice, they would've been glad to return to Treygon rather than stick it out with me at Laytrii. Here, they were constantly surrounded by people who disliked and mistrusted them. Some walked far to the side while passing them in the halls, while others stared wide-eyed or even trembled visibly in their presence.

Those too proud to show fear masked it by cold indifference or haughty disdain.

I knew the people around here were unaccustomed to having Simathe on their home turf since Ilgard himself had once told me he only rarely attended Council. However, I couldn't help feeling a little exasperated with them for their attitude. I admitted my feelings had once been similar, but spending several months among the Simathe had forced me to acknowledge that, while they were definitely intimidating, they also weren't going to pull out a weapon at the slightest provocation and go to work with it.

Hopefully that meant I'd matured somewhat. Hopefully, over time, others would do the same. As I bluntly told more than one dignitary who dared question the necessity of a Simathe presence, "If having them as my bodyguards is good enough for me, it's good enough for you." I didn't think they cared very much for my candor, but I didn't let that bother me. The more I witnessed of the prejudice against the Simathe, the more I understood why they spent the majority of their time in solitude.

During this period of my life, even as I settled into a new world, a new place, and a new role, I was often caught unawares by heart-wrenching waves of homesickness. I thought I'd dealt with the loss of my family some time ago, but how could one ever permanently deal with a grief like that? Sometimes the loneliness and homesickness swept aside during the day would overtake me at night. I cried myself to sleep more than once. Many times I'd get up the next morning wondering where I would find the strength to face the day ahead. Some days, all that kept me going was the knowledge that, somewhere on Earth, my family loved and missed me and that there were also people here in Aerisia who loved and believed in me.

And then there was Ilgard.

I wanted him to come back; I didn't even try to deny it anymore. I knew if he were here, I would actually have someone who would pull no punches while giving me the advice I needed. He might make me mad, but hey—at this point, I half-wished I had somebody around at whom I could blow off some steam. Also, if he were here, that would be another reason to keep going and not give up. Precisely why that was, I couldn't say, but I knew it was true.

He didn't come back though, and the weeks went by without a single word from him. If the Simathe here knew something, they couldn't or wouldn't tell. It was up to me to keep myself occupied, which wasn't too hard, considering everything I had to do. Along with everything else, I went back to weapons training on a daily basis with one or more of my Simathe guards. I knew what Ilgard had once told me was right: I needed to learn to defend myself on every level, so we made use of the Ranetron's practice facilities for our training.

Sometimes the Ranetron themselves or Lady Tey would be there. I observed the Cortain Pronconcil with admiration. She was strong, but she was also clever, quick, and nimble. Watching her, I realized the key for a woman to defend herself physically against a man was more a matter of outthinking and outmaneuvering him than physically overcoming him. Clearly, she knew what she was doing since she could more than hold her own in any of the mock battles she entered.

In the evenings, with only Risean or Rittean present, I practiced the things Aureeyah and I had worked on in the privacy of my own bedroom suite. I still felt unsure about all this—the very concept of these skills was so foreign and new. However, as the days went by and I kept trying, I gradually grew more comfortable calling on my magic, bending it to my will, and exploring its depths. I still kept someone nearby who would be able to help, should something go wrong, though.

I remained uncertain what to do or think about the Adragon. They were often about the palace and consistently showed me nothing but extreme deference. To the casual observer, they seemed to want nothing more than to please, but were they a little too eager? Something about them just didn't sit right. Their shapeless clothing— the same for men and women—the loud, hacking cough they all suffered from, and their continual uncleanness didn't help form a good impression. I also found it really weird how they always wore those deep hoods whenever they passed into direct sunlight.

I'd finally questioned Lord Raycold about this, and he told me, "Great Lady, my people's village lies in the perpetual shadow of a mighty mountain called Zor. The sunlight is kept from us by its high peaks and never shines with full strength upon our homes. Since we rarely leave our homeland, we are a people unused to the brightness of this place. That is why we wear these hoods to shade our eyes and skin."

As he spoke, his voice was sincere and his smile endearing. I didn't contest his story, although it seemed pretty farfetched to me. On the other hand, I reminded myself, maybe it was true and I was simply being unfair again.

All that aside, the way the Adragon glided about the palace in those shapeless robes and deep hoods, generally silent except when overtaken by one of their horrible coughing fits, unnerved me. Like my Spinner friend, I couldn't quite bring myself to like or trust them, although almost everybody else saw only their devotion to the Great Lady and their willingness to serve wherever needed. Were Elisia and I the ones being duped, or were they? Were we being harsh and overly critical, or were they being naïve?

More and more I found myself wishing the Simathe High-Chief were here to help me decipher this quandary. On top of that, though, I also found myself worrying about how long it was taking him to arrive. Was he all right? What was he doing? When would he come back to me?

Chapter Seventeen

Rumors

"You know, nobody came to see me today," I remarked to Cole and Chief Captain Norband one day, several months after my arrival in Laytrii. "As a matter of fact, this past month things have slowed way down, and this is the fourth day in a row nobody's come. Isn't that weird? I can't imagine why. I mean, has my breath gotten really bad lately?"

We were walking in the palace gardens, a beautiful spot in the central courtyard, placed directly in the middle of the sprawling palace itself. The setting reminded me of an ancient Roman villa, with doorways and balconies surrounding the enclosed retreat. The Living Tree stood in the center of the gardens, with flowers of every color, shape, size, and variety blooming all around. Shrubs and fantastically trimmed hedges framed the flower beds, and watery music played from numerous ornamental fountains. All in all, it was veritable paradise, and my favorite escape in my new home.

Neither man said anything in reply, not even to the bad breath joke—which they probably didn't get, anyway. The silence was broken only by the sound of their boots crunching on the crushed gravel paths.

"And it was the funniest thing," I rattled on, stooping to admire a lovely purple blossom. By now, I was pretty well used to their silence, having learned long ago that even when making no replies they were listening to me, nonetheless.

Usually.

"You know Rosean? She's been serving me the whole time I've been here at Laytrii—since the very first day, actually. I thought we'd gotten to be fairly good friends, but lately I've noticed she's been acting really weird. She won't hardly speak to me or look me in the eye. She always seems in a hurry to get out of my room, too. I tried asking what was wrong the other day. She said nothing, but I could tell she was lying."

A look passed between the two men. It was over my head since they were both taller than me, but I caught it out of the corner of my eye. Rising, I swiveled to face them, hands on my hips.

"Okay, guys, what is it? I saw that look. You know something you're not telling me."

Another exchanged glance. I couldn't tell if they were discussing something in their mute, telepathic ways or if both were waiting for the other to speak first. As senior officer, Norband finally took the lead, saying slowly, "There have been rumors, my lady, of something amiss."

"Rumors? What sort of rumors? What's amiss?"

The Simathe Chief Captain went on, choosing his words carefully, I thought.

"Whispers abound that perhaps you are not the Artan at all. That a mistake was made in bringing you here. There are even allegations that you..."

"That I what?" I prompted warily when he hesitated.

"That you walk in shadow and are secretly of The Evil."

My mouth dropped open. "*What?*"

"It is true." Cole nodded. "Some say you were planted by the Dark Powers to overshadow the advent of the real Artan."

At first, I was too shocked to think, speak, or move. I just stared, unable to comprehend what I was hearing. However, as comprehension dawned, my immobility was swiftly overtaken by anger.

"And people actually believe that? After all I've gone through, after all that I've lost, after all I've been made to sacrifice for them? They'd actually listen to that crap? Who could be telling those lies about me, anyhow? Why would they tell them? Why? *Why?*"

The rage fled on the last word, replaced by stinging pain. I was hurt. Who could possibly hate me enough to spread such vicious lies? Who had I wronged that they would despise me so much?

Cole must have seen what I was feeling because he stepped forward, laying a hand on my shoulder.

"Trouble not yourself, my lady. As the Chief Captain says, they are merely rumors of rumors. Whispers in the dark."

"They can't just be rumors of rumors," I protested, throat tight. "It has to be more than that. I mean, the number of people coming to see me has totally dropped. And Rosean's been acting so strange… Clearly people are believing there's some truth in it."

The warrior squeezed my shoulder sympathetically.

"Never fear, my lady. We will deal with this. These lies will be quelled."

I sighed unhappily. "Yeah, but maybe the damage has already been done. Besides, how do we figure out who's been starting them? Who do we even look for?"

He didn't bother trying to reply. There were no ready answers. With a final squeeze, he released my shoulder. "Fret not, my lady."

"Aye, we will see to this," Norband promised solemnly.

I looked from one to the other, knowing they would indeed do everything in their power to make sure these lies were stopped. But would it be enough? The origin of rumors already this widespread would have to be difficult to trace. The realization left me depressed as well as angry and hurt. Who would do such a thing? And why?

* * *

Shortly afterward, I made my way from the gardens, head drooping. I felt mentally and emotionally weary, defeated, sore, bruised, and battered. Dejection dogged my footsteps, sending hard questions racing around my brain.

Who's my friend and who isn't? Who can I trust? If Rosean, who's known me since the first day I arrived in Aerisia, now distrusts me, who'll be next? Rittean? Garett? Elisia? And who could be spreading these rumors, anyway? It has to be a person, or persons, of some status for people to believe them so readily. Which means it must be somebody people trust, consider reliable.

The fact remained that Aureeyah had suspected the possibility of a spy at Laytrii. If she was right and there was a spy, was he or she linked to this incident? Could the spy be the one starting the rumors, or could they be allies?

Oh Ilgard, I mused sadly, wrapping my arms around myself, more than half-wishing he were here to talk this over with. *If only you were here. You'd get to the bottom of this; I know you would. You could tell me what to do and who to trust. You wouldn't listen to these rumors...you'd know I couldn't ever do or be what they're saying. Wouldn't you?*

Surely he would. Surely our *Joining* bond, if nothing else, would tell him I was innocent of these terrible charges. Surely when it came down to it, I could count on this man to back me up, if no one else.

For more than an hour I meandered through the maze of palace hallways, with no particular destination in mind. Cole and Norband followed but, sensing my mood, said not a word, maintaining their usual stoic silence. I didn't have the heart to try breaking them out of it, like I sometimes did. Cole, anyhow. The Chief Captain I tended to leave alone. Of all the Simathe I'd ever encountered, I believed he was the hardest and most uncommunicative.

Passing a beautifully carved casement on the west side of the palace, I happened to look out, noticing as I did that the sun was beginning to set. Memories of that first meeting with Aureeyah flooded my mind, of how she'd called Aerisia the land beyond Earth's sunsets. The reflection pricked my numb heart, and I stopped to watch the colors change in the sky. Bracing my hands on the windowsill, I leaned my weight on them, lifting my chin and inhaling deeply of the fresh evening air.

Although the world outside this window was beautiful beyond belief, secretly I was wishing I could somehow fade into that sunset right now, cross whatever barriers kept our two worlds apart, and find myself once more home on Earth, with all the dangers and difficulties of this new world forgotten. Where I could simply be myself and not have to worry about being judged as to whether I was evil or whether I was good.

Artan shmartan. My family wouldn't care jack about any of this. They'd be happy simply to have me *around. That's all that ever mattered to them.*

It'd been so long since anybody had responded to me as *me*, without any preconceptions or expectations of me as the Artan, that I half-wondered if I'd even know how to relate to people anymore who knew me as simply Hannah

Winters. Not as Hannah Winters from Earth, the fulfillment of an ancient prophecy.

Might as well get used to it, I told myself glumly. *Until you get home again, if you ever do, it's gonna be this way.*

The thought was far from cheering. I supposed I was at a very low point just then. I didn't know what might have come of it all, had what happened next not happened when it did.

Movement below in the outer courtyard caught my eye. I shifted my focus to see a Simathe warrior walking past, leading his ebony Restless in the direction of the stables. Everything about him was familiar: the set of his shoulders, the broad scar lining his cheek, visible even from the window. And yet he wasn't one of the men who'd been staying with me here at the palace. I racked my brain, trying to think. Then it hit me.

"Cole, Norband, look! It's Lord Contrey," I exclaimed, pointing down at the man. "They're back!"

Sudden, bright joy flooded my being, driving away the gloom. I knew if Lord Contrey was here, so was his High-Chief. And if there was anybody in this world—this crazy, mixed-up world—who not only knew me as the Artan, but also me as Hannah, it was him. Maybe I'd once resented him having this knowledge; maybe part of me still did. But right now, I simply needed reassurance, and I had to go to him.

Even as, at my excited cry, the two warriors stepped forward to take a look, I ducked by, dashing down the hall. Servants, Council members, and noblemen alike stared in astonishment as I flew past, but I didn't care. The excitement welling in the pit of my stomach drove me forward, telling me to hurry before I lost my nerve, hurry before I second-guessed myself, hurry before I overthought this, hurry before this moment was gone forever.

Finally, I made it to the main hall. I didn't slow but tore through it and then the huge, thick, double doors safeguarding the palace entrance. Slipping outside, I pulled to a stop at the top of the stone steps leading down into the outer courtyard, searching eagerly.

Where is he?

There! I saw him, still too many paces away, leading his own mount toward Laytrii's stables. At the mere sight of him, all worries, doubts, and fears instantly fell away. He was here. All of a sudden, I knew everything would be all right.

"Ilgard!"

I called out to him. At the sound of his name he paused, turning toward me.

Not content to wait, I dashed down the steps and flew across the courtyard, relief and happiness giving wings to my feet.

Chapter Eighteen

Reunion

As they journeyed toward Laytrii's palace, her presence strengthened with every passing mile. The void created by her absence was beginning to fill; the effects of the *Joining*, dimmed by distance and time, restored themselves. Soon he would see her again, and, seeing her, would be able to lay aside the disquiet of not being there, watching over her himself. The sensations were, he knew, a derivative of their *Joining*, but that did not make them any less real.

At last, they passed the gates of Laytrii's palace. He could feel her now as strongly as in the unbelievably intense moments when they'd first been bound together. He detected sadness, worry, dejection, and wondered over the cause. Within her, consuming her, he interpreted a deep longing for something—no, someplace—else.

Then, a quick burst of excitement.

The Simathe lord, having already dismounted, was leading his horse to the stables when he felt her approaching. She paused, called his name. He turned.

She stood at the top of the palace steps. A light breeze teased the fine curls escaping from her upswept hair and stirred her hem about her ankles. The pale green sleeveless overdress, laced up the bodice, was worn over a simple white skirt and a blouse with long, full sleeves. The color heightened her complexion, while the sprig of tiny white wildflowers tucked behind her ear set off her dark hair.

She stood still like that for only a moment, a moment that would be branded forever in the Simathe's memory. The light of the setting sun splashed against her skin, burnishing it gold, glinting off the hidden flames in the dark depths of her hair. Then she was off the steps, running toward him.

This was the last thing he had expected her to do, but, dropping the reins and leaving his mount, he began walking toward her. He progressed only a few steps before she was there, not stopping, flinging herself against him with a little cry. He heard her gentle panting, felt her heart pounding against his chest, and for a split second was unsure what to do. At last, almost of their own volition, his hands came up to clasp her shoulders, pulling her gently against him.

Time stood still as she embraced him fiercely. More than a few seconds crawled by before she finally eased back, lifting her chin so she could look into his face. He saw, then, the tears shimmering in her mismatched green and brown eyes—tears reinforcing the anxiety flooding their bond.

"My lady, what troubles you so?"

"Oh Ilgard…" Her lower lip trembled as she spoke. "Things have been so crazy around here. First the Adragon, then all these people coming to see me to tell them what to do. I don't know what to tell them—I'm no judge! I haven't even finished college! And now this— they're not coming, because they're saying I'm not the real Artan, that I'm actually a part of The Evil! Can you believe that?" Indignation flashed across her face.

"On top of everything else, I was worried about you and your men," she went on. Her fingers fumbled nervously, unconsciously, with the ties of his jerkin. "Maybe it's silly, but I couldn't help it. You were so far away, and I hadn't heard anything from you in so long. Nobody would tell me where you were or what you were doing. I wanted you to come back because I thought if you were here… Oh—" She broke off, pressing her face into his shoulder, muffling her next words. "Never mind. I'm just glad you're back."

Mystified, he held her, attempting to puzzle out the gist of her speech. The approach of his Chief Captain, accompanied by Cole, caused him to look up. Whatever they thought of seeing their Artan and High-Chief in this unusual position, they did not betray but wisely held their peace.

Of what does she speak? he questioned his subordinates silently. *Something has gone awry?*

Much, replied his second-in-command, frowning. *Your timing is impeccable. It is well you have returned.*

* * *

While he washed off the dust from his travels, the Simathe he'd left to watch over the young Artan in his absence filled him in on what had transpired during his absence: the Adragon, the Artan's visitors, the rumors. By the time he was ready to sit down with her and hear her version of events, he possessed a better grasp of what was troubling her. Some of it, anyway. Some of what she'd said earlier still made little sense, but as soon as he seated himself facing her in her own private sitting room, she unleashed a torrent of words.

Among other things, he perceived her insecurities at being thrust into the position of judge, lawgiver, and peacemaker. Perhaps it was unfair of the people to lay this burden upon her shoulders. She was but newly come into her own and had much to learn. However, it was the nature of humans to seek help from those they identified as the highest authority present; he could only warn her she should expect her role to be a complex one.

"At this point in my life, I hardly need any more complexities," she grumbled, and he hid his amusement.

Strange, but he'd thought much the same about his duty of safeguarding her.

Carrying on, she elaborated on the problem of the Adragon and of her distrust for them, which she could not quite put into words. She fretted that she might be unfairly condemning them since no one except Lady Elisia seemed to find fault with the newcomers. There was little he could say beyond reassuring her that he would personally look into the matter and not to let her feelings, either of guilt or mistrust, cloud her judgment.

"The truth will come out," he counseled her.

She was hardly mollified, but she let the matter drop, going on to discuss what he deduced was troubling her the most: the whole, sorry tale of the vicious rumors people were far too willing to believe. Underlying all this was something that troubled her even more deeply, something he sensed her gathering her courage to ask. At last, with her fingers twisted in her skirts and her eyes lowered to her lap, she said, "Ilgard, since we're *Joined*, if I were a part of The Evil... If I was bad, like that, you'd know it— wouldn't you?"

At first, he was taken aback by the halting question and knew not how to respond. Gathering his wits, he inquired gently, "Why do you ask, little one?"

Even the term of endearment slipped by unnoticed as she struggled to formulate a reply.

"Well I...I just thought that maybe, someway— through Jonase or something—the Dark Powers might've tainted me or my abilities. Is that possible?"

Her once clenched fingers were now anxiously twisting and untwisting. Leaning over, Ilgard placed his own hand atop hers, effectively stilling their movement and bringing her distressed gaze to his.

"My lady, had the Dark Powers some sway over you, we would both know it. Shadow catches no victim unawares—its followers welcome it."

"What do you mean?"

Lifting his hand, he went on, trying to explain the matter. "The seeds of good and evil reside in all our hearts. It is we who choose which seed will flourish and which path we will walk."

She frowned a little. "Are you saying that even good people—like, for example, Rittean—have an evil seed in their hearts? And even though they choose not to let it grow, the seed is still there?"

He nodded agreement. "Aye, still there and still troubling us. That is why we all sometimes speak words or commit actions we regret."

A mischievous smile bloomed. "Even you, Ilgard? Don't tell me you've ever been sorry for something you've said or done."

Unbidden, his mind flashed back to the kiss he'd once stolen from her.

"Aye, my lady," he answered solemnly. "Even I sometimes regret my actions."

Another stretch of silence as she took in all this. Then he saw the lines in her brow smooth away, watched them be replaced by a smile. She laughed softly.

"Hmmm…you know what? Off topic, but this is probably the longest conversation we've ever managed without arguing. Momentous occasion, right? We should probably make a note of it, so when we go back to hating each other, we'll have something to look back on."

Where had that notion originated?

"My lady, I have never hated you," he said.

She blinked, taken aback. "You haven't?"

"I have not."

"Oh, c'mon. I know you had to have hated me. Disliked me intently, at the very least."

Rubbing his jaw, he considered her protestations.

"Nay, neither have I *disliked you intently*. I have resented my duty toward you, perhaps..."—and here he chose his words carefully—"but I have never hated or disliked you."

"Isn't it all pretty much the same?"

His gaze was direct. "No."

She pursed her lips, dropping her gaze once more to her lap. "Well, I all but hated you," she admitted, almost inaudibly. "I also disliked you intently as well as resented you."

"But my lady is past that now."

She peeked up through her lashes. "Well, I'm not gonna lie and say you'll never make me mad again or get on my nerves, but I definitely don't dislike you the way I used to."

That was putting it mildly, considering how she'd flown at him in the courtyard. When he thought of it, he was still amazed she had done that publically, despite everything that troubled her.

"Ilgard," she went on, after another brief conversation lapse. "Now that we're on better footing, may I ask you something? Something I've been wondering about for a long time?"

"As you wish."

Tilting her head to the side, she considered him carefully. "Do you—well, all the Simathe, really—do you all, like, want to live forever? Don't you ever think about death and sometimes just sorta wish it would all end?"

The warrior-lord shrugged in simple acceptance.

"Long ago, I learned not to question what is or hope to change what cannot be altered."

"But that's not even human! Everyone does that, even if they know it does them no good."

Again, he simply shrugged. "What would you have me say? We are Simathe. We are not as other humans."

She bit her lower lip, frowning, contemplating this. "Then I'm sorry for you. For all of you," she stated quietly.

"Why? There is no need."

A gentle shrug. "I don't know. It obviously doesn't seem to bother you too much. But to me it seems so sad, so empty. So final."

Her eyes were full of pity, which induced a strange discomfort in him. Never in his life had he been pitied; he was not certain he cared for it now.

"You are not Simathe," he said at last, concluding the matter.

"No," she agreed soberly, "I'm not."

Chapter Nineteen

Twists and Turns

A knock on the door sounded just then, effectively ending our conversation. I couldn't say I was sorry. Right now, I had much to think about, including the way I'd acted earlier in the courtyard. At the time, I hadn't stopped to think. At the time, running to Ilgard had felt right. Now, however, seated across from this silent, imposing lord, I wondered what he thought of it all. Did he think I was crazy? Had he played along, letting me babble on like an idiot without pushing me away, just to humor me? Calm me down? Had he been shocked, affronted, scandalized?

Unfortunately, with him being what he was, there was no way to ascertain his true feelings on the incident, and I was too embarrassed to bring it up, although part of me wondered if maybe I should, if only to apologize for my behavior.

Instead, I called, "Come in," to our visitor and was thankful for the distraction.

The door opened, admitting Rosean, my servant girl. She studied the marble floor while speaking, as if its erratic silver veins were suddenly of great interest.

"My lady, the evening meal has been prepared. Do you wish it served here for the High-Chief and yourself?"

I glanced at Ilgard, a silent question, and caught the barely perceptible shake of his head.

"You may serve me, Rosean, but please have the High-Chief's supper sent to his rooms."

A nervous bow. "As you wish, my lady."

She promptly backed away, scooting out the door so hurriedly it closed on my "thank you."

I turned to my companion. "See what I mean? She's acting really weird."

"The lass is frightened."

"Well, I can see *that*. It's pretty obvious she must be listening to the gossip going around. She's freaked out just being in the same room with me."

Ilgard nodded thoughtfully but otherwise made no comment. Abruptly, he pressed his hands to the arms of his chair, pushing himself to his feet.

"If I might have my lady's permission to retire, I will do so now."

"What?" This made me laugh. "Since when do you need my permission to do anything? Since when do you ask?"

He shrugged. "You are now our ruling Artan."

His expression was utterly straightforward; I couldn't tell if he was joking or not.

"Yeah, right. And I suppose next you'll be coming to me with all your problems and asking my advice on how to rule Treygon."

"Perhaps."

I gave a very unladylike snort. "Boy, that'd be the day."

"It will."

I laughed, rolling my eyes. "Okay, you're obviously just pulling my leg. I know for an absolute fact that's never going to happen."

"Never know anything absolutely," he warned. "The world is easily toppled on end."

As if to demonstrate this truth, he reached for my hand, bowed over it, and brushed the backs of my fingers with a kiss that left my skin tingling.

"Good night, my lady."

I sat there, stunned. He was halfway out the door before I snapped upright.

"Hey, wait a sec—I didn't give you permission to retire!"

He looked back, those deep, alien eyes reflecting a subtle gleam of humor. "Good *night*, my lady."

Then he was gone, the door clicking shut behind him. I collapsed in my chair, emptying my lungs in a heavy sigh.

"And that, Hannah, is why you never underestimate anybody. Even a Simathe."

It was good advice. And I was about to get a lesson in following it.

* * *

A soft knock at my door registered in my sleeping brain, urging me to wake. Groggy, I pushed myself up, blinked a couple times, and croaked sleepily, "What is it?"

"My lady?" A follow-up knock, more urgent this time. "My lady, might I enter?"

Someone wanted to come in, I realized distantly. My brain felt fuzzy, my mouth hot and sticky. I swallowed against the dryness of my tongue.

"Who is it?"

"Elisia, my lady."

Elisia? What in the world is she wanting at this time of night?

Both her voice and her knocking had been no louder than absolutely necessary for waking me. Did she not want to be overheard?

"Come in," I called, pushing back the blankets and swinging my legs off the edge of the bed.

"I cannot my lady. Your door is locked."

"Hang on."

I got up. Grabbing a light wrap off the chair beside my bed, I slung it around my shoulders to ward off the palace's nighttime chill.

"Please, my lady, make haste!"

Her whispers were urgent, fast and low. Something was definitely wrong.

"I'm right here," I said, opening the door.

Not bothering with any niceties or greetings, the Spinner pushed past me into the room, closed the door, and bolted the lock. Next, she pressed her ear to the solid wood as if listening for something.

"Elisia, what is it? What's up?" I whispered.

"Shhh!"

She shushed me with a forefinger to the lips, continuing to listen with her ear pressed to the door. I tried listening from where I stood but heard nothing. Did she think she was being followed? Shoving an unruly hank of hair out of my face, I waited impatiently for my friend to let me know what was going on.

Eventually she pushed away from the door, grabbing my hand. "I do not think anyone is about. But to be safe, we'll talk over here, please," she said, and drew me down on the edge of the bed.

"Okay, what is it?" I repeated the instant we were settled.

She squeezed my fingers so hard I winced. "My lady, I've uncovered a terrible secret."

I felt my entire body tense. "Go on, I'm listening."

She drew a deep breath. "You may have noted my absence from Laytrii these past few days."

"Um, well…" Actually, I'd been so wrapped up in my own problems that I hadn't. "Where did you go?"

"To the Valley of Flax, home of the Spinners. In our halls, we have numerous written records of Aerisia's history. They are called *lorlin*, and I went home to study them."

"I thought you wove stories into tapestries," I interrupted. "I didn't know you kept written records, too."

"Aye, we do. Anyway, as I studied the lorlin I discovered something of weighty significance."

"What was that?"

She frowned, smoothing the skirts on her lap with hurried, nervous strokes. "You know, my lady, that I have distrusted the Adragon since first they arrived. Something about their considerably queer mannerisms prompted a forgotten memory—one which, try as I might, I could not recall to mind. Therefore, I returned to the Valley of Flax, and in a very timeworn, very aged scroll, I found—"

She broke off, surprisingly hesitant to speak it aloud.

"Well, don't stop now!" I protested. "Go on, what did you find?"

"My lady, I found proof the Adragon are not as they seem. In comparing their actions with the descriptions given in the scrolls, I came to believe they are none other than the Doinum."

"The Doinum? Never heard of them."

"Nay, few have."

She bent closer, her emerald eyes burning with intensity and…fear?

"My friend, the Doinum are adamant servants of The Evil. They are ones who have chosen to serve shadow, even from youth. Not only chosen it, but actively served it, living in the depths of a darkness so remote and so blinding, physically and spiritually, that it is as if they cannot tolerate any form of light. Not even sunlight."

"Those cloaks and hoods," I whispered grimly.

Elisia nodded fervently, pleased I was catching on. "Precisely! The lorlin mentioned these as one method by which they shield themselves from light."

"Did it mention any other characteristics shared by our friends the Adragon?"

"Aye, more still. According to the lorlin, the Doinum typically appear as the most wholesome of persons—true servants of the light, helpful to all, kind, benevolent, and generous. Nevertheless, this is only an appearance utilized to hide their true natures."

"So they're basically wolves in sheep's clothing, pulling the wool over people's eyes."

"I am unfamiliar with those expressions, yet I see how they are applicable."

"Right. So basically they appear all sweetness and light, fool people into thinking they are—and then what? What's their point?"

"According to the lorlin, they are used by the Dark Powers for many purposes: besmirching of character, undermining authority or status, assassination—"

"Wait, hold on! Are you thinking what I'm thinking?"

She nodded gloomily. "I fear so. These terrible rumors circulating about you... Doubtless, we've no conception yet of the damage already caused by their lies. Truly," she summed up, "these so-called *Adragon* must be the Doinum."

"Everything fits," I agreed.

"Aye, all things."

"Elisia." I grabbed her wrist. "Who else have you told? How long have you been back?"

"Not long, my lady. I have told only one other."

"Who?" I demanded.

"The High Elder, Lord Elgrend."

"You told him? Just now?"

"Aye, my lady." Anxiety furrowed her brow. "Whatever is the matter? The High Elder is trustworthy. Also, I passed his chambers while journeying to yours. Should I not have told him?"

"I don't know." Releasing her, I slid off the bed. "Did you see anyone in the halls? Did anyone see you?"

She also rose. "The hour is late. I saw some Ranetron; I saw Master Dilk."

"Master Dilk? Why the heck would he be up this time of night?"

"He is the Chief Steward," she reminded me, unconcerned. "His duties in a place this size are many and unending."

Grabbing her shoulders, I forced her to look at me. "Elisia, think hard. Were Dilk and the Ranetron the only ones who saw you? You're certain?"

"Why, yes, my lady. Positive."

I pressed a palm to my forehead. "Okay, I've gotta think. What do we do?"

"The Simathe?"

Lowering my hand, I stared at my friend.

"We might inform Lord Ilgard," she went on. "The Simathe and Ranetron must be informed. I only told you first because I knew you would believe me even if no others did."

"Okay, you're right," I agreed, my mind made up. "The Simathe—we'll tell Ilgard first. C'mon."

Springing from the bed, I grabbed her hand and drew her to the door. Once it was unbolted, we lost no time slipping out into the hallway. Together, we flew down the hall. My wrap slipped off, leaving me wearing only a short, knee-length nightdress. My feet were bare and my hair uncombed, but I didn't once contemplate going back to get dressed.

The Adragon, actually the Doinum. Servants of the Dark Powers. Lord Elgrend knows, and she saw Dilk. She saw Dilk…

Nope. This couldn't wait. We rushed for Ilgard's room.

Chapter Twenty

Murder

"Ilgard, open up," I hissed, keeping my voice low and my knocking quiet. "I know you can hear me in there, so open up this door!"

Trying something I'd never attempted before, I knocked down any barriers checking my stress and let the fear flooding out call to him. I was pretty sure, given the unusual nature of our bond, that he'd feel this, even if he was asleep. I was right. An instant later, his door flew open. I didn't know if he'd been asleep or not, but he was barefoot like me, and his unbound hair fell messily about his shoulders. I drew immediate comfort from seeing the blade in his hand.

"What is it, my lady?"

I dragged my Spinner friend forward. "Here, Elisia will tell you. I've gotta run."

Whirling, I sped off down the hall, hearing the Simathe's voice calling after me, demanding I turn myself around and come back, but chose to ignore it. Some inner urge told me to find the High Elder *now*, and I knew there was no time to spare. As fast as my legs could carry me, I darted through the sleeping palace, speeding toward his chambers. I turned left, dashed down a long hall, and then turned right once more. His room was at the end of this corridor.

All at once, I noticed the unnatural silence. Moonlight dripped from an open window, creating a patch of liquid silver on the floor. Other than this, the hall was dark and murky. Where were the candles, the moonstones? More cautiously, I stole past the window and felt in the wall socket where a candelabra of moonstones ought to be. It was empty, as were the silver sconces on the wall. Someone, surely with foul intentions, had removed all means of light in this short corridor.

This is all wrong.

I pressed my back to the cool marble wall while considering my next move, hardly daring to breathe, knowing my worst fears were materializing. My heart pounded madly, and my mouth was dry. Not only were the moonstones and candles gone, but so were the guards who should've been standing on either side of the High Elder's double doors.

What do I do now?

Although I listened hard, trying to hear anything that might clue me in on somebody in the vicinity, my human ears weren't picking up any noises.

Human ears?

I smiled to myself. *No longer limited to that.*

I was blessed with the power to *Become*…and in the twinkling of an eye, I was exercising some of the new skills I'd been practicing so hard in private. Basically, this involved opening up my mind to the stream of magic rippling beneath the surface of my consciousness. Whereas before it had gone untouched, unnoticed, and unknown, now—once awakened, once purposefully used—it could no longer be ignored, and I found it easily.

It was pure strength, raw magic, unadulterated power in its truest form, and the trick to using it was learning how much to take and where to direct it. I was getting better at figuring this out and now lightly skimmed the surface, dipping in mental fingers and pulling them out, dripping, wet, and cold. Taking the magic, I painted a picture with those fingertips, a picture of keener senses. Better eyesight, better hearing, better smelling, quicker reflexes. I felt the magic drape over me in a silken cocoon, experienced the heady rush of power as I *Became* what I sought. Standing my ground, I allowed myself a few seconds to adjust to these changes. Such increased hearing—I listened hard, able to discern a hundred different noises and whispers. Nothing nearby warned of danger.

Using my newfound sight and physical prowess, I glided noiselessly down the hall, encountering nothing alarming. One of the doors to the High Elder's bedchamber was slightly ajar. Placing a hand on the glossy mahogany, I pushed, entering the room.

I heard no breathing except my own but smelled an odd scent. Tracking its source, I quickly caught sight of the horrid, dark stain on the floor.

Oh no, I plead, even as I advanced forward. *Please no.*

My bare toes touched something wet, sticky. I jerked my foot aside and saw to my horror an ominous trail of what appeared to be smudged boot prints. From the smell, color, and texture, I knew what the intruder had to have stepped in.

"Lord Elgrend?"

Fearfully, I whispered his name. There was no response, but I wasn't expecting one.

Cool night air raised bumps on the bare skin of my arms and legs, while a cold tendril of fear snaked its way around my heart, squeezing hard. Uneasy, I moved toward the bed, catching sight of a pale hand thrusting its way from the tangle of blankets. Licking my lips nervously, I touched it…and gasped, snatching my fingers away. It was already cold. Stiff.

No, no…

With infinite care, I peeled back the rich coverlet. Bile rose in my throat.

So much blood.

It stained the blankets, the sheets, the floor. Up close, the odor was simply overpowering. My stomach turned, and I felt my face blanch. Fighting to maintain control, I studied the scene.

The body lay face up, eyes wide open and staring vacantly. Both legs dangled from the bed's edge as if just shifted over to stand. The long slash across the throat, down the chest, and into the stomach had ripped fabric as well as flesh, baring the victim's insides. The wound was deep, the work of a hungry blade. I stared transfixed at the grizzly sight, my limbs frozen as the corpse's, my mind equally blank.

Then there was a sound, coming from the door behind me.

I should've been afraid, but instinct took over, freeing me from emotions and pain. I whirled to face the intruder. He stood there in the doorway, the glowing moonstone in his hand casting weird, misshapen shadows on the wall and across his face. In the half-light, his eyes gleamed unnaturally bright, and I discerned the outline of a dagger grasped in his other hand, its blade still wet and dark.

"Dilk Wy' Kraux." My voice was amazingly calm. "It was you all along: a spy for The Evil, an ally to the Doinum. You saw Elisia return, heard what she told the High Elder. You knew something had to be done."

A slow, wicked smile transformed the pinched, proud features of his narrow face, but I was unafraid, sensing somehow that my strength was greater than his, even if he was armed with a blade.

"Tell me, Chief Steward," I said, pressing slowly forward. "How did it feel to murder a respected old man you've served for years? Did you enjoy killing someone who's been nothing but kind to you? Are you that sick?"

"Oh, I am far from sick, my lady, but I took pleasure in it."

There was no repentance, no sorrow, no remorse. Clearly, he was proud of what he'd done. Realizing this sealed my determination to act before he could unleash his evil on anybody else.

"That's good, Dilk." I nodded. I was closer now. "Because it's the last thing you're ever going to enjoy. In this life or the next."

The puzzlement on his face told me I'd managed to throw him off guard, giving me the advantage of surprise. Maybe he thought I'd scream for the guards or wait for the Simathe. At most, he may've figured I'd defend myself if he came at me. I didn't think he expected me to attack. He was wrong. An inhuman snarl escaped, born of virulent fury combined with a primal need for revenge. I rushed him.

Chapter Twenty-One

Passion and Fear

Desperate to find his lady, the Simathe High-Chief sped recklessly down the too-long corridors. Even though the necessity of hearing the Spinner's hasty explanation had given her a head start, the bond between them guided him toward her through the silent palace as surely as magnets attract one another. Taking stock of his surroundings, he found himself nearing the chambers of Lord Elgrend, the High Elder. Lady Elisia had relayed to him how she'd first told the High Elder her tale, but why had Hannah felt a compulsion to come here in such haste rather than go to Lord Garett or someone else ready to give aid?

Himself, he had paused only long enough to slip on his boots and tie back his hair before going after her. What the young Artan might be walking into, he did not know, and he wasn't prepared to have her go it alone. He knew he'd been right in this decision when, suddenly, he felt the shock of raw energy that he always did when she

Commanded or *Became*. He next felt a jolt of surprise, then of revulsion tinged with fear, which was followed by a steady, growing resolve. A resolve he was initially uncertain how to interpret. Only when, a trice afterward, came the realization that she was in danger did he recognize the resolve for what it was: the will to fight.

But with the knowledge of her in danger came a forgetfulness of her as the Artan, and he remembered her only as the woman he was sworn to protect, had *Joined* with for that purpose. Pace quickening, he rounded a marble pillar, running at top speed toward the High Elder's chambers. The unfamiliar taste of fear filled his mouth, and he flew toward the place where, even now, she was preparing to fight.

Almost there.

Down the hallway, he glimpsed first the formal robes of the palace's Chief Steward then saw the man's body flail as if struck by a heavy blow. He caught the glint of moonlight on a flashing blade…the man was armed with a viscous, bloodstained dagger. Her blood? Unnatural fear seized him at the thought. The warrior's long strides ate up the ground, but he could not get there fast enough.

Finally, as he was almost upon them, the warrior heard a loud cry from his charge. Again the Chief Steward's body jerked violently, the blow sending him reeling backward into the hall. The man was given no time to recover or respond before his opponent shot from the doorway, aiming a fist and then a kick at the man's head. Both blows landed, throwing him back against the wall. The

Simathe, watching, had no time to react himself before she was there again, her foot connecting with the Steward's stomach. Dilk crumpled but did not fall.

Raising a face twisted in anger and smeared with blood from a cut on his lip, he snarled, "For that I will kill you, Lady."

She edged away, balancing lightly on the balls of her feet. "Think so? C'mon then, Chief Steward. Try it! Try to kill me."

Now was his chance. Ilgard moved to intervene.

"Stay back!" She thrust out a hand but did not look at him, never taking her gaze from the man slumped against the wall. "This is my fight."

"Aye," the other agreed, "and it ends now."

Raising his weapon, Dilk charged. She dodged, leaping aside, and in the same motion hooked her foot around his, jerking hard. The Chief Steward went down but twisted violently as he fell, lashing out with the blade in his hand. Ilgard heard her scream as the weapon sliced the bare skin of her upper arm, but she refused to retreat or back down.

At the precise instant the Chief Steward hit the ground, she was there. Throwing herself on top of his body, straddling it, she grasped his knife hand by the wrist, turning the blade against its bearer. Then, with his fingers still clutching the hilt, she slashed Dilk's throat with his own weapon. Blood spurted, a crimson fountain, but she never flinched. Her eyes locked with those of the dying man, she hissed, "See the result of choosing to walk with The Evil. Now, walk in it forever!" Plucking his knife away, she drove it once, hard, into his heart.

It was only afterward, in the oddly peaceful aftermath, that Ilgard finally approached. Crouching next to her, he laid a gentle hand on her shoulder.

"My lady?"

No response. She was breathing hard, unable to tear either hands or eyes from the knife hilt protruding from the former Chief Steward of Laytrii's breast. Concerned, he tried again, digging his fingers forcefully into her shoulder.

"My lady!"

At last she turned, lifting her face to his. Her eyes were haunted as she whispered softly, "I—I killed him, Ilgard. He murdered the High Elder, and I think I would've been next, but…I just killed a man."

As soon as the battle ended, she'd released the power she held. Now the reality of what she'd done was dawning upon her. The warrior-lord knew there was no time for the remorse and even revulsion most felt over taking a life for the first time. Gripping her wrists, he pulled her to her feet, steering her a few paces from the corpse. Stooping, he ripped a strip of fabric from the hem of her nightshift then rose to bind it tightly around her arm, pleased to see the wound was superficial.

"Come, my lady," he said briskly. "The Chief Steward has undoubtedly alerted the Doinum. We must get you to safety."

A surprising calmness crept across her face, erasing the former remorse.

"No. I'll fight too."

She saw him about to protest and swiftly laid a hand to his chest, saying, "You can't coddle me forever, Ilgard. I'm the Artan. This is my destiny, isn't it? To fight? If not, why am I here?"

The logic of her words hit him like a blow. Though inwardly he cursed, the Simathe knew there could be no arguing against her. All the training with himself and his men, all the training with the fairy and the Moonkind, what were they for if not for now, this very moment?

He had protected her for so long it had become second nature. Stepping back and admitting she was ready to place herself in harm's way in defense of his homeland— now, that was a difficult thing to do. Part of him wanted nothing more than to hurry her off to a place of safety, a place where nothing ever could or ever would threaten her again. It was the curse of the *Joining*, a bond created for the sole purpose of protection. Now, however, he'd just witnessed her work. Did she even require his protection?

He curled his fingers around those on his chest, melding his gaze with hers, admiring fiercely the person she had become. Hardship had molded and trials had strengthened her. By overcoming them all, she now stood ready to meet her destiny. Knowing what he had to do, the Simathe made himself let go of her. She was ready; he must be too.

Freeing her hand, he stepped back. "As you wish, my lady."

She half-smiled at his acquiescence. "I can't believe you're agreeing to this." Then the warrior mask slipped, allowing him a glimpse of the frightened girl beneath. It was she who whispered, "You'll stay with me, won't you? Right by me? Through whatever happens?"

His blood surged, the timid, trembling question tearing painfully at something inside. Not stopping to think, he grasped her chin in his hand.

"Aye, lass," he promised, voice earnest, low. "Though the Dark One himself appear, I will fight with"—*for*, he amended in his thoughts—"you, through whatever this night may bring."

Her eyes probed his as she accepted that promise. "I know you will," she murmured simply.

With that, the girl was gone, the woman assuming her place. Time was running out, and they had to go. Whatever else occurred this night, he knew that she would never be the same. Likewise, the Simathe lord doubted he would, either. Perhaps that knowledge played into what followed.

Whatever it was, the light from Dilk's lost moonstone glinting in her mismatched eyes and frosting her hair, or maybe the passion of the moment; whoever it was, Ilgard or his lady; whoever they were—a Simathe and the Artan, he would never know. But the next second, the fingers on her chin had relaxed their hold. His hand cupped her cheek briefly before slipping down, his fingertips tracing a path over the hinge of her jaw, the back of her neck. His arm crept across her shoulder blades, drawing her body against his.

She did not resist, and it was too late to stop now…

Hesitating, he watched her long, curved lashes float closed in anticipation before finally lowering his head and letting his mouth meet hers. Shocked by what he discovered, he found himself pulled under a current too strong to withstand. It was the perfect culmination of all the desire, the appeal, the confusion, the charm, the frustration, the joy, the magic that ever he'd found in her.

It was a kiss—an actual kiss, and nothing at all like their first. It was a sharing, not a taking, and he knew that for certain when her hands slid leisurely up his bare arms, traveling slowly over his shoulders. Cupping his neck between her palms, she pressed nearer and rose on tiptoes the better to reach him. He responded instinctively, deepening the kiss and pulling her as close as he dared. She was so small, yet she fit his arms so well…

He was lost in the magic they wove, so much so that it took three attempts by his Chief Captain of reaching out to him, mentally warning him of imminent danger, before Ilgard heard. He acceded reluctantly, letting her go and reporting the news to his lady.

She simply nodded. "We've got to go, then."

"Aye." Pulling himself together, only then did he notice. "My lady, you are unarmed."

"Give me a minute," she said and stepped free of his arm, closing her eyes. Concentrating. Once more the

Simathe experienced that flash of raw energy in its purest form, and then in her hands materialized an exquisite sword of glistering steel. Its blade glimmered in the shadowy light as she arced it through the air in quick, circular motions, getting a feel for its heft and balance.

"This will do," she said. "Let's go."

Light, but she was uncommonly beautiful, standing there in her torn, blood-stained nightdress, her hair falling wildly about her bare shoulders. He'd had many visions of the coming Artan through the long years, but never one like this. Nor could any of his speculations possibly hope to compete with reality.

That is enough.

Shoving such unfamiliar foolishness roughly away, the warrior-lord stooped, seizing the hilt of the knife protruding from the dead man's chest. With a single firm tug, he extracted it, wiped off the blood on his breeches, and stuck the weapon in his belt.

With his free hand, he grasped hers.

"Aye, let us go."

Chapter Twenty-Two

Inner City Battle

Nothing on Earth—or in Aerisia, for that matter—could've prepared me for what had just taken place between Ilgard and me.

Kissing the Simathe High-Chief? Are you crazy?

Maybe I was. Okay, not maybe; clearly, I must be. Not that long ago, I would never, ever have foreseen this happening. I wouldn't have seen Ilgard initiating it or me responding. I granted that the moment had been right. There had been something in the air, something that temporarily eclipsed the mysteries, the blood, and the pain. Something that went deeper than him and me, our roles in this drama, and perhaps even the *Joining* bond between us.

Or was this a direct fruit of the bond? Had Aureeyah and Rittean been right all along? Was this somehow destined to be simply because we, a Simathe and the Artan, a man and a woman, were *Joined*?

My head hurt, and I didn't think it was only from trying to figure out that kiss. A lot more than simply our relationship had changed tonight, probably permanently. For starters, I'd not only seen my first murder victim, but I'd also killed someone. Furthermore, I'd just accepted the mantle of Artan, for real and for good. Something told me there'd be no backing out now.

Can't think about that now, can't think about that now, my brain chanted in time with my feet as we ran.

If I'd stopped to mull over any of it, any single item on the list, I'd have been hopelessly lost. Instead, I took myself back to the moment when Ilgard had vowed to stay with me through whatever we might have to face. Both his promise and his kiss—even now I could feel it on my lips—had bolstered my courage. Without another thought, I'd formed the sword in my hands; tapping into the inner force to create it had also bolstered my courage.

For the time being, fear had fled as I ran with the Simathe High-Chief toward the unmistakable sounds of battle drifting our way. Already, it seemed, fighting had broken out within and without the palace, and it occurred to me to wonder just how many the Doinum had managed to turn against us—against me, to be precise—and how many of them would actually be willing to fight.

I looked down at the blade in my hand, regretting it wasn't Laytrii's blade. The sword of the former High-Chieftess of Aerisia had become like a part of me. Since the day I'd gotten it, I hadn't used another. Heading into the unknown, something familiar would've been nice, but then...

I glanced up at the man beside me. Maybe he was all the familiarity I needed.

* * *

Slipping through a deserted servants' corridor, we entered the palace courtyard via a small side entrance. We almost made it through the eerily silent gardens before we encountered the first resistance. From the dim shadows of the enclosed courtyard, a dark figure in a shapeless robe materialized, ostensibly from the stones of the wall itself. Ilgard saw the creature before I did. Before the Doinum had time to raise its gory mace, the Simathe struck with lightning speed, slicing head from shoulders in a single, fluid motion. Clapping a hand over my mouth to keep from crying out, I watched the head fly through the air and land with a dull, sickening thump on the rich soil several paces away.

I wanted to be ill, but I clamped down on the nausea. There was no time for squeamishness, just action.

I followed the grim, determined warrior past the bleeding corpse without a word. Displaying a surprisingly intimate knowledge of the intricacies of the palace's interior, Ilgard led me through a series of narrow, winding passageways I'd never seen before, until we ultimately emerged outside into the huge open courtyard.

Oh no. No, no, no.

I gaped, momentarily paralyzed by the hideous melee. Doinum in shapeless robes, emitting animal grunts and displaying insane, animal strength, fought against armored Ranetron and a few scattered Simathe. Just as I'd feared, also recognizable among the moonlit figures were servants and more palace guards, courtiers and folk from the nearby city of Laytrii—and these were fighting *against* us.

How did the Doinum do this? What sort of power do they wield that they could convince these people to fight and die like this? I don't understand it!

I jumped, startled, when my companion gave my shoulder a hard squeeze. He leaned close to my ear and practically shouted to be heard above the noise.

"Stay with me, my lady. No matter what happens, do not leave my side."

I nodded vigorously, my sweaty hands clenching the hilt of my sword in a death grip. Panic threatened once again until the Simathe looked deep into my eyes, holding me there...and suddenly the oddest sensation of peace, assurance, and even calm stole through my veins, driving away fear and doubt. At first, I thought I really was losing my mind. I mean, who wouldn't have been scared to jump into her first battle? Who but an immortal?

When I realized that, I also realized, through our *Joining* bond, Ilgard must have been taking my fear and replacing it with his own calm assurance. He had never done this before or anything like it. Perhaps the barriers I'd knocked down earlier when I was trying to get him to open his door to Elisia and me had changed another facet of our bond. Whatever the case, I was grateful for his help and felt my heart rate slow to a steadier beat.

He must've sensed me calming. With a final hard clasp, he let me go.

"Now," he said, "we fight."

I drew a deep breath, nodded, and together we plunged into the fray.

Dread, death, and blood were all around, but fight we did, at times back to back, at times side by side. The initial onslaught of fear and revulsion nearly overwhelmed me, but all the past months of training kicked in. I reached deep within and found my magic, then I sent my senses toward my sword, the sword I'd created from this magic. *Becoming* this sword was even easier than *Becoming* Laytrii's sword, possibly because it was part and parcel to me and my gifts. I found it and *Became* it; afterward, I knew neither panic nor pain as I waged war.

Time stood still, locked in a frigid state of combat. I had little recollection of how long the battle lasted or how many I killed, but by the time the struggle ground to a slow, torturous halt, my sword was slick with scarlet. Encircling Ilgard and me on every side were dead and dying, both friend and foe. More of our allies stood than theirs, so I assumed we'd won. I also assumed the fighting here was almost at an end. All that remained were a few small pockets of resistance that were even now being dispatched.

I freed the power I'd been holding, noticing instantly how my clothing was soaked with blood and sweat. Salt was dried on my skin, and strands of hair clung to my face and neck. I used one hand to peel them off as I gave myself a hasty once-over. I was relieved to discover only a few cuts and nicks.

I was distracted from my inspection when Norband suddenly plunged by. Ilgard caught his subordinate's arm, bringing him up short.

"The palace?"

"Secure, my lord."

"And the city?"

The Simathe Chief Captain shook his head. "Turmoil. The Doinum have either turned against us or slain all Ranetron leaders in Laytrii. The men are confused; some fight for and some against us."

"What about the people?" I spoke up. "Are they for or against us?"

The warrior's ebony gaze flicked toward me. "Divided as well, my lady. The Ranetron need their High-Chief; the people their Artan."

I turned helplessly to Ilgard. "But right now, I can only fight. What good does that do? Even if I could do something more, what if it's not enough? What if people don't believe in me? What if they won't accept me?"

Disregarding the other man's presence, with a movement quicker than my eyes could follow, he snaked his hands out to catch my arms just below the wound received during my fight with Dilk. He pulled me near, his fingers biting so sharply into my flesh that I almost cried out.

"Listen well, my lady. The time to stand up and be accounted for is *now*. Do what you are able, and those who believe in you will fight for you. Tonight, you are changed. You may no longer hide behind the walls of Laytrii or Treygon, behind the Moonkind or the fairies or the Simathe. Not even behind myself. As you yourself said, those days are gone—that woman is gone. In her place stands prophecy fulfilled. The Artan. Fight, and we fight with you. You will conquer."

The fierceness of his impossibly black eyes, the urgency of his grasp, and the exigency of his words left no room for doubt. I knew if he didn't think I could do this, he wouldn't be saying these things. If anything, Ilgard was not one to sugarcoat the truth. He believed this was the time, and he believed in me. I simply had to believe it myself.

You can do this, Hannah. You can. I know it seems insane to finally and forever accept the fact that you are the Artan, but right now that's what you have to do. You have to accept it, you have to become it, and you have to win this fight.

The sun was finally rising in the east, the promise of a new day brightening the early morning sky. A new day for Laytrii, for Aerisia, for Aerisia's people.

A new day for me.

Closing my eyes, I drew a deep breath, steeling my heart and soul against the inevitable, and nodded once. Just once.

Nothing more needed to be said.

* * *

I couldn't deny that my courage failed me more than once during the heart-pounding ride toward the city of Laytrii. Already this morning I'd had enough of blood and death to last me a lifetime. I knew I was likely going into yet more and wondered how people managed to become warriors who dealt with it all the time. That, I knew, wasn't the life for me, never mind that I was the Artan.

There has to be another way, I kept thinking.

But what?

We hadn't even cleared the huge city gates before the din of battle assaulted our ears. Proving Norband's warnings true, people fought in the streets, some with and some against the Simathe and Ranetron strewn about. Doors and shutters of houses and businesses were locked tight, some even nailed shut, as those inside sought protection from the madness. I honestly couldn't believe what I was seeing. How could the Doinum have managed to turn so many against us?

Halting in front of me, Ilgard dismounted, preparing to enter the combat on foot. As he did, a thought suddenly struck me. The memory of the Simathe Chief Captain's words flashed across my mind, bringing with them an unlikely idea.

The Ranetron need their High-Chief; the people their Artan, he had said.

I think I know what I have to do, I realized, feeling excitement—a nervous but good sort of excitement—

building in my chest. Had I just found the way? The way to stop these atrocities for good?

Throwing myself off the back of my horse, I shoved my way through the warriors packed in around me, calling Ilgard's name.

"My lady?" He spun to face me.

"Ilgard," I panted, sliding to a stop in front of him. "Can you get Lord Garett and me to a really high place? It has to be a place where lots of people can see us, and it has to be quick."

He stared down at me, uncomprehending, like he wondered if I'd suddenly taken leave of my senses. Pressed for time, I grabbed his shoulders, shaking him a little in my need to make him understand.

"Ilgard, I mean it! If there's a place like that, you have to take me there right now!"

Again he hesitated, but only for a second. Something in me must have warned him this was important. He managed to snag the attention of a nearby Ranetron, commanding the soldier to fetch his lord and be quick about it. The young man hurried to obey, and Lord Garett was standing before us in a matter of moments.

The Ranetron High-Chief had lost his helmet during the fighting. His red-blond hair was matted with sweat and blood, and his face was streaked with more of the same. I wondered if I looked as bad as he did and decided dismally, *Probably worse.*

We withdrew from the struggle to quickly hash out our plans. Both High-Chiefs cornered me against the wall of a nearby wine shop while we spoke, using their own bodies to shield me from danger as I sketched out my idea to Lord Garett. He nodded approvingly.

"I begin to see your plan, my lady. There is a place we might go."

"The city square? The white bridge?"

This from Ilgard.

"Aye. Come, my lady. The High-Chief and I will take you there."

The two men took the lead, dashing down a side alley. I followed closely, guarded by Cole and a couple other Simathe. In an effort to keep as far from the clash as possible, they escorted me in a roundabout way to our destination, utilizing a series of back streets and narrow lanes. While we were lost in this confusing, complex labyrinth, the noise of the skirmish receded for a time. It grew louder again as we made a sharp turn to the left, heading back, I assumed, toward the action.

We raced out onto a broad street, running hard. Here and there were clusters of people fighting. For the most part they ignored us, being too caught up in their own senseless battles to notice any newcomers. Only a few were foolish enough to actually challenge us, and these were eradicated so quickly I was never given the time or opportunity to make use of my own weapon. I couldn't say I was sorry.

Another street, even broader than before. This one I judged to be one of the city's main thoroughfares. Now, the further we went, the more intense the fighting. By this point, we were all fighting hard to stay on our feet and stay close together. At times, the cobblestones beneath our feet were slick with blood, impeding progress. The fallen were strewn across the ground, the wounded crying out for help, their moans blending in with the general noise and confusion.

Suddenly, out of nowhere, a crazed woman with wild hair came charging straight at me. Face twisted in anger, she screamed curses at "the evil deceiver." In her upraised hand, she gripped a huge butcher knife, which she looked prepared to use.

Sheer instinct took over, and I flung a burst of raw power straight at her. It left my fingertips in the form of a dazzling ball of blue flame, striking her in the middle of the chest, and knocking her backward to the ground. Her head collided with the cobblestones, and she moved no more. Even as I turned to go, I saw the flames of my self-made weapon beginning to lick greedily at her hair and clothing. Sickened, I knew I must put a stop to this before I was forced to take yet another life, even in self-defense, of the people I was supposed to be delivering.

After a fierce struggle, we finally reached the bridge.

A rather narrow, shallow river swept through the middle of the city, speeding through in its hurry to reach the mighty Largese River a few miles beyond. This smaller river, the Coiyne, started as a stream somewhere high in the Unpassed Mountains, the location of its source a mystery to all except possibly the Simathe. As it tumbled through the midst of the city, the Coiyne became Laytrii's main water source. There were specially appointed riverwatchers whose job was to keep a close eye on the river, making sure it stayed clean. People caught emptying chamber pots or dumping refuse into its waters were heavily fined or otherwise punished.

The Coiyne not only sliced through the very heart of the huge city, but actually the city square itself. Here it was spanned by the beautiful, soaring Singing Bridge. Elisia, who'd told me all these things, had included the fact that the Singing Bridge had gotten its name from the enchanted Singing Stones, mentioned in the Artan's prophecy. They were actually discovered by builders digging the bridge's foundation.

The bridge was unusually high, designed for style and grandeur as much as function. It was tall enough to be seen over the rooftops of the city's grandest mansions; in fact, it could be seen from any vantage point in Laytrii. Slender and elegantly arched, the Singing Bridge sported fanciful scrollwork railings carved so fine they resembled lace. And although built from the same delicate pink-and-silver marble as Laytrii's palace, the bridge did appear white from a distance (hence its other moniker of the "white bridge"). It was for the middle of this vantage point that we now found ourselves fighting and running.

Chapter Twenty-Three

The Singing Bridge

Ahead of me, I saw Ilgard thrust his sword deep into a Doinum guarding the ascent of the bridge. We were only halfway up, and several more of this one's companions blocked our way. While he fell to the warrior-lord's sword, the next went to his yedin. Even as Ilgard withdrew his sword from one victim, he slammed his elbow into the face of the other. The Doinum went reeling backward. A swift kick took out the creature's feet, and then the Simathe was plunging his yedin mercilessly into the creature's chest.

The yedin, a weapon no longer than a Simathe's sword, was three pronged with razor-sharp talons tipping each prong. Because of its ease of transport and use, Simathe generally carried a yedin, along with their other weapon of choice, when they went into battle. It was a yedin with which Ilgard had killed Jonase; seeing it now was enough to bring back a host of unwanted memories. I averted my eyes as we rushed past the Doinum's corpse, not wanting to stir up further mental turmoil.

Lord Garett took out a screaming Aerisian man armed with a spear, and then we were in the middle of the bridge. With the Simathe and Garett hemming me in, I moved to the railing and looked down. Citizens and soldiers alike filled the city square, their rioting spilling out into the streets and alleyways beyond. In a few places they were stretched very far, as far as to the great gates through which we'd entered.

Had the battle not been raging, I would have enjoyed this—my first real view of the vast, handsome city. I'd been kept so busy at Laytrii's palace the past few months that I hadn't gotten a chance to visit the city. At present, however, the beauty wasn't what caught my eye, but the cruel skirmishing and killing.

I was here now. Time to put my plan into action. But how to gain their attention? Shouting would do no good. I'd never be heard above the din. Could I amplify my voice? Even if I could, would that do the trick? Would anyone want to listen to just me, even a very loud me? I couldn't risk it; I needed something impossible to ignore. Sifting through ideas, I remembered with a start the ball of flame I'd used earlier to kill the woman who charged me. Could I do something like that again? On a much larger scale?

I looked to my friends. "Get ready. I'm going to try something."

My companions exchanged glances, but I closed my eyes and shut them out, concentrating on the task at hand. Dropping my sword to my feet and stretching my arms, I opened myself up to the river within, letting it fill and engulf and wash over me like a mighty wave. Retracting my arms, I mentally caught hold of a single ripple, which I sent flowing from mind to hands. Opening my eyes, I beheld with satisfaction the large sphere of floating, shimmering, blue-white flame hovering between my hands.

Holding it there by willpower alone, I searched desperately for a spot below, any empty spot...found it, and threw! The sphere streamed from my hands like a streak of blue-white lightning. Almost in slow motion, the glittering fire hurtled toward the cobblestoned city square. It struck, and a fountain of dirt, stone chunks, and flame sprayed dozens of feet into the air, calling an effective halt to the battle. People screamed, falling back in confused terror. Some tried to run, tripped over cobblestones, bodies, or broken pavement, and fell clumsily to their hands and knees. Confusion reigned.

In the midst of it all, a strong voice beside me cried loudly, "People of Laytrii, hear me!"

At the cry, a few swung their attention our way. Lord Garett shouted the same words a second time, even louder, causing more people to look toward us. By his third call, people were glancing at each other in confusion, shifting nervously, then peering up anxiously at us. Many dropped or sheathed their weapons. Most began edging closer, assembling in a massive crowd down below. Even those previously skirmishing in streets and alleyways gathered, having heard the explosion and come running to investigate.

A relative hush fell over the crowd as former enemies, fighting to the death only minutes before, gawked up at the strange group atop the Singing Bridge: several Simathe, a Ranetron, and a half-dressed woman obviously not Aerisian. I could only imagine what was running through their minds. As for me, now that I had their attention, I felt suddenly tongue-tied and edgy. I rubbed sweat-slick palms fretfully against my nightshift before raising them to grip the bridge's solid rails. Hard.

What do I say to these people? Who am I to think I can end this insanity? Who am I to think I can lead them?

Below, someone in the crowd coughed noisily, breaking the spell fear had cast over me. Flicking a glance toward Ilgard, I caught his reassuring nod. Encouraged, I turned once more to the people beneath the bridge.

My people.

Chapter Twenty-Four

Their Artan

Clearing my throat softly, I began.

"People of Aerisia, of Laytrii—Simathe, Ranetron, Moonkind, all of you gathered here today… I am Hannah Winters. I was brought here to Aerisia from Earth, your sister land, many months ago. Most of you know this. Most of you know me as the woman said to be your Artan."

I paused, stealing a moment to draw a deep breath and study faces before continuing. By the ever-brightening morning light, I could see the people below listened intently. Also, one by one, doors and shutters were opening as folk slipped outside or poked their heads out to see what was going on. Much to my relief, I noticed no more Doinum, and hoped they'd all fled for good or had been dealt with. Permanently.

Buoyed by these encouraging signs, I went on.

"For a long time, I was unhappy to be here. I refused to believe I was your Artan. I hated Aerisia and what coming here had cost me: a life on Earth with my friends and family. Everything I knew and loved, I was forced to leave behind when I was brought here.

"But after a while, all that changed.

"First, I was attacked by The Evil, and if not for the protection of your Ranetron High-Chief and these Simathe warriors"—I gestured in turn toward each of my companions—"I would now be dead. After this, for my own protection I was sent to Treygon, the Simathe stronghold. There, I learned to fight not just with weapons, but with the power within me."

They were hanging on my every word. Though there were those who scowled in angry defiance, none dared interrupt.

"With the help of many people—the Elders, the Ranetron, Simathe, Moonkind, Spinners, and even a fairy—I learned more of what I was. Trust me, it wasn't just you who had to be shown who I was; it was me also, and it took time for me to believe it. However, today, right now, I stand before you to tell you I *am* the Artan.

"By now, I've had to fight and kill servants of the Dark Powers, The Evil, more than once. They've tried several times to destroy me by taking my life…" Here, I hesitated, debating whether or not to go on. Something told me these people needed and deserved to know the whole truth if they were ever going to trust me implicitly. Steeling myself, I plunged ahead. "And when that didn't work, they even tried rape."

A gasp of horror rose from the crowd, and people immediately fell to busy whisperings. I had to raise my volume in order to grab their attention and make myself heard.

"*They* knew I was the Artan, and they wanted to ensure my downfall before I had the chance to come into my own. In spite of their best efforts, each attack failed…until now."

I paused, letting my eyes seek out faces in the crowd. I met and briefly held gazes, making certain each and every person assembled knew what I was saying and where I was going before resuming.

"In this, their latest scheme, the Dark Powers again sent their servants to destroy me. To destroy not just me this time, but you and your city and all hope for peace and unity among us. These servants walked among us not as themselves, but hidden behind masks. They deceived us with kind words and fine actions, while in their hearts there was nothing but death. They gained our trust by pretending to walk in the light. Once this trust was given, they took advantage of it—of you—to spread lies and wicked rumors, raising questions and doubts about me.

"*Was* I your Artan? Was it possible I was *actually* a part of The Evil, using my position to take advantage of Aerisians in general? Maybe I was simply trying to overshadow the real Artan's advent.

"I don't know what all was said or what 'proofs' they showed you. But I do know this: that even many of those who believed in me were afraid to stand up and be accounted for when it came right down to it."

A third time I explored faces in the crowd. Some looked ashamed, while others hung their heads. Still others looked angry, as if they wished to argue but didn't dare.

"You see where suspicion, mistrust, and fear have brought us," I went on gently. "The Evil may not have murdered me, but their mission has been more than accomplished. Look at us—we're fighting, slaughtering each other! If that's not the work of The Evil, what is?"

Now even many of those who'd been against me were starting to look mortified. I pressed on.

"Because of our failures, not only have we ourselves served the Dark Powers, but good men and women have died who didn't deserve to. Because of our failures, the strangers among us were allowed to murder Ranetron leaders of this city as well as your High Elder.

"I want you to know it was my friend Lady Elisia, the Spinner, who had the good sense to be wary of the Adragon. She was the one who eventually unearthed our enemies' secret. She was the one who warned me that these 'Adragon' could be nothing less than the *Doinum*— ancient, devoted, powerful servants of the Dark Powers."

Another round of outraged gasps from many in the ever-growing crowd. Apparently, not all knowledge of the Doinum had vanished from common Aerisian memory.

At this juncture Lord Garett intervened, stepping up beside me and taking over.

"Ranetron of Aerisia, you have fought both for and against us this day. Having heard our lady's words, will you now unite behind your High-Chief and against our shared foe? Our enemy is not this woman beside me. Our enemy is any and all who oppose her, for, in opposing her, they also oppose the Powers we serve."

I don't think there was even one of the several hundred Ranetron dispersed about the city square who didn't raise his sword at Garett's question, shouting loud allegiance to his lord as well as to me.

"It is well," their High-Chief said, nodding approvingly. Then, "Lencon, Rayde!" He singled out two soldiers at the edge of the crowd. "Fetch one of these slain Doinum. Bring it hither for all to see.

"You there, clear a place for the corpse."

As his men and the onlookers scurried to do his bidding, I glanced at him, bewildered. "What's going on? What are you doing?"

He didn't look up from observing his commands being carried out below but replied grimly, "In death, my lady, as in sunlight, their true natures are revealed. Elisia informed me of this before the fighting began."

I didn't have to puzzle long over his cryptic statement, for just then his two warriors returned, placing a broken corpse on the ground. Jerking off its slashed, shapeless robe, they stepped away. My cry of astonishment mingled with the crowd's at what unfolded next. As soon as the soft, dawn sun touched its pale skin, the body began contracting, twisting, shrinking, hardening. Fingers morphed into claws, ears to horns, and teeth to fangs as the remains of this previously normal-looking Aerisian altered into something entirely different. Something gray, scowling, and stone-hard.

"It's a gargoyle," I breathed, awed.

"My lady?" asked Cole from behind.

I couldn't tear my eyes from the thing. "It's a gargoyle. I've seen them on Earth. Well, not real ones. Stone ones. People used to be big on making statues of them, but I never knew why, and I never knew they actually existed! I wonder…"

My words trailed off into silence as I realized I was looking upon yet one more Aerisian fact that had morphed into Earth legend. Shaking my head, I wondered if I'd ever stop finding links between our parallel worlds.

Eventually, I had to force my focus back to the job at hand. Taking control of the situation, my voice overpowering the shock waves reverberating through the crowd, I said loudly, "You see? What further proof do we need that everything I've said is true? Are you going to believe me, or will you continue serving the Dark Powers by listening to their lies?"

People glanced questioningly at one another, as if debating whether or not I wanted a verbal response.

"Well?" I pressed, forcing the issue. "Will you? Which side are you going to choose? You can't have it both ways."

At last, a lone Ranetron, young, bloody, and weary, raised his spear. "I know not where others may stand, but my choice is made. This woman speaks truth. She is our Artan, and I will follow her as such. What say you?"

"I say, aye!"

This, much to my surprise, came from Norband, who had stepped up beside the young Ranetron. The crowd shifted around him, as few seemed willing to stand close to a high-ranking Simathe. Nevertheless, in mere seconds his cry had been taken up by men and women alike, and shouted repeatedly until it echoed throughout the city square and beyond.

"And will you," I cried, "stand together, uniting yourselves with each other and with us to fight The Evil and drive them from our homes and cities when that time comes?"

The shouts of "Aye!" and "Yes!" resounded so strongly that it seemed even the great Singing Bridge vibrated beneath my feet.

My heart was overflowing as I stared at these people.

I can't believe this. I did it! It's really happening. I've truly become the Artan.

Nevertheless, if I thought I was going to get off that easily, I was mistaken. The glow of success had barely warmed my soul when an impossibly deep and loud voice slashed through the crowd's joy to issue a daring challenge.

"What proofs have you? What proofs do you offer us that *you* truly are what you claim to be?"

* * *

I was so startled I was momentarily frozen in place. Turning my head slowly, I peered over my shoulder. An astonished intake of breath, followed by a broken exclamation, fled my lips. Whirling, I pressed up hard against the railing, gripping it with all the strength I possessed. Blinking rapidly, I tried to dispel the vision before me, but my eyes opened and reopened only to reveal they were still standing there just as I'd first glimpsed them, alive and all too real.

Giants!

Chapter Twenty-Five

Challenge

That was the only word to describe the phenomenon standing beneath our bridge. I may have been up too high to accurately estimate their height, yet even from there it was easy to see they'd more than dwarf a normal-sized man.

The newcomers were fair-haired, like other Aerisian folk, and dressed alike in dark-colored breeches, leather boots laced to the knee, and long-sleeved white shirts with full, billowy sleeves. Over these they wore vests of somber blacks, browns, grays, and blues. Their leader, however, the one fronting the group who'd called out the challenge, wore his shirt open at the neck, displaying the bronze circlet clasped around his throat to full advantage. Although the object reminded me of the slave collars once used on Earth, this man was obviously no slave. Authority and confidence radiated from the tips of his dusty boots to the huge broadsword poking over his shoulder to the top of his golden head.

I shook myself like a person awakening from a trance. Cautiously, I moved to the opposite railing, where I peered down at the stranger.

"Who are you?"

"Why, I am Prince Kurban Wy' Damondule, son of High King Ergat, also of House Damondule. I am prince of the Tearkin, and I am at your service, my lady."

He offered a grand, sweeping bow, which I thought wasn't untouched by mockery.

I frowned. "Do you come in peace?"

He seemed to find the question very funny. Shaking his head, he laughed, the three tiny golden hoops in one ear swaying and the layered lengths of his burnt-blond hair brushing against his vest's stiff, embroidered collar. He was a good-looking guy, even for a giant, but I couldn't say I cared for his attitude.

"And if we do not," he demanded audaciously, "what would you do, Lady?"

Choosing to ignore the subtle insult, I reiterated firmly, "Do you come in peace?"

The cheeky smile slipped as he folded his arms mulishly across his chest. "That would depend, my lady. We have come a long journey to see if the rumors reaching even the land of the giants are true. On mission to seek out the lady Artan have we come. You are this lady?"

I nodded, brushing a lock of hair behind my ear. "Yes, I am."

"So you say. But what proofs have you to verify your words? We heard some of your speech to these city folk." His broad hand gesture encompassed the throng of Aerisians gawking openly at the intimidating strangers on the opposite side of the river. "Very pretty," the prince went on. "But what sign do you offer that we may accept you as the deliverer of our land?"

I stared him dead in the face. "Didn't you see the explosion I created a few minutes ago? How do you think I got the attention of all these people bent on fighting and killing each other?"

"Nay, Lady, we did not see. We heard something—mayhap an eruption of some sort—but we saw nothing more than the unguarded gate and unprotected streets by which we entered the city."

"You really should consider having guards stationed," he added, "to prevent strangers from simply walking in."

I bristled at that. "There *were* guards there, you—" I bit my tongue to refrain from adding "idiot."

Taking a deep breath to calm myself, I started over. "There *were* guards there, but the fighting in the city and at the palace had us all in confusion."

"Then 'tis truly a good thing for you and your people that it was only my men and me entering your city unseen and unchallenged, was it not?"

"I suppose that's true," I agreed warily.

He was smiling again. "Then we are agreed on this point, at least.

"Come, Lady, let us waste no more time. Show us you are the true Artan, and my men and I are prepared to pledge you our swords. Howbeit, if you cannot offer what we seek…"

His sentence trailed off into dangerous, foreboding silence.

"Yes?" I prompted, even though I figured I could guess the rest.

His hand shifted, going to the hilt of his mammoth sword in an understated gesture of warning. "Then we slay you as a deceiver and a servant of the Dark Powers."

"You would pass through my men and me to do so, Tearkin."

Ilgard! He shouldered up to stand beside me at the rail, his own hand resting lightly on the hilt of his sheathed sword. Below and behind us, the inquisitive crowd was deathly silent as they watched this drama unfolding. I shifted a step closer to the tall warrior, watching the giant's face to see what his reaction might be to knowing I had Simathe protection.

To my astonishment, he laughed! A huge grin splitting his face, he called out, "Ho, Ilgard, High-Chief of the Simathe. Well met, my lord! How fare you and your warriors this day?"

"*What?*" I gaped openly at the two of them. "What's going on here? You guys know each other?"

The Simathe was not smiling. "We of Treygon have lent the Tearkin our strength on more than one occasion."

I stared in disbelief at this man I'd thought I was finally getting to know, trying to process this information into my already overwhelmed brain. "Wait a minute: you knew there were giants in Aerisia? And you didn't tell me?"

He offered no apology. "The Tearkin are like the Simathe; we leave our lands only when we must. There was no need for you to know what others did not."

"What? Hold on," I sputtered angrily. "You mean to tell me the Simathe are the only ones who knew these giants existed?"

When he made no reply, I rounded on Garett. "Did you know?"

"No, my lady. I did not."

Back to the other High-Chief. "Ilgard, is it true then? Only the Simathe knew? How is that?"

"A common bond, my lady," broke in the Tearkin prince, who up till now had held his peace. "A common bond shared through the Scraggen. We were both created, as one might say, by the witch-women."

I couldn't believe my ears. "So you're saying you guys are practically cousins or something?"

"Oh, very nearly," the prince chuckled. "Ho, my friend, how do you like that?" he said to Ilgard. "You and I, cousins! I shall be certain to save you a seat at our next family gathering."

"Hardly necessary," the Simathe High-Chief declined coldly. "Get on with your business, Tearkin."

"Ah, you wound me," sighed the Prince, laying a hand to his chest. "Very well, then." Turning back to me, he said, "You have heard our request, my lady. Will you show us proofs that you are what you say?"

"Not until I know how you knew about me," I demanded. "If your lands are so isolated nobody over here knew about you, how come you all knew about me?"

"Rumors spread and word travels," shrugged the giant. "As do the Simathe, who recently assisted us in handling a problem we faced."

"What kind of problem?"

"What else but the Warkin? Their lands border ours, which, according to them, affords them the right to help themselves to our livestock and goods."

"The Warkin? Who're they?"

"They are the Dragonkind, people of the dragon," murmured Lord Garett, still by my side. "I have heard of them. They are a tribal people, whose clans lay claim to lands throughout the Western Territories. So rarely do they come into contact with any of us that I had half-wondered if they were a myth."

"Speaking of myths…" I turned a glare on Ilgard. In one morning I'd seen gargoyles and giants brought to life, and now I was calmly being told that dragons existed as well?

"You'd think *somebody* could've let me in on some of this and saved me lots of shock and confusion. Obviously I was mistaken in thinking you Simathe had no close ties with anyone. I guess it's true that no man is an island. Just wish you'd bothered to clue me in instead of having it take me completely by surprise."

The man looked right back at me with those pupilless black eyes, refusing to speak or take the bait. We were at a stalemate, until the Tearkin prince interrupted.

"I say, all of this is quite amusing, yet we still await an answer to my original question."

"Kurban, I have *Joined* with her. That should be answer enough," Ilgard stated quietly.

The giant's jaw dropped. "You jest!"

"Yeah, because the Simathe are so big on practical jokes." I rolled my eyes.

Ignoring that, he demanded of Ilgard, "Is it true, then? You believe her to be the Artan?"

"Wait a minute, he didn't tell you he'd *Joined* with me? Just what did he say?"

"When we made inquiry about the rumors of the Artan's arrival, he merely said that she had indeed been brought and that we ought to come see her for ourselves. So here we are. We only require a bit of proof before we pledge our swords to your cause."

"If I have *Joined* with her, that should be sufficient proof for even your stubborn self."

Seeing the recalcitrance that crossed the giant's face, one proving Ilgard's assessment of him was likely true, I sighed deeply.

Now that the immediate danger seemed passed, it occurred to me how tired I was. The sun had barely risen in the sky, and a bone-deep weariness had already settled in. All I wanted was to go back to the palace, tumble into bed, and sleep for a dozen years. Unfortunately, I knew that unless I did something to solve the situation on my hands, it could quickly escalate into a drawn-out battle of wills between Simathe and Tearkin. Who would win that I didn't know, and I didn't plan on finding out either.

The people gathered below still waited patiently, both inside the city square and surrounding it. They, too, needed all of this to be finished so they could bury their dead, mourn, rebuild, and go on with their lives. However, they'd heard the prince's challenge, and after the literal war last night over the question of me as the Artan, I couldn't help feeling a little more proof for them wouldn't be a bad thing.

Finally, I broke the silence stretching thin between glaring Tearkin and composed Simathe by stating simply, "He's right."

Both men slowly, reluctantly, turned from each other to me. "He's right," I repeated. "The prince is right. He does deserve proof that I'm the Artan. Everyone does."

Neither of them said a word. Ignoring their silence and the unnerving atmosphere of hundreds of pairs of eyes trained on me, I puzzled over how to back up what I'd so bravely proclaimed.

* * *

Walk in the light.
  Peace... Unity... Light...
  Light.
  Her true essence...birthed with...the dawn...

The sun. The dawn. Light. Sunlight…

As I stood there observing the dawn-painted sky, trying to determine what to do, the voices began whispering inside my head. Like a carousel they started slowly then picked up speed. Faster and faster the words went spinning around my brain, tripping over each other, mingling together, then dancing apart. And they were beginning to form an idea, something I hoped I could use.

Lifting my face to the sun, I felt the warmth of a new morning touch my skin. A smile curved my mouth.

The sun…

It was on full display this morning. Broad shafts of light pierced the filmy white clouds overhead, striking the earth in a dazzling circle of sunbeams. Once more, the sun had risen to chase away the dark of night, bringing daybreak with it. Chasing away the darkness *with* light, just as the Artan was prophesied to do.

Allowing my lashes to drift closed, I breathed deeply. Weariness melted away as I drank in the fresh morning air, tasting the scents of light, water, dust, and flowers on my tongue—the flowers that bloomed in gardens and gaily painted window boxes all over the city, the flowers that grew in fields beyond the city walls, the flowers blooming on trees both inside the city and out.

With the heightening awareness of all these things came an almost imperceptible releasing of myself to the sun and the elements and the beauty all around me. Uncurling my fingers and extending my arms, I embraced these emblems. Letting my head fall back, I permitted the light and life and energy to fill and overtake me. I *Became* them, and they me.

Chapter Twenty-Six

Sun-borne Promise

As her feet left stone and she began rising off the surface of the Singing Bridge, Ilgard, High-Chief of the Simathe, watched with awe but little astonishment. The sensations filtering to him through their bond of light, buoyancy, and warmth were merely a fulfillment of what she'd started to feel the instant she closed her eyes.

She had a point to prove, and this was it. This Artan did not simply walk in the light; she *was* the light, and she personified that as she *Became* the sunlight into which she drifted. Above the city walls, above the white bridge, high above his head, she stood in midair. She was the essence of tranquility. Her eyes were closed, and her arms extended as she welcomed the brilliance surrounding her. Her head had fallen back, and her dark hair rippled past her shoulders. With her feet pressed neatly together and her nightshift skimming her knees, she hung suspended between earth and sky.

Before his eyes, the bloodstains, grime, rents, and tears marring her clothing melted away, vanishing into the void. Her skin darkened to gold until every outline of her face was etched like a statue. People beneath her, both on the Singing Bridge and down in the city streets, stood amazed.

Ilgard did not look at Prince Kurban to catch his reaction to the miracle he had demanded. This something no one, not the Tearkin prince nor the Simathe High-Chief, could have predicted or would ever forget. They knew—everyone who witnessed it knew—this was no meager exhibition of this woman's power as the Artan, but a solemn declaration, a sun-borne promise that she walked in light. That she embodied light. That she alone was fit to fulfill the prophecy of someday passing *through the vales of shadow and despair to walk forevermore in the light.*

Even as the Simathe tipped back his own head to memorize a sight he knew would linger eternally, a feeling of weightlessness flooded his limbs. *Joined* to her, he could float with her into the sun, if only he would allow himself to be carried by her…

Shaking off the not unpleasant sensation, he planted his boots firmly on the stone arch of the great bridge, going so far as to grip the railing with both hands. Watching her, he now willed her to come down, to return to his side. She ignored him for a time, lost so deeply in the throes of her magic that perhaps she did not feel his silent appeal. Several long minutes slipped by while she hovered high above, radiating golden sunlight, rotating in a nearly indiscernible spin. Uneasy, the Simathe interjected more urgency through their bond. Would it wake her? Did she even feel it?

At last, she did. Her achingly slow spin halted then ceased altogether. Her head rose, her eyes opening, seeking his. Her mismatched eyes glowed as she awakened from her self-created spell as if from a long and satisfying sleep. She began to descend, drifting down toward him. Ilgard was only vaguely aware of his companions edging aside, of himself releasing the railing and stepping back toward the center of the bridge.

Finally, she hovered before and slightly above him. The golden lines melted from her face as her countenance returned to normal. Her arms lowered, and in her eyes he read an open invitation. He accepted it without thought, raising his own arms, molding his hands to her waist. As he did, she released the final tendrils of power, her weight falling on him to support. He did so, holding her high above him for a long moment before lowering her slowly to the ground.

A shout of victory went up from one individual in the crowd, was caught by another, repeated by another, and echoed by one more. The cries swept the assembly, fusing into a roar of happiness that shook the firmament as thousands of Aerisians joyfully seized her promise. All over the city, any still lingering in places of refuge now darted out, joining the crowd, adding their voices to the clamor. The throng swelled and, with it, his lady's joy.

Favoring him with a brief smile, the young Artan turned away. Dropping her left hand from his shoulder, she lowered it in a scooping motion and brought it up sharply to fling something into the air. A shower of golden dust and tiny gems burst, raining down upon the city square. Some threw up eager hands or held out hats to catch it. Others, tilting their faces and closing their eyes, allowed it to wash over them as though it were real rain. Children and young maidens lifted their arms as well, spinning and dancing in this enchanted downfall of gold.

She laughed with them, his lady, her relief and joy so full it overflowed, touching him, as well. In that moment, he knew beyond a shadow of a doubt that she had triumphed. She had won Laytrii to herself, and he rejoiced with her. However, in so doing, she had also shown the Dark Powers who she was and that she would not be defeated by any subtle or simple means. Glad as he was to know the Artan had come in his time, that he was privileged to share her day, he also felt an unfamiliar pang of fear.

From here, the path she walked would doubtlessly grow harder and darker. What the future might hold for them both, he could not say, but before the victory must come the battle. Before the triumph must come the struggle. There was no shielding her from it; it was her destiny. This shining moment was indeed beautiful, but how long dared he hope it would last?

Part Three
Discoveries, Dreams

Chapter Twenty-Seven

The Healing

The din of galloping hooves caught my ear.

"My lady!" someone cried. "Lady Hannah!"

From my vantage point on the lowest step of the palace's main entrance, I spun toward the cry.

"Elisia? Elisia, what is it?"

My friend, jumping off her mount before it had come to a complete standstill, ran toward me with hair askew and tears streaming down her cheeks. She was crying hard; she looked scared to death. Running headlong into my arms, she flung herself against me, clutching at my shoulders and sobbing as if her heart would break. But only for a moment. Fighting visibly to regain control, she made herself let go and step back, scrubbing hard at her weepy eyes.

In between short, breathless sobs, she choked out, "My lady, you must come. Garett has been injured!"

"The Ranetron High-Chief? Wounded? But how?"

This from Prince Kurban who, together with Ilgard, stood on the steps just above me.

I wondered the same thing myself. Upon descending the Singing Bridge, Garett had taken off with Cole and Kurban's two dozen Tearkin, all of them volunteering to assist the citizens of Laytrii in putting the city and palace back to rights. Prince Kurban, Ilgard, and I had returned to the palace. Despite my daze of happiness, my weary body was ready to collapse. I'd been planning on a bath and bed; however, I feared those plans were about to be disrupted.

The beautiful Spinner broke into a fresh torrent of tears at the Tearkin's simple question. She could barely speak for her crying.

"There w-was a-another—there were more of them," she wept. "Th-they, they were h-hidden, and—and…"

"And they attacked the High-Chief," Ilgard summarized, taking pity on her.

"Yes!" The word came out as a wail. Frightened myself, aching for her, I put my arms around my weeping friend and drew her close as she sobbed, "I fear he will die. Please, my lady, you must come!"

"But what can I do?" I asked helplessly.

"What can you do?" Pushing herself upright, Elisia swept the tangled hair out of her face and dashed away her tears with a fist. "You are the Artan—you can heal him!"

"Elisia, I'm no healer. I mean, I've never even tried it before. Shouldn't you have a physician—"

"The physician has already attended him. He says there is no hope and that my Garett must die. Please, Lady Hannah, if anyone can help him now, if anyone can save him… You must come. With my whole heart, I am begging you!"

I was hardly unmoved by her pleas, but the simple truth was that I was scared. I'd never attempted a healing before. Furthermore, this was not some stranger, but Lord Garett, the Ranetron High-Chief and the man with whom one of my best friends in Aerisia happened to be in love.

What if I can't help him? What if I do something wrong? What if I fail?

I didn't know I'd spoken these last thoughts aloud, and I jumped when a huge, heavy hand, though remarkably gentle, clamped down on my shoulder. It was the Tearkin prince. His face was empathetic, Elisia's piteously hopeful.

"My lady, you are the Artan. I have, this day, seen things I never hoped to see—things assuring my soul of that truth.

"As the Artan, all powers of goodness and light are met in you. Is not the power of health one of the greatest of these? Just because you have not attempted it yet gives you no cause to fear it. If you are skilled to heal, as I believe you are, then you must go with the Spinner and try. To try is all that she asks."

Elisia nodded fervently. "Aye, my lady. For you to try is all that I ask. If you try and succeed, my love will live. If you try and fail or if you do not try—" Fresh tears welled, yet she persevered bravely. "My beloved will die, I know this. But please, you *must* come."

I looked helplessly at Ilgard, studying his face for some clue, some sign as to what I should do. It revealed nothing. I wanted to be angry with him for not helping me out at this critical juncture, but couldn't. I knew he was holding back for a reason. I'd just shown the whole Aerisian world, basically, that I was the Artan, and now he wanted me to stand on my own two feet and make my own decisions. Although a part of me respected him for that, the frailer, panicky side moaned that independence was too heavy a burden to bear.

On the other hand, the love and hope emanating from my friend could not be denied, and I thought, *How would I feel if I were her and our situations were reversed? Wouldn't I want her to at least try?*

I knew that I would.

"All right, Elisia," I acquiesced. "I'll come. I'm not sure what I can do, but I promise I'll do my best. Just please, don't hate me if—"

"Have no fear on that score, my lady. No matter what occurs, you are my dear friend, and I will cherish you the more for your efforts on Garett's behalf." She summoned up a reassuring smile then said, "Now I will send for horses."

With that, she was gone, hastening off across the courtyard, demanding fresh horses be brought. I started to follow but felt a hand grasp my arm. Surprised, I half-turned, and Ilgard bent close, saying quietly, "Well done, Hannah."

I glanced up in surprise. Had I heard him correctly? Not only had he complimented me, but had he actually called me by my given name? That was certainly a new one, which made me wonder, again, to what extent that kiss may have altered our relationship.

"My lady!"

Elisia's desperate cry caught my attention, and I was forced to leave both Ilgard and thoughts of his unexpected praise behind as I jogged across the courtyard, heading toward the Spinner and the horses being saddled. Yet as I loped off, I heard Prince Kurban's voice as he and Ilgard descended the steps, following me close behind.

"Such love she has for him," the giant observed. "We should all be so loved."

Ilgard made no reply. Of course, he wouldn't. But as I swung up on my horse, I twisted to watch him mount his own animal, catching the glint of sunlight on his bronzed face and impossibly black hair.

You're right, Kurban, I couldn't help agreeing. *We should all be so loved.*

* * *

People rapidly gave way as our cavalcade clattered through the cobblestoned city streets. Elisia led the way, leading us down a maze of city streets until we drew up before a comfortably large inn. It was three stories, and a swinging sign out front named it *The Speckled Cock*. Here we dismounted, throwing our reins to the stable boys who came on the run to assist us.

We rushed from the brightness of the outdoors into the cool dimness of the inn's spacious common room, a combined dining and sitting area. People stood around in small groups or sat chatting at the tables, but when we entered, a hush fell and the folk fell to openly staring. Elisia, ignoring them all, brushed past the hefty innkeeper stationed at the bottom of the staircase without a word. Picking up her skirts, she took the stairs two at a time, vanishing almost instantly from view.

At any other time, I would've been tempted to laugh at the sight of this elegant woman doing something so out of character. Need, though, necessitates many things, and rather than laugh, I dashed after her, giving the innkeeper a quick smile as I darted past. This was met with a broad grin and a deep bow, which I scarcely had time to notice as I flew by. I reached the main hallway of the second floor in time to catch a glimpse of Elisia's skirts as she disappeared into a guest room. Slower now, I followed her toward the same chamber, pausing in the doorway.

She was kneeling alongside a low-slung bed, grasping a man's pale hand between both her own. The heartbreaking mixture of love, sorrow, and hope on her face was enough to make me cry as she whispered softly, "She is here, my love. The Artan is here. She will save you; I know she will."

No reply from the person on the bed.

I took a reluctant step forward, and a board creaked beneath my weight. The Spinner glanced up at the sound, panic in her green eyes.

"Please, my lady, you must hurry," she begged.

With that bit of urging, I moved closer, sinking down beside my friend in order to assess the man before me.

"We did all we could, my lady, that we did."

This came from one of the women standing on the opposite side of the bed. Looking away from Garett, I offered the twosome a reassuring smile, assuming they were probably workers here at the inn. They were dressed alike in dark skirts and red blouses under black, laced-up vests. The white kerchiefs covering their hair matched the roomy aprons protecting their clothing. Telltale bloodstains marked these aprons as well as their square, capable hands. One held a porcelain basin filled with dark water, bloodstained cloths draped over its side.

"I'm sure you did," I soothed, and they looked relieved.

The thinner one who held the basin went so far as to say, "We hope the best for the High-Chief. That we do, my lady."

"Aye," the other chimed in. "If anyone can heal him, my lady, we know it's you."

Hoping they were right, I offered a weak smile of thanks. Taking it as their signal to leave, they curtsied and headed for the door. Just before exiting, the one who had spoken first paused to inquire, "Might we be of further assistance? If there's anything we can do to help…"

Was there? I shook my head. "No, I don't think so, but please have someone stand by, just in case."

"Very well, my lady."

They left, closing the door softly.

Giving my full attention to the man on the bed, I carefully peeled back the sheet covering him and removed his blood-soaked bandages with the utmost care. A soft cry escaped. I knew I should have been strong for Elisia, whose face had gone stark white at the sight, but I couldn't help my shock. The poor thing buried her face in the warrior's blond hair in a desperate attempt not to look at the ghastly wound. I wanted to look away too but instead forced myself to study what I was contending with.

"Good heavens," I heard myself whisper, amazed the man was still alive.

He lay on his left side because his right was ripped open from hip to armpit, his innards exposed for me to see. I bit my lower lip hard to keep from gagging at the sight of so much blood, of being able to see entrails through the torn flesh.

Oh help, I pleaded, fearing I would faint.

I'd only ever received the most basic CPR training and had no idea how to deal with something like this. Gingerly, I reached for his wrist, then neck, searching for a pulse. It was so faint and erratic I almost couldn't find it. His breathing was so shallow his chest barely moved at all. Lowering my hand, I gazed fearfully at the gaping hole in his side. This man was clearly near death and could die at any second. It was a miracle he'd held on this long.

Feeling somebody's fingers brush my shoulders, I glanced up to see Ilgard standing next to me. He knelt, putting his hand under my chin and lifting it so he could peer deeply into my eyes.

"You can do this, lass."

Tears welled at the gentle encouragement. One rolled down my cheek, dripping off my chin. "I don't think I can. He's going to die. What can I do? What if I kill him myself?"

"You will not," he said simply. Using his thumb, he wiped away my tears then got to his feet. Looking down, he said, "I will wait with the Tearkin in the common room below. What you do now, you must do on your own."

After that, I had to watch him leave, helpless to conjure up an excuse that would get him to stay. He knew I wanted him there, but he'd chosen to go anyway, leaving me truly on my own for what felt like the hardest trial I'd had to face yet. Pushing down a surge of resentment, I returned my focus to the immobile form on the bed and Elisia weeping soundlessly into his hair.

Powers of Good, be with me now, I entreated silently.

Placing my hands tentatively over the gaping wound, I closed my eyes, struggling to concentrate while plunging deep within for anything that might help. A gasping breath, a choking gargle distracted me. To my dismay, I realized Garett was breathing his last, the death rattles starting.

"My lady, he is dying! You must do something!"

I refused to open my eyes at Elisia's desperate cries but gritted my teeth and fought harder to shut out the world around me. Aureeyah had never given me lessons in healing. Maybe it'd been too far beyond the scope of my capabilities at the time, but right now I wanted to curse her for it. This was no ordinary feat of magic but something far different and far more complicated. I probed the depths of my innermost being, flinging about desperately for something, anything…

A shudder rippled through my body, forceful enough to rock me to the side as I touched something new inside. I felt…*life* and at that instant realized I'd somehow tapped into a life-force. My own.

It was a desperate attempt, a last-ditch effort, a shot in the dark, but I tried it anyway, despite instinctively knowing its danger. Telling myself I had no other option, I acted. Plunging my hands deep into the wound, I opened myself up completely. I felt power racing through my fingertips, power that flowed out of my body and into the Ranetron's.

Instantly, I knew something was wrong. Using my magic before had always felt exhilarating, empowering. This was brutal. This was agony. I'd never felt such intense, draining pain. I heard my own screams as if from a distance, but, defying the pain, I held on until I felt the man under my hands jerk wildly. In spite of the suffering, relief washed over me. I knew his life was returning to him.

As the wound closed in on itself, my hands slowly withdrew themselves from his body. A final brilliant burst of agony, and they were completely free. The wound had closed without a scar. I don't know how, but I somehow managed to shut off that flow of power, of life. But it was already too late. I felt consciousness slip, heard Elisia cry out as my body pitched forward. The darkness closed in, and I swayed like a drunk, only to collapse, toppling across the insensible form of the Ranetron High-Chief, every bit as lost as he.

Chapter Twenty-Eight

Sacrifice

The first stirrings of consciousness arrived slowly. I struggled to wake, feeling as if I waded through quicksand. I had an overwhelming headache, one that seemed to branch out into my limbs, making it more like a full-blown body ache. Groaning, I forced my eyelids open in spite of the painful, overwhelming brightness all around.

"My lady?"

The voice was concerned, questioning. I struggled to bring my gaze into to focus so I could determine the speaker. A face loomed above me—a face with alien, pitch-black eyes. Ilgard?

No, can't be him.

The voice was wrong, and the face was younger, somehow.

"My lady? Can you hear me?"

I squinted, shaking my head to clear my fuzzy brain. "Cole?" The word came out scratchy and rough. Clearing my throat, I tried again. "Cole, is that you?"

The impassive features above me relaxed just a little. "Aye, my lady," he agreed, relief in his voice. "You awaken."

I tried to smile, but it required too much effort. Instead, I whispered, "Where am I?"

"In your palace chambers."

"Wh-what happened? I remember—I remember passing out, but I don't remember anything else. It feels like I've been asleep for decades."

Since nobody in Aerisia would've known the name Rip Van Winkle, I didn't drop it, but I swear, the way I felt right then, I wouldn't have been surprised to discover my hair had turned white and twenty years had vanished while I slept. I couldn't believe how heavy and weighted my limbs felt. Under the blankets, I was wriggling my toes and turning my ankles, simply to make sure they still worked.

I guessed my nap hadn't quite matched Rip's, though. After handing me a glass of water off the nearby nightstand, Cole replied slowly, "Not decades, but you have slept five days. This is the morning of the sixth."

"Five days solid? Really?" I pushed myself up on my elbows, mindful not to spill the cup. "What on earth happened to make me go out like that?"

"Easy, my lady. Your strength has yet to be restored."

Relaxing back against the pillows, I took a drink, more to satisfy him than my own thirst, and then handed him the glass. "But why did I sleep five days? Was I sick?"

He permitted a slight frown. "You do not remember?"

"Remember what?"

"The Ranetron High-Chief…the healing…"

"I remember that, Cole," I declared impatiently. "But what's that got to do with this?"

He eyed me gravely. "In restoring Lord Garett, you nearly took your own life."

At his somber statement, new memories suddenly washed over me. Memories I'd blanked out until now. Terrible memories of searing, draining, horrific pain. Memories of my life leaving me and spilling into Garett.

My life…

I draped an arm across my eyes. "I remember now. I must've done the healing wrong."

"To say the least."

Lifting my arm, I shot him a mock glare. "You didn't have to agree."

He quirked a half-smile. "You did not have to say it."

"Oh brother." Collapsing once more against the pillows, I replaced my arm, shielding my eyes from the brightness of the room, which was doing nothing to help my headache. "At least once, you'd think you Simathe could sugarcoat the truth a little. You don't have to be so blunt all the time, y'know."

"Should I dissemble then?"

Before I could respond with, "That might be nice for a change," seriousness replaced his humor as he said, "I cannot say you did not err. Nevertheless, I will confess your act showed great courage. You are no woman to surrender easily."

Slowly, I lowered my arm so I could see his face. "Wow, that's quite a compliment, coming from a Simathe. Thank you, Cole. That means a lot to me. It really does."

Another smile softened his face. "You have earned your praise, and your rest."

With that, he stood as if he was going to leave.

"Wait," I forestalled him, "how is Garett, anyway? Recovering okay?"

"Weary, but well. Resting, as you should be."

"What about Elisia? And where's Ilgard, by the way? I wanted to ask him what Council's going to do now that Lord Elgrend's gone."

"The High-Chief is...in his chambers," he replied slowly.

Was I mistaken, or did he sound almost reluctant to hand out this information?

"So can you get him for me?"

"Forgive me, I cannot."

"What do you mean, '*forgive me, I cannot*'? Cole, what's going on?" I demanded suspiciously. "There's something you're not telling me, and I want to know what it is."

Once more, I detected hesitation. However, he finally answered, "The High-Chief rests, my lady. He would not be drawn from your bedside, despite—well," he pressed on quickly, as if I wouldn't have noticed the skip, "the Lady Braisley intervened at last, sending him away to rest."

"Braisley? Who's that?"

I had to admit, I felt a bit jealous of this unknown woman who had enough influence over the Simathe High-Chief to get him to do anything. I'd been *Joined* to him for months, and I certainly didn't have that kind of hold over him.

"And what do you mean, he wouldn't leave my bedside, *despite*—despite what? Why does he need to rest, anyhow? I know you guys don't have to like other people do, so what happened to him to make this Braisley person send him away?"

Luckily for Cole, a knock sounded at the door, saving him from my interrogation. Without waiting for a response, whoever was outside opened the door just enough to enter then turned and closed the door.

Was my vision playing tricks on me? Was it the headache? Or was my visitor really white and shimmering? For an instant, the powerful glow reminded me of sunbeams striking early morning fog lying low over the lake. I blinked my eyes to dispel the haze, but it wasn't going anywhere.

"Aureeyah?"

The figure spun gracefully at my call, and I saw at a glance it wasn't Aureeyah after all but another fairy, equally entrancing. Cole stood in respect as she glided across the marble floor, positioning herself at the foot of my bed.

"Greetings, lady from Earth," she said, folding her hands at the waist, gazing down solemnly upon me.

"Uh…"

Maybe I was still stupefied from my long nap, or maybe it was how the power in me sensed the power in her like a tangible thing. Either way, I was so overwhelmed by her presence I could hardly think at first, and I couldn't stop myself from staring. She was stunning, mesmerizing, in a way even my friend Aureeyah couldn't match. Whereas Aureeyah was like forest shade on a summer day, this fairy was the arresting, impassible, snowcapped peaks of a wild mountain range.

Her sleek, silvery-white gown stopped shy of her bare feet in the front but trailed more than a yard behind her in the back. A gossamer veil, delicate and sheer as a bride's, draped from an ornate tiara that looked carved from ice. That seemed impossible, but if there was one thing I'd learned so far in Aerisia, it was that the impossible was very often possible, meaning I didn't rule out an ice crown for this woman. Her golden hair, heavily streaked with scarlet, was pulled over one shoulder but reached her waist even so, and embedded in her forehead was a six-sided snowflake that glimmered brilliantly.

The set of her face was sharper, perhaps, than Aureeyah's and her skin even paler, which made her green eyes startlingly bright in contrast to the white of her clothing and pale blonde of her hair. Her aura gave her an almost ghostly appearance, yet from her back fluttered a pair of wings, long and diaphanous and almost as tall as she. Clearly, she was no phantasm but a storybook fairy brought to life—one whose icy beauty was alluring and startling all at once.

"You've awakened," she observed, her voice a low, pleasant alto. "That is well." She stepped delicately from the bed's foot to its head, placing a cool palm on my forehead as if checking for fever. "We feared for your life, Hannah Winters from Earth."

I blinked, surprised. "You know my name."

"I know a great deal about you, including most all that has befallen you since your arrival in Aerisia," she corrected.

"Who are you?"

The fairy didn't reply right away, her face grave even though her eyes smiled. She was studying me like I was studying her, I realized. Maybe I was every bit as foreign to her as she was to me. Maybe she'd been awaiting the Artan for many years and was now looking me over, wondering if I was really it. Did I measure up? Could I ever measure up to all that was expected of me?

"I am one called Braisley," she explained at last. "My home is Cleyton, the highest peak of the Unpassed Mountains."

"You're the mountain fairy?"

"Not *the* mountain fairy, for I am but one of many. I reside at Cleyton, for from its icy breath was I born, and I am part and parcel to its strength."

"She is strongest of all fairies," Cole put in quietly.

Uh-huh. You're obviously acquainted with her, and I'm guessing she was undoubtedly in the Unpassed Mountains the whole time I was there. Nobody ever bothered to let me know that, though, did they?

I guessed I shouldn't have been surprised, since the Simathe had apparently pulled the same trick with the Tearkin giants, but it still rankled. How many other secrets and surprises were they holding onto?

"Aye, so I am," the fairy concurred lightly, moving to take a seat on the edge of my bed.

"Aureeyah never mentioned you," I said. "Actually, neither did anybody else."

I shot Cole a scowl. He shrugged in return, a gesture that could've meant the matter was out of his hands or else, *Deal with it.* Or both. Likely both.

"My name is seldom heard," the fairy replied, and I switched my attention back to her. "Many and long have been the years since I last descended to walk among mankind. Were the need not so great, I would not have done so now."

"What need?" I frowned.

"You truly do not know?"

I shook my head against the pillows. "No."

"Why, the need was for you, Hannah—for your life. To save it. Without myself, without the Simathe High-Chief, you surely would have died."

* * *

My legs were so stiff as I made the solitary journey from my room to Ilgard's that I felt like one of those old ladies shuffling along the halls of a nursing home in their bathrobe and slippers. I'd always felt sorry for them when, as a kid, I'd go with my family to visit my grandmother, and I felt even more sympathy now.

After five days in bed, I could pretty much use a cane or walker, I thought wryly. *Boy, wouldn't it be inspiring for folks to see their Artan getting around like that?*

Truthfully, I probably didn't look very inspiring right now anyway, but I was determined to make this particular visit alone and had turned down Cole's offer of help.

Besides, I figured, *the exercise has to be good for me after so much time in bed. In fact, I should go visit Garett when this is done; keep moving and stay on my feet.*

If I still had the strength, that is. Braisley had warned me I might suffer bouts of weakness for the next several days. My body had undergone severe strain during the Ranetron's healing and my own. Time would be needed for it to recover satisfactorily. How much time, she hadn't said, but with how weak I felt, I was afraid it might be awhile.

The going was slow enough that I was beginning to think I should've taken Cole up on his offer after all, but eventually I reached my destination, after stopping twice in the hallway for a brief rest. I didn't bother to knock but entered silently, closing the door after myself and leaning against it to catch my breath and gain my bearings.

The first thing I saw was the Simathe Chief Captain, seated behind a desk near the window, going through a stack of paperwork and scratching on parchment with a quill pen. Upon my entrance, he glanced up, stabbing the pen in the inkwell as he pushed his chair back from the desk. Rising, he strode over to me, saying firmly, "This is not a good time, my lady. Both of you should rest. Come, I'll escort you to your chambers."

Shaking my head, I whispered, "No. No, Norband, I have to see him. I need to see if he's okay—just have to…"

My gaze fell on the man on the bed, and I couldn't go on. Silence stretched. At last, Norband said, "Very well, my lady. I'll allow a moment. Do not disturb him, however."

I nodded in agreement, not quite trusting myself to speak. Accepting the gesture, the Chief Captain went out, leaving me alone with the sleeping man on the bed. I looked back when I heard the door close, half afraid of being in here by myself and half making sure he was really gone and Ilgard and I were really alone.

We were, and for the life of me, I couldn't figure out how I felt about that. Or any of this, for that matter. Inside was a mixed-up, bubbling concoction of emotions ranging from disbelief to gratitude, attraction to awkwardness, and everything in between. This was possibly the most delicate position we'd been in yet, the High-Chief and I, and I honestly didn't know how to respond. When I looked over at him, though, it was clear he was out, and that gave me the courage to steal closer.

At his bedside, I stood gazing down at him for a time, simply watching him sleep, and felt my heart turn over. I'd never seen him like this—off guard, asleep, as vulnerable as I supposed he could be. Beneath its bronze cast, his face was unnaturally pale, the eerie blackness of his unbound hair accentuating that pallor and the fact that he was not himself.

I felt a stab of guilt.

My fault, all of this.

Sinking onto the floor beside the bed, clutching it with all ten fingers, I debated what to do. Selfishly, I wanted to wake him up, to hear him speak and reassure me everything was going to be okay. On the other hand, I'd promised Norband, and I didn't think he would appreciate me breaking my word. The temptation was there, though. I even thought if I simply willed it hard enough, maybe he'd wake up on his own, leaving me innocent of all charges.

Then I asked myself why I was being such a baby about this. Deep down, I think the answer was that I was afraid. What if his condition was more serious than Braisley, Cole, and even Norband were letting on? What if I'd done something to permanently scar or alter him? What if, when he woke up from this, he was never the same?

That's stupid, the more rational part of my brain interjected. *You're the same, aren't you?*

I didn't know. Was I? Or had that moment in the corridor, that moment of weakness or passion or whatever it had been, changed everything, including me? It must have changed something, or else I wouldn't be in here. I wouldn't be afraid like this. Afraid that everything would've changed; afraid that nothing had changed.

"Oh Ilgard," I whispered, laying trembling fingers on the bed next to his bare arm. "What have I done? What have we done? And what on earth are we going to do about it?"

* * *

When Norband found me a short while later, I was up off my knees and in a chair beside Ilgard's bed. I had more dignity at least than to be caught weeping over the Simathe High-Chief. And I wasn't weeping—not really, although I did scrub the traces of a couple tears off my cheeks as the Chief Captain entered the room. He inquired quietly if I were ready to return to my room, and I said I was. I felt spent, emotionally and physically, and even accepted the Simathe's arm and his silent aid on the return journey.

Once in my room and alone, I sank down onto the bed, kicked off my slippers, and collapsed against the pillows. I'd hardly rooted into a comfy spot before a knock at the door announced a visitor, who turned out to be Elisia.

"I was following you from a distance and saw you on the Chief Captain's arm," she said. "I bethought myself to look in on you. Are you well, my lady?"

I gave a half-hearted nod. "I'm fine. Just...oh, I don't know."

Seating herself next to me, she touched my wrist gently. "Whatever troubles you, my friend, let it go. This is not the time to plague yourself with worry."

"No, Elisia, you don't understand," I objected brokenly, wringing a folded hankie between my fingers. "This is all my fault. My fault for making that stupid mistake."

"What do you mean?"

"I mean my healing Garett. It was stupid. Now Ilgard's the one paying for it, and—"

"Stupid?"

Indignant, my friend shot to her feet. Hands on her hips, she towered over me, green eyes flashing. "Was it stupidity that saved Garett's life? Stupidity that healed him? Stupidity that rescued the man I love? Would you rather he had died?"

"Hey now, calm down, I didn't mean that!" I protested, holding up my hands in a defensive posture. "I'm sorry for the way that sounded. I don't regret saving Garett's life at all! I'm thankful he's okay. I'm just saying the way I did it was stupid. It not only harmed me, it harmed others because of me."

As quickly as it had flared, her anger left, and Elisia was my friend once more. "Ah, you refer to the Simathe High-Chief," she observed.

I nodded miserably. "You should see him, Elisia. He's so pale and haggard looking. He's not supposed to be like that."

My fingers went back to twisting the handkerchief in my lap until my friend leaned over, laying her hand on top of mine.

"You care for him, don't you?"

I thought about protesting but didn't think it would do any good. It was very likely by now that she wasn't the only one who suspected something was going on. I wished I knew exactly what it was, though.

"Am I crazy?" I whispered.

Sure felt like I was headed that way.

"Some would say no more than me loving a soldier, a High-Chief."

I narrowed my eyes. What did she mean by that? Surely she didn't think that I...

Before I could get her to clarify, she went on, saying, "My lady, do not fret. Anyone who undertook what the High-Chief has done for you would be laid low for a time. An ordinary man could not have done it at all. And then to refuse to leave your bedside for several days and nights...naturally, he is worn. Regardless, Lord Ilgard is Simathe. He will recover in time."

"Maybe. I hope you're right." Pulling my knees to my chest, I locked my arms around them. "But he shouldn't have had to go through that for me."

"My lady, when the High-Chief *Joined* with you, he was well aware of the dangers and risks. He chose to do it despite those perils, and we all ought to be thankful that he did."

"Of course I'm thankful, Elisia. I just—I wish none of this had ever happened."

The Spinner scooted closer. Draping an arm about my shoulders, she drew my throbbing head down onto her shoulder.

"Oh, Lady Hannah, none of us has the power to change the past. It is to the future we must look."

What if it's to a future that doesn't include Ilgard? What if it's to a future that does? What if my future is limbo, not knowing what I want or don't want?

"The future can be a scary thing," I admitted softly.

"It can," my friend agreed. "It can be a terrifying thing because it can change in an instant."

Thinking of that unprecedented moment in the palace hallways, of a very much unforeseen and unanticipated kiss, I had to agree.

"And sometimes it leaves us even more lost and confused than before," I added.

She looked at me quizzically. "Do you refer again to the High-Chief? You know he will recover."

I had been, though not in the way she assumed.

"It's just hard for me to believe I was so far gone that it took both Ilgard and Braisley to bring me back," I hedged. "Was I really that close to dying?"

"Aye, you truly were," she agreed solemnly. "Even closer than Garett, if that is possible. The High-Chief gave of his own life-force to restore you, and Braisley was the means by which it was transferred. A mighty fairy indeed was required to direct a thing so powerful as an immortal's life-force."

"How did she even know to come?" I asked. "If I was really that close to death's door, I'm surprised she made it in time."

"She was at the palace by the time you were moved there. Most of us feared we were moving you there to die; yet there she was. Fairy magic," the Spinner summarized, shaking her head. "It is unpredictable and mysterious. Likely, we will never know how she knew to come, but come she did."

"And she couldn't just use her magic to heal me?"

I hadn't thought to ask her that earlier when she'd told me what had occurred. Then again, I'd been so overawed not only by Braisley herself, but also by the story she wove that I hadn't thought to ask for extra details.

"No." My friend shook her head. "You had no wound to be healed; you had a life-force to be restored. I tell you, Hannah, had the High-Chief not been *Joined* to you, you would have perished. Only through the *Joining* bond could what you gave be safely replaced. And then, his weakness after the ordeal notwithstanding, the High-Chief refused to abandon your bedside. For more than three days and nights he kept watch, until Braisley finally persuaded him that you would be equally safe in another Simathe's keeping."

"He looks so weak," I murmured, feeling tears as I thought of all he'd sacrificed for me.

"Aye, but he will recover. He needs only to rest. And you, my lady, need your rest as well. Methinks you've done too much upon awakening, considering your weakened state." She stood. "Back into bed with you."

By this point, I was too drained to do anything except comply with her gentle demands. Crawling to the head of the bed, I collapsed. Sleep rushed in before my cheek touched the pillow, and I barely heard the Spinner say as she tucked the coverlet around me, "Sleep now, and I will wait beside you. When you awaken, you must eat to regain your strength."

Eat...food... I was pretty hungry, come to think of it. Nevertheless, sleep sounded even better than eating. For now, I gave in to the siren's song and slept.

Chapter Twenty-Nine

Friends

"My lady?"

"Elisia?"

The beautiful Spinner smiled down at me. I waited for her to speak, but she said nothing, just stood there grinning like a fool.

"Okay, what is it?" I snapped, a little annoyed at having been disturbed in my reading. I'd been flipping through a thick tome, *Chronicles of Aerisia's Past*, that I'd discovered in the massive palace library, seeking information about the first Artan and what, if any, clues her life might give about my own destiny. "Why are you smiling at me like that?"

In spite of my touchiness, her smile softened. "He has awakened," came the short reply.

It took less than a second for that to sink in. I didn't have to be told twice. The book fell into the chair, forgotten, as I picked up my skirts and rushed from the library, hearing my friend's laughter behind me as I fled.

* * *

The door was partially open, and I could hear muted conversation as I approached. My heart was pounding double- time. I knew he could probably sense that, which made me even more nervous. Should I go back, wait until we were alone for this first meeting? Or was it better to do this now with other people around, delaying any potentially awkward discussions?

Since I wasn't sure I was ready to hash out our kiss and where that placed us yet, I opted for going in now.

Just play it cool, I told myself. *It's perfectly natural to be visiting him under these circumstances. Nobody but Elisia has to suspect a thing, and they won't if you don't act weird.*

That advice was all well and good, but before entering, I still took a moment to tidy my appearance, pulling out the ribbon tying back my hair and tucking it into my pocket. I wore no makeup (cosmetics, as they called it around here), and I was clothed in a simple skirt and blouse with tiny embroidered flowers around the neckline and hem, set off by a pair of plain hoop earrings. Still, with my hair down and the blouse's scooped neckline framing my customary necklace, I supposed I looked presentable enough.

Not like he hasn't seen you at your best and worst by now. And it's not like he really cares about your looks. Besides, since when do you care if he does?

Giving my head a shake to toss all these ceaseless arguments and debates aside, I mustered up my courage, knocked softly on the doorframe, and entered the bedchamber. Several people filled the room, including Chief Captain Norband, Lord Garett, Moonkind Risean, and the fairy Braisley. He'd been looking at her, but the instant I cleared the door, his head turned and those inscrutably deep eyes captured mine. Suddenly, I had to remind myself to breathe. The walls seemed to close in, narrowing until only the two of us were present. Or was I imagining things?

Regardless, relief overwhelmed me at seeing him awake and looking more like his normal self. Even though he lingered in bed, he was now sitting up, braced with pillows against the mahogany headboard. His gaze was direct, his eyes clear, and even the skin under his eyes was no longer shadowed by weariness. Except for the fact that he was still in bed, I would never have guessed he'd just undergone any sort of trauma.

Several people addressed me as I approached. I thought I made the proper greetings in return, but I admit it was hard to stay focused on acting normal with him right there, awake and undoubtedly aware that inside I wasn't at all myself. Whatever he sensed, though, he didn't betray with a look or a word. His expressionless, Simathe's face was calm, giving nothing away.

Braisley stood, motioning for me to take her chair.

"Thank you," I said, breaking eye contact with Ilgard as I slid into the proffered seat.

The flow of conversation resumed, but for the life of me, I don't think I heard a word that was said. Before long, the fairy had excused herself and slipped out of the room. In short order, the others discreetly followed her lead. The door closed behind Risean's retreating figure, and we were alone.

I smiled at the man across from me. "Hey," I began, touching his arm softly.

He inclined his head. "My lady." A brief hesitation, then—"You look well."

"Thanks, so do you," I offered almost shyly.

What on earth is wrong with you, Hannah?

There were a lot of things I'd been around the Simathe High-Chief—angry, rebellious, clumsy, ridiculous, defiant, stubborn, awkward. Shy, though—that was a new one.

When he made no direct reply, silence fell. Unsure what to say or do next, I let my gaze drift down, settling on the fingers I folded in my lap.

"I dreamt a beautiful woman, perhaps a fairy, came to me as I slept."

My chin jerked up.

"I remember…she spoke to me," he went on slowly, his attention fixed on my face. "I believe she shed tears as well. Tears for me."

My throat tightened as I stared at him. What had he heard? Did he actually remember my visit?

His eyes held mine for an endless moment, and then…softened. Reaching up, he touched my cheek ever so softly with all five fingertips.

"It was not a fairy, I think. Nor a dream. It was you?"

Hardly daring to breathe, I laid my hand across the back of his and leaned my face into his palm.

"Yes," I whispered.

"I thought as much." He fell silent then asked, "Why tears?"

What could I say to that? Because I was overwrought, feeling guilty I'd put him in that position, worried about his well-being, and, most of all, worried about this new phase of our relationship?

"I—I was concerned about you," I stammered, evading the deeper truth. "They told me what you did. How you saved my life and wouldn't leave me, even to rest. I'd just woken up, and I felt so terrible about everything. I came to see you, to check on you, and—and you were so pale, and I was afraid…"

"No, Hannah," he interrupted, voice kind. Beneath my hand, his thumb moved, tracing the contours of my cheekbone. "You need never fear for me, lass."

"I'm sorry, I can't help it. I'm only human after all."

He smiled then—a real smile which lingered before fading away as he said, "Human—yet so unlike the rest. I have never seen your like, my lady."

This made me laugh. "I've never seen yours, either." I paused, hesitating before inquiring, "Are you sure you'll be all right?"

"I am told I may leave my room on the morrow."

I smirked. "And since when do you do what anyone tells you to?"

"Braisley has spoken, and one does not lightly anger a fairy."

"No, nor a Simathe."

He permitted a brief smile, lowering his hand to the bed. I thought about placing mine inside it, imagining how it would feel to have my fingers swallowed by his. Resisting the impulse, I asked instead, "We've been through a lot together, haven't we?"

"That we have."

"And we'll probably go through a lot more, before all's said and done."

He studied my face. "As Artan, your journey has scarcely begun."

"Be that as it may," I said slowly, "and no matter what happens in the future, I want to thank you right now for everything you've done for me. I know in the beginning I resisted everything you threw out there, but I realize now that from then until the present you've been my protector, and now I'm honored to call you my—my friend."

Friend.

It didn't quite seem to cover everything we'd been, everything we were, or all of the crazy, mixed-up feelings roiling through me. There was so much more to say than a mere offer of gratitude. The time wasn't right, however. Knowing that, I contented myself with a simple declaration of friendship and went on.

"We'll probably butt heads in the future; we're both too stubborn not to, and I know I can be a brat sometimes. You've always stood by me, though, and I know I can count on you to be there for me when I need you."

His countenance changed as I spoke, his eyes regarding me in a way I'd never seen him look at anyone else. Or at me, for that matter. Hope sprang in my chest, especially when he said, "True, my lady. You may always depend on me. I'll never fail you."

Chapter Thirty

Preparations

I was on the verge of getting dressed, preparing myself for the Instating ceremony of Aerisia's newest High Elder. This was Lord Ri Wy' Joisten, a former member of Council, elected to lead by his fellow council members. Tonight, Lord Ri would be formally welcomed as Aerisia's newest High Elder in what I'd been told by my friend Rittean would be a "surpassing grand event, especially with the Artan in attendance."

"Yeah, I'm not too sure about that," I'd answered wryly, thinking of the handful of formal occasions I'd attended in my former life back on Earth. Basically those had included junior and senior prom and a couple of weddings. I was pretty sure none of them would even come close to the splendor of an Aerisian Instating ceremony, and I couldn't deny my nerves as I waited on Rosean to come help me dress.

While I waited, I sifted through memories of poor Lord Elgrend, the High Elder who'd welcomed me to Aerisia the day I arrived. I actually didn't have many memories of him, as the only opportunities I'd had to get to know him were during the past few months here at the palace, and I'd been so busy then that there was little time for friendly socializing. I did regret having to miss his funeral, which had been held a few days after his death while I was sleeping, recovering from Garett's healing. In fact, Ilgard and I had turned out to be some of the very few not in attendance for this last veneration of a great man. Even though I hadn't personally been well acquainted with him, I knew by reputation that Lord Elgrend had been much honored and much loved.

Council, meeting as soon as Ilgard was up and about, had quickly gotten on with the business of choosing a new High Elder. Ordinarily, the office of High Elder went from parent to child, but Lord Elgrend had married young and lost his wife to illness after only a few months of marriage. Since Lord Elgrend had never remarried or produced an heir, Lord Ri was chosen to assume his role, while a respected and prominent Lord of Lands and Ranetron veteran, Lord Hornst Wy' Justley, had been selected to receive Lord Ri's seat at Council. Lord Hornst would also be officially welcomed into his new position during tonight's festivities.

"My lady?" A knock at the door interrupted my musings. My servant girl, Rosean, slipped into the room. "I am come to help you dress," she said.

"Sounds good," I agreed, and she was off scurrying about the room, retrieving my gown, fetching my shoes and silk stockings, and laying everything out in readiness upon the bed.

Earlier, she'd been one of my first visitors once I was able to receive any, bringing with her profuse apologies for having ever doubted me. Or she tried, anyway. I'd cut off her explanations and regrets with a hug and a, "Forget about it. Everybody makes mistakes. It's all in the past."

That had gone a long way toward soothing matters, but I still felt she was treading lightly around me. I didn't know if she was afraid I'd change my mind and have her packed off to the kitchens as a scullery maid or maybe come up with some other punishment. I was sorry the relative easiness we'd once shared was gone, but hoped in time we'd get it back. I couldn't worry about all that right now anyway, since I had to hurry up and dress.

I'd already bathed and had spent the past half hour outside on my balcony in an attempt to coax my hair into drying faster. Sometimes I really missed the modern conveniences of Earth, specifically little amenities such as blow-dryers that I'd always taken for granted. At any rate, my hair was now only a little damp, so I sat absolutely motionless in a chair by my dressing table as Rosean first applied cosmetics then began the process of arranging my hair.

Once that was done, I pulled on silk stockings and then stood to slip into my gown. Next came my shoes, which Rosean knelt to fasten for me. I dabbed a rich perfume, a gift from a visiting dignitary, onto my throat and wrists, allowed the servant girl to sprinkle a few drops onto my hair, and went to the mirror for a final check.

I could hardly believe the image that presented itself.

Rosean had done a masterful job with my hair, threading it with seed pearls before twisting it into an intricate knot on the back of my head. Several thicker curls fell from the artistic weave to drape over my left shoulder, while a few wisps floated around my pearl earrings.

The Spinners had outdone themselves with my gown, which had been created especially for tonight. A shimmering silver-white, it hung in clean, simple lines to the floor, where it pooled softly at my feet. The flared hemline was embellished with tiny pearl-pink flowers and the off-the-shoulder neckline with soft, draping folds of chiffon. Wispy sleeves of the same material fell to my fingertips, and the back of the gown was laced up with silver ribbon. Matching slippers and pearl jewelry completed the look. Staring in the mirror, I felt red-carpet worthy, if not quite Artan worthy.

Don't know if I'll ever feel worthy *to fill those shoes.*

"You look lovely, my lady." This from Rosean, who had come up behind me, her reflection meeting mine in the mirror. She reached up to tuck a stray hair into place, saying, "Doubtless you will be the loveliest woman present."

I shook my head, picturing Elisia the Spinner and Lady Tey. "I doubt it, Rosean," I said, turning to her. "But thanks for the compliment."

Stifling any would-be protests with a quick hug and a sincere "thank you," I made my way to the door, leaving the servant girl free to ready herself for the upcoming festivities.

Aerisian custom dictated the new High Elder enter the Instating ceremony escorting the greatest lady available of either rank, wealth, position, or beauty. This was in homage to High-Chieftess Laytrii who, centuries past, had actually created the office of High Elder. Tonight, as the Artan, I had been chosen to play this role. As soon as I left my room, there stood Lord Ri, resplendent in formal robes of deep violet trimmed with gold.

"My lady…" He sketched a deep bow. "There are no words to describe how honored I am that you are here with me at this time."

Touched, I replied, "Thank you, High Elder. I'm honored to be here."

"Not High Elder, not yet," he warned playfully, offering me his arm. "Let us refrain from early use of the title, lest it call down bad luck upon us. Although," he added as an afterthought, "with the Artan by my side, I believe all bad luck will surely stay away this night."

"Let's hope you're right," I agreed. "I think we're all due for a break."

I knew I was. Nevertheless, the way things had been going, even if tonight turned out to be peaceful, I sincerely doubted the respite would hold.

Chapter Thirty-One

The Instating

His eyes met hers as he knelt to place his hands atop those of Lord Ri, swearing his allegiance to the man, Pronconcil to High Elder. The Simathe High-Chief had to force himself to turn his attention to the new High Elder, to look away from his lady's captivating gaze…a task he was lately finding ever more difficult. Upon completing his oath, he rose, resuming his former station between the Cortain on his left and Spinner on his right. The Ranetron High-Chief, situated on Lady Tey's other side, now stepped forward to make his own declaration to Lord Ri.

The Instating ceremony was nearly complete.

After swearing the fealty of himself and his men, Lord Garett would move back into place, the last to pledge. Afterward, all that remained was for the new High Elder to make his own solemn oath to the people of Aerisia, in which, as head of Council, he swore to lead, guide, and direct them with honesty, justice, fairness, and mercy. To do all in his power and wisdom to restrain the hand of The Evil while championing the cause of good.

Lord Ri Wy' Joisten delivered the words solemnly and slowly, taking care that each syllable was pronounced distinctly and clearly. The ceremony was complete. However, before any congratulations could be offered or cheers raised, the newly instated High Elder did a new and unprecedented thing. Turning from the people, he slowly lowered himself to the floor, genuflecting before the woman at his side. Taking her right hand between both of his, he peered up humbly into her face. Speaking loudly enough for all to hear, he said, "And to you, my lady Artan, I pledge every assistance it is in my power to give, both this evening and for the remainder of my life. Ever have the High Elders looked for the promised Artan. Now you have come, and with all the influence of my station, I vow to assist you as you rid this land of the Dark Powers and the taint of The Evil. This I swear to you, upon my honor as a lord of Aerisia and my oath as the High Elder."

To end his speech, the man bent over the hand he clasped, pressing a kiss upon it to seal his vows.

Ilgard, watching the young Artan closely throughout, saw as well as felt the rising of her emotions. After she had been doubted and scorned as Artan not many days past, to have the new High Elder publically align himself with her was cause for tremendous relief. Though she restrained herself, he could see tears glittering like dewdrops in her mismatched eyes as she stooped to pull the new lord of Aerisia to his feet. Together, facing the people they both served, the pair was met with loud, raucous cries of tribute.

They descended arm in arm from the dais where the ceremony had been held to the floor of the Grand Chamber, passing between the lines of Council and Pronconcil members bordering both sides of the steps. All were cheering, lending their voices to the happy cries of the throng. Save himself. Still, as she passed him by, he caught the scent of her perfume and could not help noticing that tonight she was beauty itself.

First Council, then Pronconcil, fell into step by twos behind the lead couple, descending to the ballroom floor in similar fashion. Ilgard found Lady Tey at his side. The Cortain Pronconcil, lovely in summer-sky blue, graced him with a fleeting smile as she accepted his proffered arm for the descent. At the bottom of the staircase, they parted ways, she going to the other guests, and Ilgard taking up a stationary post against the far wall. With the ceremonies over, the festivities would now begin. Rather than join in, he contented himself by playing the onlooker, letting his eyes follow the progress of his lady as she wove in and out among the crowd.

His Chief Captain soon joined him, fixing himself silently at Ilgard's side. Like his lord's, Norband's eyes were also constantly moving as he observed the throng, alert for any signs of danger.

Should you not be at her side?

I sense no danger to her person.

To this Norband made no reply, accepting the assessment as it was stated. Ilgard felt a measure of surprise, even so, when the man next remarked casually, *She is very beautiful tonight.*

He did not ask who his friend meant, though he did question why he would say such a thing. Did he seek a reaction? Or was he merely remarking on the obvious? Rather than seek an answer, he contended himself with a straightforward agreement.

Aye, that she is.

His Chief Captain fell silent then, busy with his own thoughts and watchcare, leaving his High-Chief to his.

Ilgard found his eyes straying again toward the place he had last seen the young Artan. She stood there still, situated between two slender, fluted columns, chatting with her friend Moonkind Rittean. Raising her chin, she laughed merrily at something the other woman said, and he could hear the chords of it even from here. The soft light given off by moonstone chandeliers and scores of candles illuminated her profile, highlighting her smile. She reached up to brush the hair from her face, the movement graceful in its casualness.

His Chief Captain's words rang true. She was indeed lovely this night—to him, breathtakingly so. Perhaps it was the peculiar color of her hair and eyes, marking her clearly as a child of Earth. Perhaps it was remembering how she'd come alive in his arms when he had kissed her during that rare moment of self-surrender. Perhaps it was knowing that she had visited him when he was laid low, that she had cared enough to come, had cared enough to shed tears. Perhaps it was all this that set her apart and made her so beautiful.

The things he had once failed to notice or had outright ignored could not be overlooked now. His mind was so entwined with her that he could scarce tell where he ended and she began. Nor could he say how this had occurred. Was it the *Joining*? Surely that was a part of it, but could not be all. The *Joining* alone did not explain how this woman from Earth had managed to ensnare him, making him think and sometimes even act in such uncharacteristic ways.

The answer to his questions came soon after as she chanced to turn his way, catching his eyes upon her despite the distance and crowd separating them. Rather than frown, turning away in cool disdain or with a shiver of fear as an Aerisian woman might have done, she waggled her fingers in an inconspicuous, playful little wave and smiled. Such a beautiful smile, and only for him. He could feel its warmth from across the room and found himself faced with the temptation of smiling in return.

Even when her attention slipped, flitting back to her companion, his did not vacillate. Impervious to anything else, he kept watch on her during the next few hours as she wove through the guests, chatting with visitors, accepting tidbits of food and flutes of wine offered by busy servers, or stood aside to observe the dancing. At one point he followed, undetected, as she slipped away from the Grand Chamber and into a side hall on some private mission. To his amusement, once out of sight of any milling guests, she sank down onto an elegant chair and kicked off her shoes to rub her feet before slipping her footwear back on and returning to the gathering.

Witnessing that, he hid a smile. There she was, the long-awaited Artan, embodiment of prophecy and legend, whom many, including himself, had rather expected to arrive like a goddess in human form. Instead, she was simply a girl from another realm, a girl who made missteps, grew ridiculously stubborn, and whose feet hurt at celebratory occasions. She was the Artan, bold and brave as a dragon, yet so very human, too. And that, he realized, enchanted him more than all the magic and power she possessed.

Chapter Thirty-Two

Under the Moon

Standing off to one side of the vast, gorgeous Grand Chamber, I surveyed the intricate dance patterns winding about the ballroom floor. The gowns of the women and richly embroidered tunics or coats of the men made for a swirling sea of color. The dancers wove in and out, spun, dipped, curtsied, and bowed in elaborate configurations too difficult for me to decode. Although the scene was a far cry from the dances I'd attended back home, it was fascinating to watch, and I half wished I was more adept on my feet so I could join in.

Smiling, Elisia, in a gown of green velvet that brought out the color of her eyes and red sheen of her hair, whisked past me on the arm of Garett, who was dressed in muted tones of red and black. The air was stirred by their passing, and I rubbed my bare forearms to ward off goose bumps.

"Cold?"

The deep voice caught me off guard, making me start. Turning my head, I looked up into the face of the man I'd been trying all evening to sneak glimpses of.

"Ilgard, hey, don't you look nice all dressed up?" I approved.

He really did. To say he and his clan weren't fashion conscious was a major understatement, so to see him wearing something other than functional tonight was definitely a change. His white shirt beneath a dark coat set off the bronze and black of his skin and hair, and while he still wore boots and a sword, they were more decorative than what he typically wore. Along with his customary earring, glimmering around his neck was a gold medallion portraying what looked like the tower at Treygon where we'd been *Joined*. I liked the look, but maybe I was comparing him to some of the other guys in attendance.

Whereas the clothing of many men tonight was tasteful and masculine, others were wearing some pretty strange stuff. Their women's was equally bad. I didn't even have anything to compare some of the strange clothing choices I saw tonight to, but Rittean had assured me that most of the more outlandish sorts were worn by visitors to Laytrii who had different customs, manners of speech, and styles of dress.

I didn't doubt it. Apparently the Instating of a new High Elder was a momentous occasion. Already this evening I'd spoken to several people with unfamiliar names and accents from unfamiliar places. Of course, my knowledge of Aerisian geography was limited, to say the least, but it didn't take a genius to figure out tonight's event had drawn many visiting dignitaries.

Speaking of dignitaries, the one standing beside me took my compliment in stride—meaning he said nothing at all. I hadn't really expected a response, and lifting the wine flute I held, I had brought it to my lips for a sip when out of the blue he said, "You are exceedingly beautiful tonight."

What?

Startled, I inhaled some wine, which made me cough.

Did he really just say that? In front of a room full of people, no less?

I tried to hide both my shock and coughing by pressing a napkin to my mouth and turning my back, but several heads still turned our way. I smiled as best I could and waved to signal I was okay.

Definitely not going down as my classiest response to a compliment.

"You are well?"

The Simathe's question cut into my self-berating as he reached over to slip the glass from my hand. I drew a few deep breaths to calm both the coughing and my racing heart.

"Uh, yes, just fine, thanks," I croaked, dabbing at my chin with the napkin and hoping there was no wine on my face.

He handed back the wine flute. "Perhaps you have had enough."

"I'm not drunk!" I declared, embarrassed. "I just swallowed wrong, that's all."

He saw right through the fib. "Of course…which is why I do not give compliments."

Had I offended him? I felt terrible until I looked up into his face and saw actual humor in his eyes.

Oh, he's making a joke.

I felt some of the humiliation slip away and quipped, "Maybe if you did it more often, it wouldn't come as such a surprise."

"Perhaps I shall."

"Yeah, I can see that happening."

He fell silent then, and so did I, but that didn't mean my mind wasn't a beehive of thoughts, most of them along the lines of, *I can't believe he just said I was beautiful!*

True, he'd at least intimated it once before, but that was under the sort of circumstances where a person could easily slip up and say things they didn't mean. Or didn't mean to say. This, however, had been said while he was healthy and in full command of his mental faculties. It couldn't have been a mistake, and it wasn't like he was given to flattery or fawning. Which meant…what? That he was softening toward me, even as I was falling for him?

Uh oh. Are you?

I'd told Elisia a few days ago that I cared for him, but caring for and falling for were two very different things. This was the first time I'd dared admit the latter, even to myself, which made me wonder if he could decipher what I was thinking. Suddenly, he was standing much too close and the room was much too warm. My cheeks felt hot, and I quickly took a sip of wine to conceal what I could of my face as well as to calm my nerves.

This is insane! You can't think about this now; you can't do this now. He's immortal, and you're the Artan. Besides, he's Simathe, remember? He's not for you. He's not for anybody. It doesn't matter that he kissed you or said you were beautiful. That's hardly a marriage proposal. What are you, twelve? You've got to get over this.

The wine flute still at my lips, I glanced at him from the corner of my eye, trying to gauge what, if any of this, he might be picking up on. Unfortunately, his consistent Simathe demeanor gave nothing away, but, as if feeling my perusal, he shifted, looking my way. I dropped my eyes hastily, but I knew I'd been caught in the act. Fortunately, he chose not to comment on it, remarking instead, "You do not care to dance?"

I couldn't figure out if he was making polite conversation or trying to ease my embarrassment over all the inner turmoil he must be sensing. Regardless, tilting my head to the side, I peered up at him. "Do you?"

"I do not dance."

"I do. Well, truthfully, I like dancing, but I'm not very good at it. I don't know the steps to what they're doing anyway."

"You did not dance on Earth?"

"Oh, I did, but it was nothing like this. These kinds of dances have been out of fashion for years."

"Strange. Then how is dancing done on Earth?"

I shook my head, grinning. "Oh, you wouldn't believe me if I told you. Let's just say the good folks here would be pretty scandalized by what passes for dancing back home."

He gave me a look that I interpreted as him not being able to figure out why I thought scandalizing people was funny. Maybe it was nerves, maybe it was the wine, but that struck me as even more funny. For a fleeting moment, I considered really scandalizing the Aerisian muckety-mucks in attendance, not to mention the Simathe High-Chief, by asking him to dance. But that was a bit too wild even for me.

To get things back on course, I said, "Is it just me, or is it getting hot in here? I think I'm going out in the gardens to cool off."

"I shall accompany you," he offered.

It was no more or less than I'd anticipated. Handing my drink to the nearest server, I wove my way through the crowd, heading toward the nearest side exit. The Simathe warrior-lord followed as I left the noisy, stuffy ballroom, exchanging it for the peaceful calm of the palace gardens.

Out here, moonlight flickered down through towering hedges, ivy-grown arbors, and the limbs of the Living Tree, casting shadows that swayed and dipped like the dancers inside. We walked in silence for a time, the only noises being the sighing of the breeze, the rustle of leaves, and the crunch of our footfalls on gravel paths. Although part of me was almost painfully aware of the man beside me, the other part was relieved to be away from the eyes and attention of so many who'd come to meet or simply look upon the promised Artan. Never in my life had I expected to achieve any sort of celebrity status, yet here I was, in as unique a position as I supposed it was humanly possible to be.

Wonder if this is anything like what A-listers go through back home, dealing with the paparazzi all the time. If so, I can feel some sympathy for them now.

I suppose the peace of the gardens and the privacy of darkness had put me in a reflective mood. Out loud, I mused, "Life has gotten so crazy lately. When I first came to Aerisia, I thought you all were insane for believing I was the Artan. Now, against all odds, I've accepted that's who I am and what I'm supposed to do. However, now that I've been pretty much officially instated as the Artan, it sort of feels like life has slowed down, and I don't know what I'm supposed to be doing. I thought my destiny as the Artan was to be battling the Dark Powers."

"You've not had your fill of war lately?"

"I didn't mean that the way it sounded," I laughed, chagrined. "I wouldn't mind a break. It's just people keep talking about the Dark Powers and how they're harming Aerisia. It isn't like I haven't seen any of it—obviously, I have. They've made several attempts on my life. On the other hand, practically everything I've seen so far has centered on me. Even the Doinum probably wouldn't have crawled out of the woodwork except they were trying to get to me.

"So I guess what I'm trying to say is: how are the Dark Powers affecting the rest of the land? Are they really intent on hurting other people or just destroying me? Maybe all of this would be solved if I simply...went home," I shrugged. "Maybe that would be the best way to protect Aerisia, so nobody around me can get hurt."

"You cannot mean that."

His tone was so serious, almost reproachful, that it stopped me in my tracks.

"Why can't I mean that? What if I'm right?"

"You are not."

"Well." That took me aback. "And how would you know?"

"Because you have been shielded from the truth," he declared bluntly.

"I've been—no, you're not serious."

I could tell by his face that he was. My ire rose.

"You mean to say that you, and whoever else was involved, have been keeping bad news from me? Like—like I'm too much of a child to handle it?"

"Not a child, no. We simply agreed not to overburden you."

I couldn't believe this, and yet I could. Even back at Treygon, hadn't I noticed the discussions, the meetings I wasn't let in on? Hadn't I felt there was something in the air, stirring behind the scenes?

I squared my shoulders, trying to keep calm, but my voice was icy, tight. "Okay, so when, exactly, were you planning on telling me all this?"

"The news was not mine to tell. In truth, Council made the majority of these decisions."

"You're a member of Council," I pointed out.

"And rarely attend."

"I'm not buying that you couldn't have let me in on this if you'd wanted to. We've been *Joined* for months. You knew better than anyone how I was progressing, but you still didn't think I was ready to know?"

"I knew, yes, but what would you have had me do? Interrupt your studies with the fairy to tell you of Warkin raids on Tearkin lands—not mere thieving raids, but raids of murder, blood, and fire? Mayhap I should have informed you of the sea pirates preying on merchant vessels or the Dark One having been seen in the Thorn Wilderness. Should I have distracted you from learning what you *had* to learn by such tales? By stories of Village Teron being overwhelmed by smugglers or the assassination of Deveron's Portex?

"The hands of the Dark Powers are ever at work, and we knew not how much time you had to master your gifts. Your learning was paramount, so I handled some of these matters and others the rest, leaving you to study, concentrate, and grow. It was deemed better that you wait until you could face the Dark Powers themselves, than worry yourself over single attacks about which you could do little."

That was an uncharacteristically long speech coming from a Simathe. I couldn't deny he'd made his point, but I was still angry and unwilling to give in. All of the information he'd imparted was a bit overwhelming, so I latched onto the one thing I did know something about, protesting, "Kurban didn't mention anything about the Warkin killing anyone. He only—"

"Because I forbade it," Ilgard interrupted shortly. "Knowing he would sail to Laytrii to see you for himself. I bid him hold the truth close."

Frustrated, I gritted my teeth. "This is absurd. How can this world trust me to be their Artan when they don't trust me to know what I'm fighting? How are *you* ever going to trust me as the Artan when you've been one of the main ones keeping secrets from me?"

Before he could object again that Council had made most of the decisions, I held up a hand, ticking off items on my fingers.

"First, there was the existence of the Tearkin. You never bothered to tell me that. Then Braisley. Was she there in the Unpassed Mountains the same time I was at Treygon? Never mind, I'm sure she was. What next? Oh yeah—that these raids and who knows what else were going on all over Aerisia. Apparently, I wasn't mature enough to know that either. Boy, I'd just love to know what else you've been hiding."

Some of his eerie Simathe calm slipped a bit at my acerbity. "I am the Simathe High-Chief; I tell what I choose to whom I please."

"Oh, so what are you then, the self-styled power behind the throne? That's certainly what you're acting like."

"As you are acting like the child you profess you are not," he rejoined. "If you wish to be treated as the Artan, you must act like the Artan."

"Maybe I would, except there is no other Artan and nobody to show me how to act! Sorry, hon, but in case you've forgotten, this is it. I am the Artan. It's me. Period. End of story."

He gave me a dark look. "And there is no other Simathe High-Chief save me and no other man to whom you are *Joined*. I know this land and its darkness better than you. You should trust my judgment rather than take offense."

I hated how calm he could remain, especially when on some level I knew I was being ridiculous. That only irritated me more.

"I'm so sorry, then. I'm so sorry I don't measure up to what you thought the Artan would be. I'm sorry I take offense and act irrationally. I know you wish the Artan was someone better, braver, and smarter than me, but this is it."

"That is only what you think you know," he shook his head. "I would have you no different than you are."

The firm, quiet assertion brought me to a standstill, dissipating my head of steam.

"No way. You wouldn't?"

"I would not."

"But—but after all the arguments we've had, after all the things I've said to you—heck, after the way I just talked to you!—you still don't wish I was different?"

"I do not."

This was almost too baffling to wrap my head around. "But we just had a huge fight! I bet nobody argues with you like that."

A smile flitted across his mouth. "True." The smile vanished. Soberly, he said, "You do not fear me, Hannah. How many can claim that?"

"Yeah, well, once I got to know you, I figured out you're not so scary," I admitted gruffly, scuffing the gravel with the toe of my slippers. "To be perfectly honest, I guess there's not a whole lot I would change about you either."

"Truly?"

I looked up from the gravel path and into his face— that face I'd once found so hard and so alien. What was it about him that had changed? Or was it me and my perspectives that had altered?

"Truly. I can't imagine you any different, Ilgard, High-Chief of the Simathe."

Where the boldness came from to admit that, I didn't know. Tonight had been a crazy emotional upheaval of almost tears to mischievous humor to reflection to anger and now to frank, personal honesty. The very air was charged with the changes between us, the moon reflecting in the unfathomable depths of his black, black eyes. Under that gaze, my heart pounded with a funny mixture of anticipation and fear.

I didn't know what to do, to stand my ground or flee, and because he could be so difficult to read, I couldn't predict what was going through his mind. There were several things I might've guessed he'd do. What I did not expect was for him to look down and reach for my hand, enfolding it in his. Shivers rolled down my spine at his touch, which felt exactly as I'd imagined it. His hand did swallow mine, engulfing it with gentle strength. I could feel the ridges of callouses on his fingers and palms—callouses I wanted to trail, trace, and explore.

He lifted our clasped hands into the air between us, saying nothing, his eyes fastened on our intertwined fingers while mine were fastened on his face. Beneath the silvery white of my gown, my chest was rising and falling rapidly as I waited for him to speak. At long last, his eyes came up to claim mine.

"Hannah," he said quietly, and for the first time, my name on his tongue was a caress.

"Ilgard—"

I don't know what I meant to say and would never figure it out. Brisk footfalls on the path heralded an intruder, someone who, by the sound of his or her footsteps, was advancing toward us with a purpose in mind.

"My lord?"

It was Norband. At the sound of his voice, our hands fell apart. His hurried footsteps made us retreat. By the time he approached, we stood a safe distance apart, looking as if nothing more had occurred out here in the moonlight than a casual conversation between peers. Only we knew different. That interrupted moment was one that would haunt us—or me, at least—for a long time to come.

Chapter Thirty-Three

Traitor?

"Your pardon, my lady," Norband stated first with a quick bow, "but I must trade words with the High-Chief. With your permission…"

I nodded in mute agreement and stood watching as the men moved off into the gloomy darkness of a tree with drooping, fluttering, overhanging branches. The wind whispered through those wraithlike branches, ruffling my skirts and curls, yet not a whisper of conversation could I overhear.

A gray, dark cloud trailing wraithlike fingers scudded ominously across the moon. Even the music inside had changed to a slow, haunting melody. I shivered at the unexpected sense of dread that stole into my soul, snatching away the euphoria of a minute ago. The way the two Simathe lords stood there not speaking, and yet knowing they were, only added to the eeriness of the scene.

From the open doorways beyond, I heard a woman's giggle: cheerful and bright, though muffled by distance. There was light there, people and laughter. I cast a longing glance toward the Grand Chamber, debating how much longer this meeting would take, and if it would be rude to slip back inside and wait there.

I decided to give it a few more minutes and, with nothing else to do, found myself studying Ilgard's shadowy form in the darkness, remembering how awed and frightened of him I'd been at the beginning. If anyone had suggested then that I might come to develop feelings for him, even over an extended period of time, I would have called them every kind of fool. The idea that it was actually happening was still foreign enough to boggle my mind, even if my heart was seeing things more and more clearly.

As if merely thinking about him was an audible request for his attention, he turned to me now, casting a glance over his shoulder, checking on me before resuming his absolutely silent conversation with his Chief Captain. Feeling the warmth of his care, I remained where I was, trying to ignore that growing sense of unease and the slight chill carried on the breath of a nighttime breeze. Despite keeping myself warm by mentally replaying that handclasp and the way he'd said my name, I was about ready to call it quits by the time the two men broke off their talk. Norband returned to the palace with purposeful strides, while Ilgard came to me.

"Walk with me," he said, grasping my elbow and leading me down a secluded garden path, overshadowed by night-blooming trees. I felt that sense of unease growing until my stomach set to churning. What in the world was going on?

We halted at length in a small clearing, where the white gravel path beneath our feet gave way to a circular stone mosaic depicting the Living Tree. An elaborately carved stone bench surrounded by carefully groomed rosebushes sat to one side of this mosaic: a picturesque alcove obviously intended as a haven for lovers. Ilgard, however, did not invite me to sit, so I remained standing as he pulled something from an inner pocket of his coat, uncurling his long fingers for me to see it.

"Uh...I don't get it," I said, glancing up from the object he held to study his face. It was grim, hard, in the moonlight.

"A riverwatcher pulled it not an hour past from the Coiyne. It was given to my Chief Captain who passed it to me."

"But what is it? I noticed you wearing one tonight."

Indeed, what Ilgard was showing me was another gold medallion. It was a little smaller than his, perhaps, but similar in every other respect.

"Look closely. You see the design?"

"I noticed that earlier, too. It's the tower at Treygon where we were *Joined*, right?"

"It is."

"So…what does it mean, that it was found in the Coiyne? And what is it, exactly?"

"It is a Talor, the tower's name and also the medallion's. It is given to each Simathe who chooses the warrior's life."

"I see. So what's it doing here?"

Despite the shadows, I could see his black eyes narrow and his stone-set face harden. There was no trace left of the man with whom I'd verbally sparred, the man who'd professed he preferred me as I was, the man who had held my hand. No, this was Ilgard as I knew him best: implacable, hard, warlike. A Simathe, and their chosen leader.

"Nothing good, be assured of that."

I wasn't satisfied with his reply. "I realize it means nothing good, but judging from your reaction, I'd say you know more. Tell me," I implored, laying a hand lightly on his sleeve. "Please don't keep this back from me. I think I have the right to know."

He said nothing for a while and I waited patiently, staring up into his face, wishing he would allow me to share his thoughts like another Simathe, wishing I had the ability to do so, wishing I could at least guess what he was thinking.

"I suspect," he answered finally, pronouncing each word with deliberate slowness, "it means there is a traitor among the Simathe."

My eyes drifted down to the medallion in his hand. His fingers curled about it, tightening—as if by squeezing the object he could squeeze the life, or the treachery, from its owner.

"How do you know?" I heard myself whisper.

"Because this Talor was not lost in the river. It was placed there."

"How do you know that? Maybe it was genuinely lost."

"A Simathe does not lose his possessions."

"Maybe it was stolen."

He snorted. "Nor are they stolen from him."

"Fine!" Exasperated, I threw my hands in the air. "So it wasn't stolen from him and he didn't lose it. I still don't get how you know this means one of you is a traitor."

"Because it was placed in the river in an attempt to conceal it."

"Conceal it? Why? To hide the evidence?"

"Precisely."

"But the evidence of what?"

"An exchange of tokens, the sealing of a vow. A promise given, the Talor with it."

"So what you're basically saying is whoever owns this Talor gave it to someone else to seal a bargain they'd made, and then the other person was maybe close to being found out and tossed it in the river. That's a pretty elaborate theory based off a medallion found in the Coiyne. I mean, why would anyone do that? Everyone knows the riverwatchers—"

"Sometimes fail."

I shivered, rubbing my forearms. "You could be right, but what if you're not? Ilgard, this is a big deal! You can't accuse one of your men of being a Benedict Arnold on such flimsy circumstantial evidence. This is all pretty slim, you have to admit. It would never hold up in a court of law."

"There is no court of law. *I* am the law. I know whereof I speak."

"Okay, I don't doubt that," I soothed, rubbing a palm over my brow. "But I still think you could be mistaken. You might be making something big out of nothing at all." I dropped my hand onto its opposite arm. "After all, accidents do happen."

Several long, heavy seconds crept by, and when at last he spoke he didn't even directly address my concerns.

"My lady once told me she trusted me."

I frowned, not comprehending the switch in topics. "I don't see what that has to do with this."

"Either you trust my judgment in this matter, or you do not."

I winced. "You're not making this easy on me. After all, we had a pretty heated discussion not very long ago over the whole matter of trust and you concealing things from me. Now you want me to put my blind faith in you? Over something like this?"

He waited, saying nothing, until I affirmed carefully, "I do trust you. I just want you to…use caution, that's all."

His eyes, unblinking, held mine in their black grip. At last he nodded, slowly.

"As you say."

"So you're not going to take this and run with it? You'll be careful?"

I could tell that annoyed him. "I know my own men, lady."

"Apparently not very well!" I shot back, frustrated with the whole stupid mess. "You're so willing to take this and make such an issue out of it, but you won't even give one of your own men the benefit of the doubt when it comes to being a traitor!"

"There are other things."

"Yeah, like what? More secrets you've been keeping? Imagine that. Well, c'mon, then. Out with it. I want to hear everything."

"I've told you enough."

With that cryptic statement, the man actually had the audacity to turn his back on me and walk away. I stared after him, temporarily frozen in shock, but he didn't make it far before I recovered my wits. Picking up my skirts, I ran, catching up to and managing to scoot around him on the narrow path where I stopped, blocking his way.

"Wait a minute, you—" I punctuated each word with a finger jab to the chest. "I want the whole story. You can't start this and not finish it!"

He regarded me with cool authority. "What you know will suffice for the present. Now you know to be on your guard."

"Against who? You won't even tell me who I should be on guard against!"

The frost in his eyes was frightening, his icy tones even more so. "Against all, save myself."

I felt like I'd been sucker-punched. "What are you saying?" I breathed, thinking of Elisia, Rittean, Cole, Kan, Contrey, Garett, Kurban and others. Surely they were trustworthy, weren't they?

"Time will tell, my lady. Now, stand aside, please."

I moved woodenly to do as bidden, a feeling of numbness creeping into my bones as I watched the Simathe High-Chief walk away.

Chapter Thirty-Four

Disclosures

I returned to the party, but my heart was no longer in it. As if sensing my mood, most folks were content to leave me alone with my brooding thoughts for company. Over and over again I replayed the scene in the palace gardens, my thoughts chasing each other in circles like a puppy playing with its tail until a headache blossomed that refused to go away.

Was Ilgard right? Could one of the Simathe really be a traitor? How was that possible, without anyone else knowing? True, Ilgard had claimed there were other things, but what? He had to be blowing this out of proportion, because I couldn't think of a thing. The harder I tried, the worse my headache became. Eventually, I could stand it no longer, and slipped away from the revelry for good.

Back in my room, I readied for bed alone, not bothering to send for Rosean to help. I sighed as I hung my beautiful gown inside the towering wardrobe, running a hand wistfully over its glossy fabric. The evening had begun on such a high note, only to end like this. I felt like Cinderella after she'd fled the ball, the magic having worn off at midnight, leaving her stuck with a pumpkin, rags, and mice. At least she'd had a glass slipper as a memento. I retained only good memories, partially soured by bad.

Pulling the pins from my hair, I dropped them listlessly onto my dressing table. The string of pearls followed next, and my carefully upswept hairdo tumbled down about my shoulders. Miserably, I brushed it out, wincing at each yank of the silver-backed brush on snags and tangles.

Way to end the evening. I should've brought a glass of wine with me to help me unwind.

But there was no wine, so I climbed into bed, eager to lay my aching head on a cool pillow and lose myself in sleep. Unfortunately, just I got comfy, a knock sounded at the door, disrupting my plans of forgetfulness and rest.

"Who is it?" I called, suddenly wary as the memory of Ilgard's warnings flashed in my brain like the red and blue lights of a police car.

"Rosean, my lady."

"I'm already in bed, Rosean. I don't need anything else tonight. You can go."

I started to slide back under the blankets, but she stopped me by saying, "My lady, I bear a message from the Simathe High-Chief."

Ilgard?

This halted my attempts at getting into bed. Regretfully, I kicked away the inviting covers and pushed my weary body off the mattress. Getting to my feet, I went to open the door.

"Begging your pardon, my lady." The servant girl bobbed a quick curtsey. "Lord Ilgard desired I convey his request for your immediate presence in the Great War Room."

I dropped my forehead against the doorframe. "Did he say why?"

"He did not, my lady."

Taking a deep breath, I exhaled a sigh. "Okay. Tell him I'll be there in a minute. And Rosean?"

"My lady?"

"Have someone bring me a cup of tea, will you? Make sure it's very hot and very strong."

"As you wish, my lady."

While the servant girl scurried away to do as bidden, I slipped back inside my room to get dressed.

* * *

"What is it now?" I asked shortly, upon entering the so-called *Great War Room.*

Lord Garett, Prince Kurban, Norband, Ilgard, Risean, Lord Ri, Lady Tey and another Cortain who, judging from her half-armor and sword, had been on duty somewhere, were all seated around one end of the ridiculously long central table running the length of the room.

This immense chamber was shaped like a rectangle, and its expansive walls were covered with an assortment of weapons and tapestries, most of them depicting blood-soaked war scenes. Many included two different women, both dressed in white. These, I assumed, were probably High-Chieftess Laytrii and the first Artan.

Two more Tearkin stood at ease behind their prince, and one now stepped forward to pull out a chair for me. After I'd settled myself next to the head Cortain with a quiet "Thank you," he scooted in my chair in for me, then resumed his position beside his comrade.

As if waiting for me to be seated before answering my question, Lord Ri, stationed at the head of the table, now began to speak.

"My lady, distressing tidings have been brought this eve."

I cut a glance across the table toward Ilgard and his Chief Captain. Surely they hadn't spread their suspicions of a traitorous Simathe. Not on such flimsy evidence, which mostly seemed speculation to me. As expected, they both ignored me completely, and the newly proclaimed High Elder continued speaking.

"Reports have reached our ears concerning a planned attack upon the city of Shayle."

"Shayle? Where's that?"

"Shayle is a seaport, my lady. It lies at the head of the Largese river, precisely at the juxtaposition of river and sea," Risean took it upon himself to explain.

"And I'm assuming it's important?"

"Vitally. Whoever is master of Shayle is master of the Largese—Aerisia's foremost river and vital to all watertrade. Watertrade, as you may know, supplies much food and goods to the city of Laytrii. Were The Evil to conquer Shayle, they could cut off all watertrade, as well as use the Largese to transport their own ships and men downriver."

I scrubbed a hand down my face, so tired even my jaws ached. "Great. So what happened? Did this army just appear out of nowhere?"

The High Elder and the Moonkind Tredsday exchanged troubled glances. Watching them, I noticed everyone present except myself and the unknown Cortain were still wearing evening clothes, suggesting they'd left the party and come directly to the Great War Room for a meeting.

Strange. Guess this message about the attack on Shayle really did just arrive.

Risean looked away from the High Elder after Lord Ri inclined his head, granting the elderly Guardian permission to speak.

"For some time past, ni nokestrin, there have been attacks upon various villages, estates, towns, and farms throughout Aerisia. While some have been repulsed, others, alas, were successful. The Evil has been gathering an army. With each raid, they disembowel the land in their quest for supplies, and as each day passes more of those with shadow in their hearts join their forces, binding themselves in service to the Dark Powers."

Inside, my ire rose. If not for Ilgard's admission in the palace gardens, this would have all come as a pretty nasty surprise. Instead, coupled with the information Ilgard had already leaked, it helped put the pieces of the puzzle together. Clearly, Aerisia was not as peaceful as I'd been thinking. Obviously, I'd been shielded from a lot.

"The Ranetron and Cortain have managed to put down a number of these raids and quell some of the rebellion," Risean was saying. "However," he grimaced, spreading his hands as if in apology. "They cannot be in all places at once."

"I see," I said calmly, although the sick sensation of dread was returning with force.

The Evil...gathering an army. For some time now. Is this what I've felt coming, ever since those days at Treygon? The tension on the air, the something that no one would talk about?

"And now they're strong enough to attack Shayle, a major city?"

"That is what we fear. This is not the first attack of the kind, but it is unquestionably vital to their cause if they wish to campaign against Aerisia."

My stomach was churning. It was hard to put my thoughts in order and process all this.

"So how did you find out about the attack on Shayle?"

"A detachment of Ranetron encountered the main body of this army. They fought bravely but…"

"But?" I prompted gently, when it became apparent Risean was reluctant to carry on.

"They died bravely, as well."

This from Garett, who offered the words with sorrow, yet dignity. His face was guarded, but a deep sadness darkened his eyes. I knew his men's deaths weighed heavily upon their High-Chief.

"I'm so sorry, Lord Garett," I said gently. "Your men will be honored. I promise you their sacrifice won't be forgotten."

"I thank you," he said, and the subject was dropped as Risean now picked up the tale.

"From this battle, a handful of Ranetron survived," he said. "One of them was briefly taken prisoner by The Evil, before his remaining comrades managed to free him. While in camp, he heard many whispers of Shayle. From this, we have surmised their intent."

"Unless that was a diversionary tactic," I pointed out.

"Of course, we have considered this. Scouts have already been dispatched to locate the army, follow it, and report on its whereabouts."

"Good idea. So did the Ranetron that survived have any other news?"

"There is more," the new High Elder responded solemnly. "And it is the most appalling news of all. So dreadful is it, that my tongue falters to speak it aloud."

"That bad? What could be worse than The Evil plundering villages, attacking cities, raiding the countryside, and gathering an army to march on Shayle?"

"It is worse, because word was brought that this army does not consist merely of drocnords and men. Cistweigh and Warkin also ride under the black banner."

"Cistweigh? I'm not sure I've ever heard of them."

For some reason, every eye in the room suddenly turned to Ilgard.

Weird. Why do they want him to explain?

The Simathe lord leaned forward, placing folded hands on the tabletop as his dark gaze fastened on me.

"You have met the Cistweigh, my lady, though you knew it not at the time."

"I have?"

"Aye, lass." His face was grim. "Jonase."

I felt myself shrink at the mere mention of his name. "Jonase was a—a Cistweigh? No one ever told me that before. Who, or what, exactly is a Cistweigh?"

Terse, uncomfortable silence met the question. I didn't know it, but my fingers were clutching the table so hard my knuckles had turned white. Memories of Jonase always put me on edge, but to know there were more of him, or rather, more *like* him…I could hardly stomach the idea.

It was Risean who took up the challenge.

"The Cistweigh," he began carefully, compassion in his eyes, "are great ones who dedicated themselves long ago to the service of the Dark Powers. Because of mighty deeds done during their lifetime, their spirits were permitted to live on after death."

"You mean they're like...like ghosts?" I stammered, my tongue thick and unresponsive.

"Nay, sweeting. A ghost is a spirit returned from the dead—a shadow of its former self. The Cistweigh differ in that, after their own bodies perish, their spirits inhabit the form of another."

My throat closed off. "They take another person's body?"

"Not a living one, child. They take the body of one already deceased."

I stared at him in horror. "But—but why do that instead of just reviving their own bodies?"

He shrugged gently. "I suppose it is a price they must pay. To gain immortality, they must surrender their own forms, taking that of another who has already perished."

"So you're saying they're basically a living corpse?"

That would explain the cold that had always heralded Jonase's presence—the wintery chill of death. It would also account for the other signals: the strong odors of decay, of rotting flesh.

"And you mean to tell me," I brushed a wisp of hair nervously behind my ear. "I was almost—almost raped by one of them?"

At those horrified words, I saw the Simathe flinch as if struck by an unseen blow. Squeezing my eyelids tightly closed, I fought for control, determined I would not break down in front of these people. The attack, after all, had been a long time ago, and it had been foiled. I didn't have to let this break me.

I will not let this break me.

Inhaling a shuddering breath, I reopened my eyes to find the Simathe watching me closely. Better than anyone, he understood what I'd gone through, for, in a very real sense, he'd experienced it, too. He knew…Ilgard knew, and he would have done anything to have spared me from the ordeal, despite the fact that the whole thing had been largely my fault. At any rate, it was now over and done with. Jonase was dead.

Or was he?

Something in my brain clicked as I summoned up the old Moonkind's phrase, *To gain immortality.*

Immortality.

Immortals.

Were the Cistweigh immortals like the Simathe? Impossible! With my own eyes I'd seen Jonase's dead body. Surely he was dead. He had to be.

I made myself ask anyway.

"Are…are the Cistweigh really immortal? I mean, they can be killed, can't they?"

"It is written in the lorlin," Risean rushed to clarify, "and told by the Spinners, that after their first death—the death of their own body—the Cistweigh are granted three lives-which-are-not-lives by the Dark Powers."

"Three lives? And which one was Jonase living at the time?"

"We cannot be certain, child."

"Then it's possible I might…see him again?" I groaned.

Risean frowned sympathetically. "It is not impossible."

"No," I whimpered, dropping my face into my hands. "No, no, no. It can't be. It just can't."

Again I was fighting tears, fighting for control. From her position next to me, Lady Tey made bold to place a hand on my shoulder.

"Never you fear, my lady. You are the Artan, and he cannot harm you now. Your power is stronger than any he might possess."

To my surprise, her words brought swift encouragement. Reassured, I scrubbed angrily at my tears. "You're right, Tey," I agreed. "I *am* the Artan, and I can defend myself. If Jonase and I ever do meet again, he'll be the one to regret it. Not me."

She smiled fiercely in return. "Aye, just so."

Buoyed by the Cortain's consolation, displaying more composure than I actually felt, I turned once more to Risean.

"Jonase didn't just attack me that one time in the Unpassed Mountains. There was also the *mind attack*, I believed you called it, my first night in Aerisia."

"True," he acknowledged. "Because the bodies they occupy are not strictly theirs, the Cistweigh's spirits can sometimes depart their forms to plague the minds of others."

"But I defeated him then, after a fashion," I went on. "So I must have used magic without knowing it, because he left all of a sudden when I ordered him to. What

273

happens to people the Cistweigh mind attack who can't fight back?"

Risean lowered his eyes. "There is no record of any surviving the ordeal. In the aftermath they were discovered dead, their heads split open like melons, their brains scattered about the floor."

A shudder coursed through my body at his graphic language, but I forced myself to concentrate. To think.

An army. An army of The Evil. Attacking, pillaging, plundering. Killing, butchering, looting. Growing. For how long? How long has this been going on? How long has it been bad? Surely longer than the few months that I've been here.

"Tell me," I said, voicing my musings aloud, "how long has all this—these attacks by The Evil—been going on?"

The new High Elder, Lord Ri, frowned as if trying to fathom the rapid switch of topics. "Warring with The Evil and evil ones has always been a constant on some level, my lady. That is why the services of the Ranetron, Cortain, and Simathe are so valued."

"Yes, I realize that. But you said something like the raids have been stepping up, growing worse. And now an army has materialized."

"They have, without doubt, worsened since your arrival, child," Master Risean replied. "The Dark Powers, knowing you had come to resist them, have hurried their pace to resist you. However, this latest deterioration is merely an outcome of what has been occurring for more than a score of years. Since that time, greater numbers of warriors have been required to manage the peace you see us enjoy. Yet now I fear even this is not enough. War is coming."

"Okay, wait, hold on, this is a lot to process," I begged. "A score is twenty years, isn't it? I'm in my early twenties, which must mean things have been slowly but surely growing worse since around the time I was born. Which means the Dark Powers must've had some idea back then that the time of the Artan was approaching."

The words tumbled out faster as pieces of the puzzle fell into place.

"They have to force the issue now. They've attempted several times to kill me, and failed. Once they tried rape to break the prophecy. If Jonase had succeeded, it would have been over, because that's what that part of the prophecy means, doesn't it? *She will be untouched by man?*

Now that the Dark Powers have failed with both rape and the Doinum, they're going to have to force things to come to a head. Which, as you said, means a war we have to fight. A battle we have to win."

I paused, glancing around the table, meeting each and every pair of eyes belonging to the people assembled.

"Can we fight them? Together, can we defeat The Evil and overthrow the Dark Powers?"

"The purity of Light grant that it may be so," Lord Ri intoned like a prayer. "May they aid, strengthen, and fortify our arms and hearts for all that is to come."

"Aye, fight we will or die trying," Garett vowed, and I knew he was remembering his massacred warriors. "If we must perish, then we will acquit ourselves so bravely that even in victory our foes will taste defeat."

Murmured assents and accompanying nods met the Ranetron High-Chief's words. Ilgard was the last to be heard.

"The men of Treygon are likewise committed to this cause. For as long as there are Simathe, we will fight against shadow and evil."

He stared right at me as he spoke, and I knew he was making this promise to me, personally. I knew also he wasn't merely pledging his assistance for this time, for this war. The Simathe were immortal, which meant what he was undertaking was an eternal vow of resistance to the Dark Powers.

The old Moonkind, Risean, knew it too.

Smiling, he said, "Do you know, my child, that you have this day begun to fulfill yet another element of the Artan's prophecy? ...*and she shall unite those long hated with those who long have feared them,*" he quoted softly. "Though the Simathe have long been at peace with Aerisia, they were never brethren. You, Hannah, are changing this as surely as you are changing our world." His eyes gleamed with fatherly pride. "Daily, you prove yourself to be what I have known you were since the day of your birth."

Chapter Thirty-Five

Lineage

Tilting my head, I smiled a quizzical half-smile. "Since the day of my birth? How would you know anything about my birth?"

He chuckled. "Why, I have watched over you from afar since the day you first commenced your journey of life."

He had? That was news to me!

"Do you remember," he stimulated my memory, "the tree stump split, as was thought, by lightning, where you first beheld me?"

"The one in Mr. Cutter's field? Sure. He told my dad that it happened—" I stopped, blinking at the old man in wonder. "...a little over twenty years ago."

"Ah," he smiled, "you begin to understand. It was not lightning struck the tree. I marked the place when your father chose to dwell there, that it might not be lost or forgotten, should anything untoward befall myself."

"Why you?" I demanded, not unkindly. "What have you got to do with me? Why were you the one to watch over me all these years? And why did you mark it when my father moved out there? What does he have to do with any of this?"

Leaning back in his chair, he surveyed the others in the room. "I must ask for your patience, my friends, as I digress from the topic of war to tell our Artan an important tale she is now ready to accept." When no one argued, he turned to me. "Forgive me for not imparting this sooner, but you must understand I did not deem the time right nor your heart ready to receive it. I tell you now because you have fully accepted the mantle of Artan, and I would not have you go forth against the Dark Powers without understanding your lineage and why you were chosen to withstand them."

I nodded in acquiescence, my spine tingling with anticipation. At last, the mystery of why I had been chosen as Artan was going to be revealed. This was a subject I'd never stopped wondering about, although outwardly I'd let the matter drop, ascribing it to nothing more than a random pick of fate. Now that I knew there was more to the story, I was eager to hear, so I tamped down any resentment that may've popped up about yet another thing these Aerisians hadn't thought I was mature enough to handle, determined to hear the Moonkind out before judging his decision.

"Many years ago," he began solemnly, "one of our own folk, a powerful Moonkind Tredsday, loved a Scraggen.

Of all the magicworkers and mighty Scraggens who ever have been, she was far mightier than most. And, being yet in her youth, her beauty was unmatched and the potential for her power nearly unlimited.

"Nevertheless, the Moonkind's love for this woman was forbidden. Not all Scraggen serve the Powers of Good, you see, and though they may not walk openly in darkness, well—there is a proverb in Aerisia concerning those who live in half-shadows like a Scraggen. Also, while the way of the Moonkind is to follow the Peace of the Moon, most Scraggen live only to serve themselves, and will go to whatever lengths, good or tainted, to further their ends."

"And this Scraggen, was she like that too?"

"She was. Sadly, the Tredsday who loved her could not see this. They wed in secret, for his people could not accept their love. However, he was besotted, and she possibly hoped to find a method of taking his powers for herself. But after a time, when she found this an impossibility—for the powers of the moonstone and the Moonkind may only be used by the Moonkind and their kin—she…ended their union."

"You mean she killed him," I supplied.

Deep sorrow crossed the old man's face. "Aye, she killed him. But not before…"

"Before…?"

"A child. A child had already been conceived. She would bear his child."

"A baby? Did she have it?"

"She bore the babe, aye, knowing a child of Moonkind and Scraggen magic might be wondrously powerful indeed. Yet, unable to risk her tainting the child with darkness, the Moonkind conspired to spirit the infant away and conceal it in a place she could not find it."

"You mean Earth?"

"Aye, I mean Earth. As the ways between Aerisia and Earth are closed, only we Moonkind retain the ability to pass between worlds, using such as magic as once took us from our home on the Moon to a new life in Aerisia.

"At any rate, there was the child sent, knowing it would be safe from its mother. In this new land, he was found by strangers and taken in to be raised in a place—I believe on Earth it is called an *orphanage.*" The Moonkind stumbled slightly over the foreign word. "There he dwelt until obtaining the years of young manhood. Upon leaving, he found a vocation and took a beautiful bride, by whom he has since fathered several children."

He stopped, leaving me speechless and frozen in place. At the word "orphanage," my mouth had fallen open. This baby, found on the streets and raised in an orphanage…there were few orphanages left in America, but I knew someone who'd been raised in one…someone who'd married a beautiful woman, by whom he'd had several children…

Risean knew I was thinking. Looking me straight in the eye, he said, "It is true, Hannah. You know it now. The child was your father, though that is only part of why you received the powers you wield."

As if that wasn't a big enough bombshell, he went on to say, "The Scraggen in the tale, your grandmother, was the direct descendant of High-Chieftess Laytrii's younger sister, Anea. Both of these women, High-Chieftess Laytrii and her sister, Anea, are said to have been descendants, again direct, of the sister of Artan, herself. This means not only the Scraggen, but you, Hannah, are closely linked to both the High-Chieftess and the first Artan. Which also means the potential for great power, great good, was in this mighty Scraggen, had she but chosen to use it. Alas, that she did not."

I'd sat stunned throughout this recital, a plethora of questions zipping through my brain. Gathering the wits to give them voice, I stammered, "You're saying, I'm related to Artan, Laytrii, the Scraggen, and the Moonkind? Did this Moonkind, my grandfather, have any prominent relatives I should know about?"

A hint of paternal pride glinted in those tropical water eyes. "You may think so, if you wish. This Moonkind was my eldest brother, Ren Wy' Curlm, many years older than myself. When he perished, the mantle of Tredsday was passed to me. You, therefore, are both my great-niece, and cousin to my own daughter, Rittean."

A ton of bricks couldn't have hit with more force than those words. I looked desperately into his face to see if he was telling me the truth (he was), and felt my eyes well with tears. Instantly, any animosity I might have held toward him for taking me from my home was scrubbed away. The world melted away until there was only the two of us.

"You're my family?" I whispered, my throat so tight I could barely force the words out. "I—I…"

I couldn't speak. The next thing I knew, Risean had risen from his seat across from me and shuffled around the table, putting his arms about me and pulling me close. I buried my face in his shoulder, clinging to him like a lifeline while he stroked my hair in gentle caresses.

"I know we are not the family you left on Earth," he murmured, "but I love you as my own granddaughter and Rittean loves you as a sister. Besides us, you have many other relations, people of the Moon, whom you have not met. You have a family here, my child, a family willing to love and accept you as one of our own, should you permit it."

"I don't know what to say. I mean, you don't have any idea how much this means to me," I exclaimed tearfully. "I knew my father grew up in an orphanage and had no family, my mom pretty much had no family, either, and the relatives she did have lived so far away we hardly knew them. All my life, I wanted grandparents, aunts, uncles and cousins like other people, but never had them. Not until now, at least."

His smile was beautiful. Taking the empty seat beside me, he dropped a kiss on my forehead then leaned his brow against the place he'd kissed me.

"How difficult it has been to hold this secret close," he said, "when I longed to embrace the granddaughter of the brother I lost so long ago. Nevertheless, the Moon whispered I should wait until you were ready, so I did, though I confess it was not easy."

"I understand," I whispered.

Amazingly, I really did.

We set up and broke apart, but I gripped his hand hard, not wanting to lose physical contact so soon with my new family member. He smiled in understanding, allowing me to hold onto him. There were so many things I wanted to say, so many questions I was dying to ask. Part of me wanted to jump up right now and have him take me to meet my new relatives. Part of me wanted to be alone to think all this through. The sensible part of me, though, understood these things would have to wait. I needed more information; I needed a final summary of this tale, so I asked, "So you're my great-uncle, then, and Rittean is my second cousin. I'm a quarter-Moonkind, and related to all those other people. But how did you know *I* would be the Artan? And what happened to my grandmother, the Scraggen?"

The light in his eyes dimmed, if only temporarily.

"I am sorry to say that after your father was taken from her, she went mad with anger and grief. For a time, she used her magic to wreak havoc upon all she saw. I can tell you little of it, for I was a mere youngling in those days, and the years would be many before I was competent to assume my brother's role of Tredsday. I only recall that she wrought a very great and terrible destruction. The Simathe lords will remember better than I."

He glanced at Ilgard and Norband for confirmation.

"It is so," the Simathe Chief Captain stated simply.

He didn't elaborate the point, and I didn't ask. I wasn't particularly curious to know the details of my own grandmother's reign of terror.

The Moonkind resumed his tale. "In the end, warriors were sent against her to halt her wickedness. However, when they reached the place she ought to have been, they could not find her. She had quite vanished, leaving behind no traces of her whereabouts. Some thought she'd slain herself, and others that the Dark Powers took her. I do not know. I know only that it was a very long time ago. She has not been seen nor heard from since, and I am content to let her vanish into the past."

I smiled sadly, regretting how even a story that could bring such happiness could also hold so much pain.

"I'm so sorry you and your family had to go through that," I said. "I'm sorry that you lost your brother at such an early age. Sorry—"

"No, my child, do not be sorry," he interrupted kindly. "Grief dims with time, and my brother left behind a beautiful legacy. How proud he would be to know his own descendant is Aerisia's long-awaited Artan!"

"It's pretty incredible," I agreed. "Tell me, did you always know what I would become?"

"I did not, but as soon as I was able, even from my youth, I made it my business to look after my brother's offspring on Earth. Furthermore, as I contemplated your ancestry, your family line, the thought gripped my soul that here—here was a chance for prophecy to be fulfilled, especially when I realized the magic your father *could* have held had passed him over. Such a powerful legacy must eventually be passed on, I knew, so I waited with eager anticipation for your father to produce an heir.

"First was born a son, and no fulfillment of prophecy for him. Then came a daughter, and hope flourished anew."

"Sammie," I interjected. "That would've been my older sister Samantha, or Sammie, as we've always called her."

"Yes, Sammie," he echoed. "I know her name well, for upon her birth I watched for signs, but saw nothing. Nor did anything occur in the months following her birth that led me to believe she could be our Artan."

"Then what told you it was me?"

His beautiful, blue-green eyes twinkled beneath snow-white eyebrows.

"Ah, with you, it was a different matter entirely. Upon the birth of your sister I had gone to Lord Elgrend, the High Elder, and told him all. Between ourselves, we agreed to abide in secrecy, waiting to see if anything should come of it all. Needless to say, nothing did. But when you were born, I did not send for the High Elder; he sent for me.

"Bringing me into his inner chambers, he showed me the necklace of the Artan, which he had safeguarded since the day of his Instating. Never before had it changed, but that day—the day of your birth—it came to life. The stone of the necklace began to glow, to change color, to burn as if from hidden flames. When I saw that, I knew then, as I know now, that here was the omen for which I had waited. My hopes were fulfilled, my life's dream complete. The Artan was born."

Chapter Thirty-Six

The Singing Stones

With a fingertip, I touched the stone hanging around my neck, suspended upon its ropelike golden chain. Was it my imagination, or did a mild warmth emanate from it now?

"After that visit with Lord Elgrend, you knew that I, the Artan, was born," I recapped. "Did you tell anyone else about my birth? How did you know when my time had come, the time for you to come get me?"

"So many questions," he smiled, shaking his head. "Well, that is to be expected. You've earned the right to your answers.

"When the Artan's necklace burned," he went on, picking up his story, "the High Elder and I still informed no others. We wished to wait a time in order to be perfectly certain. By the morning following your birth, the stone of your necklace had reverted to its normal state. We wondered if we had been wrong, though shortly afterward The Evil's violence began to increase, as if the Dark

Powers themselves knew of your birth and had begun plotting your defeat.

"Even so, I was convinced we'd not been led astray, and I continued to observe you from afar. The day another line of the Artan's prophecy was fulfilled was the day I knew for certain it was time to fetch you. I found myself once more with the High Elder in this palace. An urgent message summoning the both of us was sent by the Keeper of the Stones."

"Keeper of the Stones?"

"The day the Singing Stones were first uncovered, they sang," Risean explained. "They had not done so since, although a new Keeper of the Stones had been appointed each year by Council to keep watch over them. For all knew when the Singing Stones again did sing, the time of the Artan drew nigh."

"And the message from the Keeper was that the stones were singing," I guessed.

"Correct," he agreed. "The Singing Stones *did* sing that day, sing as they had not sung for hundreds of years. That same day your necklace, unchanged for so long, manifested itself as it had on the day of your birth. By this, I knew the day had arrived. Fate had deemed you ready to begin your task.

"The matter in its entirety was brought before Council, whereupon it was determined that I should be the one to bring you to Aerisia. Some, possibly, doubted then, but none would now. All, my child, know you for what you are: the woman who will fulfill all legends and prophecies concerning the Artan. The woman who will deliver our land from the powers of darkness."

His story concluded, the old Moonkind drifted into silence and I leaned back in my chair, lost in thought. It was Lady Tey who broke the silence. I'd pegged her long ago as a person of action and someone who didn't like waiting around. She proved me right by asking bluntly, "What do we do now?" Like the others present, I gave her my full attention. "The Artan is aware of her history. She is ready to fight and we have all pledged her our aid. Now, *do* we fight?"

Everyone turned to me. It was so crazy, seeing people far better acquainted with politics and war looking to me to make the final decision, but I suppose, as Artan, it was my right. I took a deep breath and squared my shoulders before saying the words that would undoubtedly change all of our lives forever.

"Yes," I declared grimly, giving my new uncle's hand a firm squeeze. "We fight. We have no other choice."

* * *

My footsteps were slow as I trudged back down the hall toward my bedroom. Rubbing the back of my neck, I massaged it gently, so tired I could've dropped in my tracks and went to sleep right then and there.

After my proclamation, our meeting had fallen into making plans. Story time was over: the decision to go to war had been made. Campaign strategies must now be formed, and all of the tactics, policies, and procedures that went along with that discussed. Risean and I had mostly sat and listened during all this, since this was neither of our area of expertise. With the exception of Lord Ri, the High Elder, the rest of those gathered had spent their lives in and around warfare and battle. By tacit agreement, we left matters in their capable hands.

The meeting was still going on when I left, but I'd already decided I could be of little use at this point, and should probably catch up on my sleep while I had the chance. I was more than happy to leave Aerisia's war leaders to their preparations as I unwound, undressed, and slipped into bed for the second time tonight.

Chapter Thirty-Seven

The Dream

Light. It came so quickly.

"Oh man," I groaned sleepily, throwing an arm across my eyes. "It can't be morning already. Feels like I just went to bed."

A strong breeze, warm and fresh, wafted over my body, stirring my hair. Surprisingly, the breeze was fragrant with scents I knew well: rich soil, fields of wildflowers, damp leaves, a morning rain, a mountain waterfall, a forest of pines and aspens, the mountains themselves.

"There aren't any mountains that *close," I puzzled out loud. "So why do I smell them? I'm in a marble palace surrounded by a courtyard and high walls. I shouldn't be smelling of this."*

But I was.

"Is this some crazy new reaction to my magic?"

Removing my arm, I raised my eyelids and sat up...in a field of tall grasses and bright, happy wildflowers. I was not in my bed. It was gone. My bed, my room at Laytrii's palace, and even the palace itself had completely vanished.

I pushed myself up to my knees, looking around. "What's going on here?"

That breeze again. It rolled over and around me, teasing my nostrils with the combined mixture of familiar natural fragrances, lifting hairs, and caressing my skin. My skin...

I looked down, finding myself no longer dressed in the silk nightshift I'd worn to bed, but a pair of frayed jean shorts and a skimpy red tank top.

"What the heck? These aren't Aerisian clothes."

They weren't. They were Earth clothes, but not any I'd likely have worn in my former life. Besides, Earth was another place, another world, another lifetime, another Hannah ago.

"I don't get it. What am I doing here?"

Getting to my feet, I turned in slow circles, taking everything in. I could tell from the altitude that I was high in the mountains. Cliff and crags were all around, mountains and valleys rolling into the horizon as far as the eye could see. I even stood on a wide escarpment. At its edge, the flower-studded pasture ended abruptly, tumbling into empty nothingness. It would be a very long drop to the rocky borders of the crystal-clear lake shimmering far below.

Behind me was forest. Slender aspens covered the face of another rising hillside, steep and adjacent to that on which I stood. Car-sized boulders were scattered throughout the field and trees, rugged polka dots spotting the face of the ground. I lifted my face. The blue sky stretched on forever, upheld by soaring, snowcapped peaks. White clouds obliterated the tallest *from view, wreathing them in veils of fog. Higher than even the mountains could reach, the sun shone brightly. The weather was perfect.*

I knew where I was. I was home. Colorado, the mountains and the sky. The forests and stones.

"I can't believe it—I'm home! I'm home!"

In senseless delight I spun around, my arms flung out as far as they'd go, snatches and phrases of the old John Denver anthem, Rocky Mountain High, beating in my brain. I didn't understand this miracle, but I was giddy with joy, deliriously happy with the sun on my bare shoulders and the green grass tickling my bare legs. Singing aloud, now, I spun around and around. Faster and faster. The world spun with me, singing too, and I was so incredibly happy...

Until the ground shifted under my feet. The field tipped sideways, making me lose my balance. I cried out in alarm. Fell. Then I was sliding, sliding faster and faster toward the edge of the plateau. Only the brink and empty air awaited me. A scream tore from my throat as I hurtled helplessly toward the rim, knowing there was no escape if I went over.

Somehow, my fingers managed to catch rock just as I slipped over the edge, preventing a deadly plunge. My body hung helpless, suspended in midair. The wind, playful and comforting mere seconds ago, now transformed itself into a sly monster. It tore at my fingers, seeking to pry them from the rocks to which I clung. Gritting my teeth, I hung on with all my strength. Realizing it couldn't get me that way, it changed its mode of attack.

Rushing against my dangling body, it battered and rocked me, shifting me first from side to side, then back and forth—ruthless, hard, and fast. I screamed, but it had no mercy. In one fell swoop, a relentless blast of air, it blasted me so hard that my body swung out and up. The world spun crazily as the invisible monster carried me in a complete circle over the rock I so frantically clutched. As I swung down and around, it finally managed to rip my fingers from their grip.

I didn't fall; the wind didn't want that. I was its plaything, and it tossed me about, high and low, to and fro, just as it would a fallen leaf. My cries for help went unnoticed as this devilish gust toyed with me. When it eventually tired of its game, it carried me in a straight rush across a little valley and directly toward the sheer, gray side of a mountain. The wind intended to hurl me into it, and I would die. There was no escaping my fate. The cliff was so close, and drawing nearer with every second.

No, I didn't want to die! But—"Die, die, die…" the wind whispered gleefully.

Flinging out an arm, I made a gallant if vain attempt to create a buffer between that unforgiving stone and my body's vital organs. I closed my eyes, praying for a swift end. My fingers touched stone, and…passed through.

Shockingly, the whole mountainside opened up, swallowing me alive. I hit a stone floor and rolled. Down and down I went, powerless to stop the plunging spirals. My momentum was carrying me toward a black hole, directly in the middle of the floor. I shrieked for help as I dropped helplessly into its black depths…

And found myself once more in bed. My bed. In my own room.

No, wait. It was my bed and my room, but not in Aerisia. Not in Laytrii's palace. It was my bed and my bedroom…at home. At my home in Westman, Colorado. What was I doing here, back home on Earth?

Freeing myself from the ivory duvet, I climbed off the bed. My bare toes touched softness; I stood on a thick green carpet. The walls were white, the décor golds, creams, and ivories. A bookcase crammed with books and knickknacks stood against one wall. Framed pictures of myself and my family hung above my dresser, and music emanated from the stereo on the bedside table. My bare toes curled into the carpet, relishing its warmth.

"Mmmm….nice and cozy."

I ran my hands over the sleeves of my flannel pajamas and hummed along with the music. The song—it reminded me of someone, someone with black, black eyes. Someone I cared for deeply. But who? I didn't know anyone like that. Did I? I couldn't remember, but all of a sudden it didn't matter. I was home and I was safe. Everything was normal. My family was here, my life, and—

"My family."

As the thought struck, I whispered the words aloud. "My family!"

If I was here, they must be too. I had to go see, had to go find them. The impression seemed important as life itself, although I couldn't say why. It was almost as if I hadn't seen them in a long time. Didn't know why that was, but, heeding my instincts, I pivoted, dashing on eager feet out my door and down the long hallway. Peeking into each bedroom I passed, I checked quickly for my parents, brother, and sisters. The rooms were all empty. No matter. They must be downstairs.

I flew down the carpeted steps, heading for the first story of the house. My hand gliding over the varnished, wooden banister, I called out, "Mom? Dad? Harli Jean? Hey, where are you guys?"

There was no answer, but a light shone from the living room. Were they there? Skidding across the tiled foyer, I burst into the room, eager to greet my family...

And saw a coffin. A long, black coffin in front of the brick fireplace. Another perched under the window. Yet another had stolen the spot where the entertainment center used to stand. In all, there were five coffins scattered about the room. Not counting me, there were five people in my family...

"Oh no."

With hesitant steps, I moved toward the coffin nearest me. A huge clock was carved right into the middle of its shiny lid, a clock whose hands were broken, hanging at odd angles. On my first attempt to grab the lid, my sweaty fingers slid right off. I tried again, managing to grasp the wood and lift, flinging it back to reveal—

I screamed, stumbled backward, bumped into the coffin behind me and screamed again. I wanted desperately to run, to flee. Every instinct cried out I should escape this terror. Yet I had to know. I had to know!

Like a maniac, I dashed about the spacious living room, flinging open every last lid of those shiny coffins, each one decorated with a clock with broken hands. To my horror, inside each coffin, on a bed of white satin, reclined the remains of a family member. While some bodies were almost totally decomposed, others were nearly intact. In each case, enough survived for me to identify the corpse: by its hair, its clothing, its shoes... A diamond wedding band on a skeletal finger—that was my mother. This was my family. And they were dead, all of them dead—except me. Five coffins, a clock on each, and six people. I was the only one left alive.

"No!"

The word was the wounded cry of a mad animal. Fast as I could, I fled that terrible room. Out of my house I ran, out of the front door and straight into the open arms of...Ilgard?

Pulling back from his embrace, I glanced up into his face. The man was Simathe, all right: I knew it by his black hair, his clothing, his hard warrior's body. But he had no face. Where should have been pupil-less black eyes, straight black lashes, a mouth, a nose, cheekbones—was nothing. I cried out, stumbling away from the apparition, even as one of its arms rose, a bloody dagger clutched in its hand. Tripping over a loose stone, I twisted violently as I fell, doing all I could to evade that knife. I struck the ground on my stomach, and the scene changed again.

The Simathe was gone, and I was in the dining area of a nursing home. An old lady in a wheelchair held a gun pointed straight at my heart. She cackled gleefully, her finger tightening on the trigger as she wheezed, "Don't be afraid, honey. Granny will take care of you. Good care. It'll all be over in a second."

The gun fired, the bullet leaping from its barrel in a flash of red-orange flame. Just as it touched the fabric of my shirt, I was gone—

The horror went on and on. I found myself standing with a horde of pirates on a wooden ship, battling for our lives against a massive sea monster carved from the ocean itself. Then I was sword fighting a woman with weird, olive green eyes. Next, I was in a graveyard, kneeling at the foot of an open grave. A figure rose from the grave, floating on mist. In its arms it cradled a tawny, headless kitten. The corpse reached for me with fingers that decomposed before my eyes. I fled...

In each scene, just before death struck or evil touched me, I vanished. I was there and then gone, transported into another place of danger and torment. My reactions grew slower, and I grew more and more weary until I could barely stumble away from whatever I faced next, let alone wonder what could possibly be happening to me. And why.

In the end, I found myself huddled in the dark corner of an empty, dark room. My head was buried in my arms and my face pressed against my knees. "If I'm very still," I kept thinking, "maybe they won't find me. Maybe I can hide in here. Maybe they won't find me."

That old saying, "You can run but you can't hide," beat against my brain like a carpenter's hammer on a roof. The din was so loud I could hear nothing but it, and I trembled as I understood its truth. I'd tried running, I was now hiding, but neither defense would do me any good. They would find me. As sure as the sunrise, they'd come.

Who "they" were, I still didn't know. I only knew I would give anything for them not to find me. They would, though. It was inevitable. When they did, I'd have to fight them. I'd have to fight and win, or else I would die.

"I don't want to die," I heard myself whimper. "Please leave me alone, I don't want to die."

They wouldn't. I knew that when I heard the footsteps. They were coming. The darkness in which I cowered melted into a dim, ghostly glow. I could hide in the shadows no longer. They were here, upon me. The time to stand up, to be accounted for, was now.

So I stood. Pushing myself to my feet, I stood upright, facing them, each and every one. They were all there: every evil I'd encountered in this strange world of madness. The woman with olive green eyes, the corpse with the headless cat, the ugly old woman in the wheelchair, the decomposing bodies of my family, the faceless Simathe. The sea monster made from the sea, and even the evil wind were there. I'd escaped before, but they meant to have me now. To kill me. To mutilate my body, rend my flesh, and drink my blood in wild celebration.

I saw no way to defend myself, yet something inside refused to quit. Something in my soul encouraged me to stand, to fight, to acquit myself bravely and well. Even as they advanced on me, step by tortuously slow step, I looked about wildly for a weapon of some sort. There was none. Nothing I could use to defend my own life lay close at hand. My heart sank. Was this it? Was I really going to die this horrible death?

One of the creatures—the olive-green-eyed woman— suddenly snarled, leaping back as if she'd been stung. By what? There was nothing, nothing at all that I could see...

My gaze dropped to my feet. One stood upon a patch of white moonlight, the other golden sunlight. The creatures seemed afraid to approach, as if they feared the light.

Light.

The light.

Sunlight and moonlight.

I turned slowly. There was an open window in the wall behind me. No glass. Beyond it, the sun and moon hung next to each other, huddling low in the sky. Their light poured over me in equal strength, dividing my body down the middle in two even portions of color, white and gold. They were light, and light was power. With these I could defend myself, defeat those seeking my life.

Stretching up arms that trembled, I reached for them, the sun and the moon. Wonder of wonders, they came to me, floating willingly from the sky to rest in my hands. A disc of white and a disc of gold, both the size of a basketball, but weightless. Eternal.

In my hands I held light, light and power. I whirled to face my enemies. Seeing my weapons, they knew the tables had been turned. I was now the aggressor, and they the defenders. I was the huntress, they the hunted. They were about to die, were powerless to prevent it.

Pivoting, they reeled, trying to flee. I threw my weapons. First the moon, then the sun. My enemies shrieked piercing, inhuman cries. The light obliterated, engulfed, overwhelmed, destroyed them. Some burst into flames, while others dissolved from the magic and heat. A deafening explosion caused the four corners of the room to implode. I stumbled backward, casting up a hand to shield my face. The backs of my knees struck the windowsill. Losing my balance, I tumbled backward through the open window, but felt no fear as I hurtled into open space. Somehow, I knew I was going home.

Chapter Thirty-Eight

Shared Visions

My body convulsed, jerking hard. The violent motion rocked me awake, snatching me from that dangerous world of dreams. I bolted upright in my bed, glancing wildly about the darkened bedroom. Salty sweat poured from my face, stinging my eyes and dripping off my chin. My eyebrows and hairline were damp with it, my silk nightgown soaked, and the linen sheets tangled about me.

Dreams can't hurt you, I tried to reassure myself.

Cold sweat oozed from every pore, proving me a liar.

Oh, but they can. Dreams can most definitely hurt you.

At least, this kind could. Instinctively, I knew that particular vision had been no ordinary dream. It had to have meant something, but what?

I lingered in bed for a moment or two, indecision holding me captive. What should I do? Go to Ilgard? I could hardly believe such a distressing nightmare hadn't brought him to my side. Tell Risean? He knew some magic, of course, but did Moonkind magic cover dreams? Should I keep the whole thing to myself? Of all my options, that felt the least right.

What should I do? Think, Hannah. There's gotta be something...

Then the answer hit.

Braisley. Go find Braisley. Tell her everything. She's Aerisia's most powerful fairy, and probably knows more about magic than all the Moonkind combined. If anyone can help you with this, it'll be her.

Obediently, I climbed off the bed, the perspiration drenched sheets and coverlets swiftly chilling in the cool, night air. It was still black outside. I didn't know how long I'd slept, but it couldn't have been more than a few hours. The sun would probably rise soon. Whatever the time, I had to find Braisley. Somehow, I knew she would help me with this.

I didn't bother to change out of my nightgown, but reached for a robe to cover it up. A woman wandering the halls at night wearing only her nightshift was surely going to be questioned. A woman wandering the halls at night in a nightgown and robe might be dismissed as having a purpose. Before heading for my door, I also paused to slip on a pair of low-heeled, backless slippers.

I was relieved to come across no one outside my room. Relieved, but surprised. Where was Ilgard? Why hadn't he come? Where were the Simathe and Ranetron guards normally posted either just outside my door, or at opposite ends of the corridor? I saw nobody but the customary palace guards as I rushed through the silent hallways, and half of them were asleep.

That's certainly odd.

I couldn't help thinking Lord Garett was going to have their hides in the morning if he found out about them sleeping on the job, but I didn't have time to stop and wake them up.

Maybe it wasn't their fault anyway. Everything was peaceful and quiet; perhaps *too* peaceful and quiet. It was almost like a sleeping spell from a fairy tale had fallen over the palace, draping its occupants in a warm, drowsy cocoon. Where would it have come from, though? I didn't sense any threat or danger, so couldn't ascribe it to the Dark Powers.

Maybe Braisley can tell me about this, too.

Speaking of Braisley, I quickly discovered she wasn't in her room, although there was nothing particularly surprising about this. Fairies were provided suites on the basis of being honored guests, but they didn't necessarily require beds, sleep, food, or anything else a human guest might need. Which meant not finding a fairy in her bedchamber in the middle of the night was really nothing to fret over. The main thing worrying me was figuring out where the heck she'd gone. For all I knew, she might have returned to Cleyton, although I didn't think she'd do that without telling me goodbye.

Looking about her room, I tried to work out my next course of action. There wasn't much chance anybody else would know where the fairy had gone, so I scratched the idea of asking the servants. Briefly, I considered giving up and going back to bed, but I was wide awake and, honestly, the risk of falling asleep and suffering a second nightmare wasn't all that appealing.

There must be some way to find her.

Just like that, I knew. There was. All I had to do was call on my magic, open myself up, and look.

I tried. Unlocking myself, I let power flood me, while simultaneously visualizing the missing fairy in my mind's eye. Nothing came to me.

Strange.

Frowning, I closed my eyes, concentrating harder. Still nothing.

Rats! What am I doing wrong?

Another flash of inspiration. Maybe I needed more than to simply visualize her. Maybe I needed some kind of physical connection. To touch something of hers, as well as see her in my mind. Accordingly, I gave the poorly lit room a hasty search, but nothing leapt out as being useful. In fact, if I hadn't known the chamber was hers, I might've thought it was unoccupied. The bed was perfectly made, the furniture exactly aligned and in place. There was no clothing, toiletries, or jewelry scattered about.

My eyes finally lighted on the massive, ornate bed and came to rest. If Braisley had used this room at all—and I knew she must have—then the possibilities she'd sat or laid on the bed were pretty good. It might be a tenuous connection, but it was the best I could come up with.

Moving to the bed, I leaned over it, splaying both hands on its rich, embroidered coverlet. Once again I tried what I'd attempted before: closing my eyes and visualizing the beautiful fairy, carefully recalling every detail of her appearance, while reaching inside for that spring of power...

The vision came, flooding me with force. An image of Braisley appeared in my mind's eye, sharp and brilliant as the fairy herself. It wavered, growing fuzzy at the edges, but I clutched the blanket tightly, straining after her. The conjuring blanked out in a sheet of snowy white, then returned, changed to the room in which I stood.

This is it, I thought, elated with success. *I've done it!*

Sweeping out her open door, the image passed into the hallway and spiraled down the corridor. It was lethargic at first, but rapidly picked up speed, racing along the route she must have taken in a tunnel vision of dizzying velocity. Dizzying, that is, until it slammed up against a closed door with a jarring impact I physically felt. Pausing, it drifted easily through the door and down a flight of winding steps. At the bottom lay an immense, underground chamber, completely dark except for the shimmer of Braisley's aura. I searched in vain for further details, but the visualization winked out before I could figure out where she was.

My mind back in my own body, I pushed myself up from the bed. I may not have known exactly where she was, or what room she was in, but I felt some inner instinct associated with my seeking vision leading me to her. I felt it, identified it, and heeded it, hoping I'd soon have the answers I sought.

* * *

The door was old, its wood blunt, thick, and scarred. Iron bands stretched across wooden panels, huge black nails meshing the two into a sturdy entranceway. The metal bolt hung open; someone was inside, someone who either had a key or the power to open a lock without a key. Braisley? I was sure my quest to find her would end here, beyond this door, down a zigzagging flight of stone steps.

I took them quickly, hardly noticing the how the walls were damp and slick beneath my hand. The stairs went down and around, twisting and turning, yet I didn't slow. The night vision I'd summoned up guided my steps and quickened my pace.

Before long, the dancing radiance of an aura flickered on the wall before me. My pace picked up again. Rounding the final bend, I halted at the top of the last dozen stairs leading down to the chamber floor. There she stood, her ghostly white aura filling the vaulted chamber. Unconsciously, I released the power, no longer needing the night vision. With it, the aura rather blinded me.

Slower now, I descended the final steps, my slippers thumping and my robe whispering against stone with every movement. Once at the bottom, my slippers clattered loudly on the floor, the echoes discordant with the vault's cool stillness. I slipped them off, gliding barefoot toward the heart of the glowing light.

"Braisley?"

She stood behind a waist-high table. Its thick, lined column was about three feet in diameter, while its top was a round marble slab whose width was twice that of the pedestal. Scattered across the surface of this slab were at least two dozen Stones ranging in size from the tip of my pinky to a man's fist. The Stones were a wild rainbow of colors: red, pink, lavender, indigo, yellow, green, orange, blue, and every shade in between. The colors of the sunset. Without being told, I knew what they were—the prophecy's fabled *Singing Stones*. I knew, because I heard their music in my own mind.

"Braisley?"

Although I'd easily tuned out the music, I wondered if the fairy was having problems doing the same. She stood transfixed with her hands spread over the Stones, her eyes fastened on one large, red Stone resting in the center of the tabletop. I hesitated, half afraid of disturbing her. Need, nonetheless, outweighed caution, and in the end I found myself standing across from her, the table between us as I called her name a third, fourth time.

"Braisley? *Braisley?*"

Her body gave a sudden quiver, her eyes darting from the Stone to my face. I was surprised to see a sheen of perspiration dampening her porcelain features.

"Braisley? You okay? What's going on?"

"I was…I had—had a vision."

The jumble of words trailed off awkwardly as she glanced away, fumbling with the delicate folds of her gown. For my part, I was taken aback by seeing this powerful, serene fairy so discombobulated. Edging around the table, I stepped to her side, placing a hand on her forearm. She stopped fidgeting and looked at me with wide green eyes tinged with fear.

"Braisley? What is it, what's wrong? What did you see in your vision that's got you so upset?"

Reaching up a pallid hand, she touched my cheek, as if reassuring herself I was really there.

"I beheld you, Lady Hannah. I saw you in strange places, attired in strange clothing. You were near death myriad times, yet it was never allowed to touch you. In the end, you were victorious and escaped."

I gaped at her. "You can't be serious! I had a dream tonight just like what you're describing. Something told me to come find you and tell you about it."

Her gossamer wings halting their agitated fluttering, the fairy regarded me carefully, her surprise and fear dissolving into calmness.

"Then so you must. Tell me all that you saw, all that you dreamt."

So I told her, told her everything, leaving nothing out. She listened closely, not saying a word throughout the whole recital. At its conclusion, she nodded evenly, her hands now folded at her waist.

"Your dream and my vision are one and the same. All was as you've described."

"But how's that possible? How could you have a vision of *my* dream?"

"It is nothing so mysterious, lady. The stronger one's magic, the more probable they will experience significant visions. Ever have I been subject to this. At times these dreams are my own. At other times, they are likenesses of visions dreamt by those such as the Moonkind, my sister fairies, or even the Scraggen. Their power attracts mine, and for a time our minds meld in sleep."

I slacked a hip against the stone table. "That's unbelievable. Nothing I've ever dreamed has felt so real or had the weird sequences or elements this one did. What do you think that means?"

Placing her hand over one of the smooth Stones, she rubbed it gently with her palm.

"All dreams have meaning. Whether it be the recalling of a forgotten memory, or a secret yearning for a lost love...all dreams have meaning and thus a place. However, there are dreams—certain, singular dreams—whose interpretations, could they be unlocked, would reveal mysteries of the future. Perhaps your dream was such a dream."

"So you think it was trying to tell me the future?"

"Who can say?" The hand on the Stone stilled. "Perhaps this dream predicts what will or could be. Doubtless it was powerful, for it shared itself with me as well as with you. Yes, yes I believe a dream this unique must contain a meaning of great importance."

"And have you not noticed," she continued, her fingertips now trailing idly from Stone to Stone, "the strangeness of this night?"

"You mean how there were no guards outside my door? Or how Ilgard didn't come, even though this dream made me wake up sweating and shaking? There's no way he couldn't have felt that."

"Just so. The potency of this dream has disrupted the night's peace for some, while others it has sunken into slumber. The High-Chief may have been taken in the latter manner, and not allowed to waken. The guards outside your chamber in the former: compelled by reasons unknown to depart their posts. When one with your power is beset by such dreams, the night hours are often altered for those in close proximity."

"Wow, I didn't know that. I had no idea things could change for other people just because they're around me."

She glanced up, eyes hooded. "To put it simply, my dear, you are a facilitator for change."

I wasn't sure what all she meant by that, but chose to let it go, asking instead, "So, this dream of mine...can you interpret it?"

"I cannot," she replied with a sad sort of frown. "Though I can sometimes interpret a mysterious sweven, the significance of yours is hidden from me. However, that does not mean I cannot tell you where you may seek answers."

I felt my pulse pick up. "Really? Where is that?"

The fairy closed her emerald eyes as if in pain. "I fear to tell you. You *will* go, Hannah, and I'll not be able to prevent you."

"Is it that bad?"

"Nay, my lady, it is far worse," she sighed. "But I suppose you must know."

Chapter Thirty-Nine

Trapped

Although her back was to the darkened staircase, Braisley was not surprised to hear the echo of booted feet racing lightly down the stone steps. Soon they would reach the bottom. When they did…

Sighing, she picked up the smallest of the Singing Stones, rolling it lightly between thumb and forefinger, seeking comfort from its magic. The footsteps reached the bottom stair. Stopped. There came the faint rustle of clothing as he bent to retrieve the slippers Lady Hannah had left behind. He advanced, slower now. Braisley could hear the gentle slap of sword against thigh with each step he took.

Straightening her shoulders, she braced herself inwardly and outwardly for the inevitable confrontation. Knowing it was unavoidable, she changed her mind about waiting passively. Taking the initiative, she replaced the Stone and spun to meet him. He took her actions in stride, his black eyes flickering over her with such scant heed that she might have been another of the vault's furnishings.

Braisley was fully aware of what he sought. She also knew that even though the darkest corners yielded their secrets to the Simathe's incomparable night vision, the High-Chief wouldn't find his lady in this place. Nor anywhere else, for that matter. Again, the fairy steeled herself for the inevitable conflict when he discovered this for himself.

Maintaining her silence, the fairy noted the warrior's half-dressed appearance, bespeaking of a sudden awakening to find the Artan gone. Their *Joining* link had led him here, but further he would not go. As soon as he accepted her absence, the questions were not slow in coming.

"Where is she, Braisley? Where is my lady?"

"Not here," Braisley answered evenly.

"Then where?" the High-Chief demanded, terser this time.

"I don't know."

It is the truth, she soothed herself, for she really did not know the Artan's exact whereabouts at this precise minute.

"You don't know?" Soulless black eyes held her in a hard, unforgiving grasp. "What reply is this? Do not presume me a fool, fairy. You know full well where she has gone. Her presence lingers in this chamber, but no further. You know why," he added accusingly.

"I have told you, I do not—"

"I will not hear that again!" He cut her off with a terse hand motion, effectively slicing away her protests. "You know—tell me!"

There was naught to be gained by concealing the truth any longer, Braisley decided at last. Her mind made up, she confessed bravely.

"Lady Hannah has gone to a place where you, my lord, cannot follow."

His expressionless face changed little, unless it was to grow harder.

"What place?"

She lowered her eyes to the floor. "She has gone to the Underworld."

The silence of death met her hushed words. In the deep stillness, the fairy could hear the rush and intake of both their breaths. Long seconds dragged by, yet she did not look up. When he finally spoke, his tone was dangerously calm.

"The Underworld?"

"Aye, Lord Ilgard. The Underworld."

"Where?" he demanded brusquely, ire clearly rising. "Where in the Underworld?"

"The Vale of the Dreamers."

Another long silence. When she finally dared to look, Braisley peeked up to see the Simathe's wicked eyes narrow with wrath. His was face inscrutably hard.

"Nay, fairy," he breathed. "You are mistaken. Even to the Underworld will I follow her."

He said no more. Dropping the slippers to clatter on the floor, he spun on his heel to leave.

"Don't be a fool, Simathe!"

Her words lashed out in the empty hush of the vault, arresting his progress. Taking advantage of the slight hesitation, Braisley moved swiftly, throwing herself into his path. When he shifted, making as though he'd steal around her, she flung both hands against his torso as if to physically restrain him.

"Ilgard, my lord, wait. You know not the way, nor will I tell you. To follow her would mean only bitter results for both you and her."

"Have you not heard, fairy?" he growled. "I am Simathe: an immortal. The Underworld holds no terrors for me."

"There are other forms of death besides death of the body. You have heard the tales: even an immortal, such as yourself, may make a misstep and find himself consigned to an eternity of living death."

"While a mortal would simply perish. Out of my way, Braisley. Though I seek help from another to gain entrance, I will follow my lady."

With that, he sidestepped, pushing around her and heading for the staircase. The man was impossible. Unreasonable. He'd not heeded, just as she'd known he would not.

"My lord, I must ask you to stop," Braisley called after him.

He kept going as if he'd not heard, his left foot now on the bottom step.

"My lord, I like not to do this, but if you refuse to listen—"

Her warning ignored, she was left with no other choice. Before he managed the first stairwell bend that would take him from sight, the fairy flung out her right arm, fingers opening wide to release a bolt of pure power. It caught the fleeing warrior, ensnaring him in a white blaze that slammed him mercilessly against the stone wall. Fixed there, his arms pinned to his sides by the power circling him in a flaming ring, the Simathe struggled fiercely to break free. For all his writhing and twisting, his furious straining, the magic—the fairy—proved too powerful.

Slowly, Braisley moved up the steps to face him, barely maintaining a mask of serenity when he shouted at her, "What have you done? Release me, release me at once!"

"I cannot, my lord."

She stopped before him, outwardly as unbothered by the spectacle as a marble statue, though inwardly she hated this, and quailed from the sight.

"Braisley, let me go. Release me!"

A note of panic had crept into his voice, but it was more than being held captive that had put it there. His next words were a confirmation of that fact.

"I cannot feel her, Braisley. She is not there, I cannot feel her." He thrashed harder against the restraints. "What have you done?"

Something twisted inside at his torment, at seeing one of the immortals lose their famed control, but Braisley heard only the Artan's soft begging: *Don't let him follow me, Braisley. Please. Whatever happens, don't let him come after me. I'd rather die than have anything happen to Ilgard. Do something, anything; just don't let him follow me to the Underworld.*

And the fairy of Cleyton had given her word.

Shifting, she leaned against the wall for support, its slick dampness barely registering against her folded wings. Already, the strain of imprisoning one as mighty as this was making itself known. Were he an ordinary human, this would be far less difficult.

"Calm yourself, High-Chief," she said. "I gave the lady my word that I would not allow you to follow her. It was her wish that you remain here. I have temporarily blocked your bond so that, until she returns, you will neither feel her nor know her whereabouts. It is the only way I can be assured that, should you break free of me, you cannot go after her."

He would have none of it. "Release me, fairy," he ordered furiously. "At least restore our bond, allow me to feel her."

Sweat shone on his temples. His lips were bloodless against the bronze of his face as he exerted all his strength to throw off her restraints. Mentally, the fairy was aware of him straining equally hard against the blocked bond, struggling for a way to reopen it.

She shook her head. "I cannot, my lord. You know this. If I did—"

"It would be better for us all."

"I cannot!"

She let the stairwell take more of her weight, shocked by the effort necessary to sustain both the restraining ring and the shield over the Simathe's *Joining* link. A fairy's power was not meant to be used in this way. Most, outside their vales, couldn't have done it at all. Fortunate indeed that she was Aerisia's strongest fairy. For, if she found this task so difficult, could another have even executed it?

The Simathe wrenched violently from side to side, muttering vile curses against herself, her sister fairies, women in general, and any with the ability to wield magic. The need to open the bond, to fill the void her shield inflicted, provided a fresh, wild strength born of sheer desperation. Nevertheless, Braisley held firm, concentrating all her power, hoping fervently she could persevere until the lady returned. The future of all Aerisia depended upon a swift conclusion to the Artan's perilous Underworld journey.

I take a deep breath, feeling as if I'm poised on the brink of infinity, of eternity, of destiny. I don't know what awaits me on my journey to the Underworld; I only know that it's a journey I have to make. Somehow, it's tied to my fate as the

Artan, so I must walk the path unfurling before me to find out how and why.

The doorway stands open, a welcoming blaze of light that bids me enter and lose myself in its warm interior. Turning, I cast a final look at Braisley, fairy of Cleyton, who stands by the marble table holding the fabled Singing Stones. Her face calm, her carriage regal, she dips her head in an undecipherable gesture that might be reassurance I'm doing the right thing, encouragement, or a farewell. Maybe it's all three.

This is it! I tell myself, *and step into the light. Bright colors shimmer around me, pastels seep into me, and bold darks consume me. Time shudders to a standstill as I surge forward three steps, feeling like I'm wading in Jell-O. Then I'm through. The light and colors vanish, and before I have time to twist my neck and glance behind me, I hear a soft whisking noise. Braisley's doorway is gone.*

I'm in the Underworld, and what awaits me in this place is anybody's guess.

LOOK FOR BOOK THREE, *AERISIA: FIELD OF BATTLE*

ABOUT THE AUTHOR

Don't believe all the hype. Sarah Ashwood isn't really a gladiator, a Highlander, a fencer, a skilled horsewoman, an archer, a magic wielder, or a martial arts expert. That's only in her mind. In real life, she's a genuine Okie from Muskogee, who grew up in the wooded hills outside the oldest town in Oklahoma and holds a B.A. in English from American Military University. She now lives (mostly) quietly at home with her husband and four children, where she tries to sneak in a daily run or workout to save her sanity and keep her mind fresh for her next story.

For a complete list of all Sarah's works and the links to find them, visit her website at www.sarahashwoodauthor.com.

To keep up to date with Sarah's new releases, sign up for her newsletter. You can also follow her on Bookbub, or find her on Facebook, Pinterest, Instagram, and Twitter.

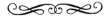

BOOKS IN THE *SUNSET LANDS BEYOND* TRILOGY

Aerisia: Land Beyond the Sunset
Aerisia: Gateway to the Underworld
Aerisia: Field of Battle

Made in the USA
Columbia, SC
20 October 2020